TIM TRAYLOR AND THE STAR MARSHAL
NEILL HOSKINS

SHODAN SEA

To my parents, who always encouraged me to read.

Thanks to John Jarrold for your shrewd and insightful observations and to Lee at bookediting.co.uk for your keen eye and helpful suggestions.

Table of contents

One
Discovery

T im was halfway down the cliff when he slipped.
His hand lashed out automatically, grasping
onto a crumbly ledge. He made it, but the
sudden jolt lanced pain through his shoulder and he
cried out. His feet scrabbled to find any kind of hold
that would take the pressure off his arms. Thick drops
of sweat ran into his eyes, blurring his vision, and the
sun's heat on his neck felt like a slap. *Stupid, stupid,
stupid,* he thought. What had possessed him to try
such a tricky climb in the middle of the day? It would
have been so much easier to go for a swim.

A few feet below was a ledge just wide enough
to stand on. He edged down. Changing his grip, his
hand brushed against something sticking out from the
cliff face. He rubbed away some of the accumulated
dirt and saw the gleam of what looked like gold.

He dropped down onto the rock shelf and took a
moment to get his breath back. Stretching up, he tried
to pull the object out, but it was stuck fast in the sun-
baked earth. He took out a house key; maybe he
could dig the thing out with that. *Don't drop it*, he

murmured to himself. He'd only had the key a couple of months, a present on his twelfth birthday and a sign he could be trusted more. A little thing, and nowhere near as impressive as his mountain bike, but it made him feel more grown up. Two minutes of digging and prodding and he was able to yank the object out.

It was bigger than he had realised, nearly the size of his hand. A movement below caught his eye. Frankie, the family dog, was nosing around on the seaweed-clad rocks at the base of the cliff, having sensibly taken a safer route down. Tim didn't want to leave him on his own for long so he pocketed his find and concentrated on getting down as quickly as possible to examine it.

Five minutes later he jumped the last foot down onto the pebbly shore. He fished the object out of his pocket and whistled to Frankie, who trotted over wagging his stumpy tail. The thing definitely wasn't gold, despite its colour; it was much too light. Some kind of metal though. It was wedge-shaped, roughly five inches long and engraved with flowing, wavy lines. There was a curved, hollowed-out section on one side.

Probably just junk. I should bin it. He was about to fire it out into the sea when he stopped.

His fingers were tingling as the object lay flat in his palm and he could have sworn it was vibrating slightly. What could it be? His dad would know what it was. He crammed it into his pocket, clipped on Frankie's lead and headed back along the beach.

Half an hour later he was walking up the path to his house. He hesitated as he unlocked the door. Perhaps he should hold off showing his find to his parents? They were bound to ask a lot of questions and when they realised he'd been on a dangerous part of the coastal path they'd hit the roof. It would be better to hang on to it for a couple of days while he came up with a better story.

Darting up the stairs into his room, he slipped the object beneath the mattress. Time for a nice, cool shower and then he'd see what Mum was rustling up for tea.

***

'No, I've no idea. Never seen anything like it before. It was at the base of the cliff?'

'Yeah, just the end sticking out. It caught the sun,' Tim answered, trying to sound nonchalant. It was three days since he'd returned from the climb and he was sitting at the kitchen table with his dad. The man asking the question was Alan Henderson, a neighbour and reporter on the local paper. Tim wasn't sure what to make of him; he always seemed friendly enough but could be nosey if he got the chance. When he wasn't chasing down the news, Mr

Henderson was a metal detecting enthusiast, so Tim's dad thought he might know what the object was.

'If you like I can take a couple of pictures of this and run them with an article in the paper, mystery object found kind of thing, and we'll ask if anyone knows what it is. If we don't get a response after a couple of weeks, we can try the museum,' Mr Henderson said as he sat back.

Tim exchanged a glance with his dad, who nodded. 'Yeah sure, why not.'

Mr Henderson said he'd pop back later with his camera, and his dad saw him out. Tim stayed back. He felt unsettled but couldn't think why. Neither his dad nor Mr Henderson had mentioned any kind of tingling sensation that Tim always felt when handling the object. Perhaps it just affected him. But why would that be? What if it was radioactive and only kids could detect it? No, that was silly. There was probably a simple explanation, and most likely he'd find out next week when the story appeared in the local paper.

Two
Contact

Tim saw the note the moment he wandered into the hallway. It was too early for the post so he'd assumed it was junk mail but, as he scooped it up, he saw his name, handwritten. He didn't recognise the handwriting but something about the letter made him feel uneasy.

He'd had the dream again last night. Third time in a row, always the same. He was running, running hard across a desert wilderness, the wind was howling and the whipped sand stung his face, but he knew he must keep going. Someone else ran beside him, but he couldn't see who they were, and then he was wide awake, safe in his room, and everything was all right. Just a stupid dream, but it seemed so real that he half expected to shake the sand from his shoes before getting dressed. And now this note. He waited until he was back in his room before opening it.

Tim,

I very much want to examine the object you have found; I believe it could be of great importance. It's vital you keep it safe. I don't want to alarm you, but you could be in danger. I can explain more when we meet. I will be on the beach where you found it at dawn tomorrow morning. Please do not speak about this with anyone else.

Until then,

G.

'As if!' Tim muttered and crumpled the note into a ball before firing it into the wastepaper bin. G was obviously some kind of weirdo. They'd been coming out of the woodwork in the week since the paper published the article about him and his mystery find. All sorts of people had emailed and written in with one wacky suggestion after another as to what the artefact was, or could be, but the upshot was nobody seemed to know. It remained an unidentified relic.

Maybe one of his mates had written the note to wind him up, Tim wondered. Could be Josh's work, though the handwriting was different. Well, he wasn't going to be fooled. He wouldn't even mention it when he saw him. Might be best not to say anything to his parents either; they'd only worry. He slid open the drawer on his bedside table. The object was still there, lying on a sheet of bubble wrap. He resisted the urge to pick it up and slid the drawer shut.

Three
Nerissa

T im knew something was wrong the moment he opened his eyes. It was much too light. He'd said goodnight to his parents and gone to bed hours before but it couldn't possibly be morning yet. He rolled over and picked up his Casio watch. The LED display read 3.00 a.m. Then he saw the drawer of his bedside cabinet was partially open. He pulled it fully out and peered in. The relic was gone.

Flinging the duvet aside, he perched on the side of the bed. Maybe his parents had come into his room and moved it, or Cate, his sister. But why now? The light outside grew brighter. He could feel his heart pounding in his chest. He was going to have to look.

Creeping closer to the window, he drew the curtain, blinking against the glare. His breath caught as he saw the girl.

She was glowing, actually glowing with light. She was around his age, dressed in dark blue satin pyjamas and her long black hair was tied back. She smiled and beckoned to him. Tim's hand shook as he opened the window. Before he could speak, she turned and walked away.

Tim jumped out. Being on the ground floor, he was able to land on the lawn easily. The girl paused, looked back over her shoulder, smiled, and silently sprinted away.

'Wait!' he called as he ran after her. There was nowhere to run; where did she think she was going to go? He'd almost caught her when there was a blinding white flash and he stumbled and then pitched over. Light dazzled him and it took a few seconds for his vision to clear. Little balls of colour danced in the air wherever he looked.

'Next time close your eyes.'

He jumped, startled at the unexpected voice.

The girl had gone and he was in a small, cream-coloured room. Utterly bewildered, he stood up. The walls were perfectly smooth and appeared to be made of metal. Ahead was an open door. An old man moved into the doorway. Tim stepped back. His eyes darted around the room, but there was no other way out.

'Don't be afraid.'

The stranger's voice was rich and deep. He was tall with long, grey, wavy hair and had the weather-beaten look of someone who spent a lot of time outdoors. He wore dark blue coveralls, like a pilot's.

'We meet at last,' he said, and smiled.

Tim was struck dumb. Where was he? Where was the girl? A spike of fear lanced down his spine and he backed further away from the old man, who stood there calmly regarding him.

'It's OK, don't be frightened. I mean you no harm. I'll explain everything. Did you get my note?'

'Note?' Tim croaked. For a second, he thought the old guy had him mixed up with someone else, but realisation struck, and his stomach lurched.

'You wrote that note? You're G?'

'Yes. My name is Garrantius Neva, but please, call me Gar-ran. Welcome on board the Scarab,' Gar-ran said, smiling.

Tim's jaw dropped. Surely he was dreaming? This couldn't be real, could it?

'Who are you? 'Where are we?'

'I will explain, but first I want to talk about this, and where you found it.'

Tim gasped. The stranger had his relic! He lunged to grab it but checked himself; the man might have been old, but he was still bigger than him. He looked strong too.

'It's mine.' Tim clenched his fist. He was tempted to make a grab for the relic and leg it through the door; there must be another way out somewhere. The stranger seemed to catch his mood and held up his hands.

'I know this must all seem very peculiar to you, but I had to bring you here because I believe you could be in danger.'

'Danger? What kind of danger? I haven't done anything.'

'I know, but that doesn't matter now. We don't have much time, so I'll be quick. It will seem crazy, but please listen.'

Tim opened his mouth to object but thought better of it. What choice did he have really? He was trapped, for the time being anyway, and despite his fear, he was curious. Nothing like this had ever happened to him before. There was one thing he needed to know though.

'What happened to the girl? And please, where are we?'

'The girl's fine. You'll see her in a minute. You're aboard my ship, the Scarab, and you're safe here. Come, I'll show you.' He moved into the corridor beyond the doorway and gestured for Tim to follow.

Tim hesitated. He looked around again, but there was still no other way out. Taking a deep breath, he followed Gar-ran through the door.

The corridor was L-shaped and they walked to the bottom end. Tim ran his fingers along the smooth, pale grey walls. Definitely some kind of metal. They stopped in front of a closed sliding door made of two panels that met in the middle. Fixed to the wall on the right was a square tile made of what looked like black glass. He watched as Gar-ran placed the palm of his hand on the tile. Immediately it changed to dark blue and the doors slid open with a faint hissing sound.

'Wow.'

The first thing that caught Tim's eye was the big, black, curved screen on the far wall. Strange symbols and characters flashed across it at incredible speed. Below was a console filled with a staggering array of switches, buttons and levers, many of which pulsed with different colours. Immediately in front of this were two high-backed, black leather chairs and a third central chair behind. He couldn't help smiling; it was like something from *Doctor Who*, but much better. His eyes flicked to Gar-ran as he moved to the central chair.

'Is this some sort of control room?'

'Yes, I call it the command hub. Now, as for the girl, it's time the two of you were introduced. Nerissa?'

'Yes marshal?'

Tim whirled around. The room was empty apart from the two of them, but he'd heard a girl's voice very clearly.

'Our guest was wondering where you'd gone.'

Gar-ran was smiling now, but at what Tim couldn't tell. He edged back towards the doorway.

'I'm always here,' Nerissa said.

Tim's gaped as the girl's smiling face appeared on the big screen.

'What ... what's going on?' he mumbled as he gazed at her.

'Nerissa is the ship's computer,' Gar-ran replied, as if it was the most natural thing in the world.

Tim tried to speak but the words wouldn't come. Nerissa's face filled the screen and he felt his cheeks burn as she smiled at him. *Stupid, she's not real.* But he couldn't take his eyes off her. He realised Gar-ran was still talking.

'... She's highly sophisticated, almost sentient in fact. She can project herself into a 3D form that looks like a real person. Normally the form wouldn't look so young, but I had to find a way to encourage you on board, and I thought the image of an attractive girl of your own age would be useful.'

'You tricked me,' he blurted out. To his own ear he sounded sulky, and he stopped himself from saying more as he didn't want to sound like a baby in front of the girl, even if she was just a fancy computer. He snorted and shook his head.

'This is getting too weird. What do you want with me?'

'Don't be angry, Tim. We didn't want to trick you, but we need your help,' Nerissa said. She looked troubled now and Tim turned to Gar-ran.

'Help with what? I don't even know you, and you still haven't told me where we are.'

'I can do better than that. Take a look at this.' Gar-ran moved to the control console. He smiled as he exchanged a look with Nerissa, and Tim felt his face flush again. *Are they laughing at me?*

Gar-ran turned to him as he pressed a small blue button. Immediately Tim tensed up. *What now?*

Nerissa's face vanished and was immediately replaced by a clear screen. Somehow, a part of Tim knew that if he looked out, nothing would ever be the same again. He wavered. His leg began to tremble and he was afraid he would topple over, but he had to see. Keeping half an eye on Gar-ran, he moved to the screen and peered through.

It took him a second to realise it, but there, way down below, was his house, so small and distant and just one of many wrapped in the surrounding streets. Far ahead he could see the tiny lights of the cars on the coast road and just beyond was the sea, black as an oil slick in the moonlit night. His head swam and he had to look away.

SPACESHIP! I'm on an actual spaceship! It was unbelievable, and yet there he was. Then another, darker thought tore through his brain and his legs wobbled. If this really was a spaceship, that would mean that Gar-ran wasn't human, and if he wasn't human, he had to be ... alien. He suddenly felt sick and horribly alone. What could he do? There must be a way out. He took a few deep breaths and felt himself calming a little, but when he found his voice it was barely a whisper.

'How? ... How is this possible?'

'Here in the Scarab, we can go anywhere,' Gar-ran said, offering Tim a sympathetic smile. 'Let me explain why you're here. Please take a seat.' He gestured to one of the black chairs. Feeling stunned, Tim took the furthest chair, positioning it so he could see the doorway. Gar-ran took the far-right seat.

'Tim, what I'm going to tell you will seem hard to accept, but it's important you have an idea of the bigger picture, and what's at stake.' Gar-ran paused and Tim, realising this was his cue, slowly nodded.

'Your planet, Earth, is in a part of the Milky Way galaxy known as the Orion spur. The spur is an offshoot of a much bigger section of space, which here on Earth is known as the Perseus arm. Earth is the only planet in your solar system with advanced, intelligent life. But this system is just one of many in the galaxy and many others also have planets, and worlds filled with intelligent life, not all of it friendly, just like here on Earth.'

'Whoa, stop there. Other worlds?' Tim felt really scared now. This old guy must be nuts, but then how did he have this ship? How could he even be here? *Unless I'm hallucinating or something.* That could be it. Somehow, he'd become ill during the night and he was imagining all of this. In a minute his parents would come and wake him up and he'd be safe back at home. He screwed his eyes shut and willed himself to wake up, but when he opened them again, he was still sat there in the chair.

Gar-ran smiled faintly and reaching into the top pocket of his flight suit. He withdrew a silver hexagonal disc on which was engraved the image of a planet cradled between a pair of huge hands. It reminded Tim of a sheriff's badge. He didn't know whether to laugh or run.

'I'm a star marshal. We're a galactic order formed over a thousand years ago dedicated to watching and protecting different areas and beings of the galaxy. Your world is in my area. However, I'm from further away. A planet called Cathrox, in the Metallin system, also part of the Perseus arm, but very distant.'

Tim stared at Gar-ran and then all around the room. He rubbed his face hard but nothing changed. New thoughts seeped into his head.

'How do you even understand and speak English?'

Gar-ran laughed softly. 'All marshals have to learn languages, as we travel widely to help maintain law and order. We come into contact with different races and civilisations. I've been familiar with several Earth languages for some years now.'

'Oh.' It made sense in a weird way. 'Is this all to do with that thing I found?'

'Yes. Take a look at this.' Gar-ran tapped another button on the console and the view disappeared, replaced by an image of a golden orb.

It was faded and the lines were indistinct, but there was something familiar about it. Tim could feel his heart was still thudding away like a bass drum but, moving nearer, he saw the orb was formed from four quartered pieces. Each looked very similar to the thing he'd found.

So, what is it? If only his dad and Mr Henderson were here, they would know what to do. *Hang on.* If Gar-ran was showing him this, it could mean that he wanted the orb thing for himself. He still had Tim's piece. Maybe he had the other parts already. He turned to look at Gar-ran, who was watching him expectantly.

'You see?' Gar-ran said.

'I think so. It looks like I found a piece of whatever that is,' Tim mumbled.

'Yes, exactly.' There was a bright gleam in Gar-ran's eye as he stared fervently at the screen. His sudden intensity made Tim nervous.

'The dimension bomb. A legendary weapon crafted from the rarest metal. It's been lost for centuries, no trace of it anywhere, until now. You've found a missing piece, I'm sure of it,' Gar-ran said, his eyes still fixed to the screen.

A new idea stole into Tim's head. Maybe Gar-ran was a collector of old artefacts and curiosities, someone who travelled all over the place hunting down rare items to add to their hoard. *I could sell it to him.* No, that might just complicate things. Maybe, if he gave the piece away, he could make a clean break from this weirdness and go home.

'Do you want it? You can keep it now that I know what it is. I'm not bothered. I won't say anything about this place.' *As if anyone would believe me.*

'Tell me,' said Gar-ran, looking serious. 'Have you seen any of the reports on the news about the disappearances in Snowdonia?'

24

It wasn't the response Tim had been hoping for. He shrugged. 'Urm ... yeah, I've heard a bit. My parents were talking about it. Two climbers went missing and then some girl who was hiking. Maybe they just got lost?' His voice trailed off as another disturbing thought hit him: was Gar-ran planning to go there? Would he force him to go with him?

Gar-ran shook his head slowly. 'I think it's worse than that. I've found evidence that a portal has been opened, a gateway to another dimension. Some things have come through, bad things, and I'm afraid it will get worse, much worse, unless we can stop it.'

We? Tim felt his gut tense. What was this old guy talking about? And why was he including him in whatever was going on?

The picture of the orb dissolved and Tim flinched at the sight of the face which appeared in its place. He turned away, but the image of the huge, curled horns and blackened skin was scorched into his mind.

'Mephango, the world slayer,' Gar-ran said, his voice low. 'A demonic entity of enormous power; bringer of destruction and death.'

Tim bolted for the door. He didn't care about the relic now, he just wanted out of there, back to his nice warm bed, his family, and his safe, uneventful life. He was halfway down the corridor before he skidded to a halt. Nerissa stood there, her big dark eyes and raised arms imploring him to stop. *She's not real. You can run right though her,* he told himself as he shut his eyes and put his head down.

He stopped just in time, his face inches away from her. Slowly she placed her hand on his chest, the air sizzled and Tim yelped and jumped back, as much from surprise as from the tiny electric shock that was her touch. She smiled apologetically.

'Tim, I know this all sounds crazy. You don't know us, and we've brought you here in the middle of the night, and it's all new and scary, but please listen to what the marshal has to say.'

Tim glanced back; Gar-ran was standing in the doorway of the command hub. There was nowhere else to go. What was he thinking anyway? Even If he'd managed to get outside, they were hundreds of feet up, and he was only in his pyjamas.

He shrugged and threw his hands up. 'OK, OK.'

Back inside the command hub, he refused the marshal's offer of a seat. 'What's this all got to do with me though?'

'That's what I was about to explain,' Gar-ran said as he sat down. He looked tired and, for a moment, Tim felt a twinge of sympathy for him.

'Something happened a long time ago on another world which caused disaster, and I'm afraid that unless it's stopped, a similar thing could happen here on Earth.'

'What are you talking about? What happened?' Tim slid back towards the door; he wasn't sure if he could bear to hear any more. Gar-ran held up his hands placatingly and Nerissa's face appeared on the screen. She smiled again. He felt silly just standing there, so slowly walked back and sat down.

'It started with a group of scientists in the Vothrun system, which is also within our galaxy, the Milky Way, but many light years from here. The Vothruns were a highly evolved, very clever people. Perhaps too clever. Their scientists were working on a secret project to prove the existence of other dimensions. Eventually they succeeded, and opened a gateway to another realm. At first, they were overjoyed; it was an amazing breakthrough. But soon they realised that it was much harder to close the barrier than to open it. Things started to come through. Bad things. At first, they could handle them, but then HE came though.'

Out of the corner of his eye Tim could seem the demon's head displayed on the viewing screen. He looked down and then back at Gar-ran and was alarmed to see the old man had grown pale and there was a distinct tremor in his right hand. Suddenly aware he was being studied, Gar-ran sat up straighter and continued the story.

'His power is unreal; he nearly destroyed everything. He seemed invincible, until it was discovered a certain very rare metal, if fashioned into a weapon, could defeat him.'

The golden orb appeared on the screen again. Tim fidgeted in his seat; this was getting more and more intense by the moment. Aliens, demons, magic weapons, and he *still* didn't know what it all had to do with him.

'So, a weapon was crafted,' Gar-ran continued, his voice low. 'But, by the time it was ready, it was almost too late; many were dead or lost, and it fell to a young apprentice called Terius to stand against the demon, and against the odds, he won. Mephango was defeated, forced back to his own dimension, and Terius and his world survived.'

Tim gazed at the piece of the relic that Gar-ran still held. He struggled to corral the thoughts pinging through his head. He took a breath and looked Gar-ran dead in the eye.

'This is nuts. First you tell me there's other worlds out there, then you say that this demon thing is going to come here and he's got to be stopped. But even if this is true, what can I do? I'm just a kid. What does it have to do with me?'

'Because you found this.' Gar-ran waved the relic in Tim's face. 'You found this for a reason. It's no coincidence. This piece and the other pieces have been lost for centuries but now, at a crucial time, a segment has come to you. Somehow, you've been chosen, but the rest of the pieces must be located and brought here before it's too late.'

'Too late for what though? I don't understand.'

'The previous disappearances in Snowdonia have occurred when there is a full moon. The next full moon will be a supermoon, and whoever has opened the portal has warned that Mephango will come again at that time. That can't happen, and whoever is behind this must be found and stopped.'

Tim wasn't sure how to respond. He felt a growing pressure to say something but it just didn't seem real, although clearly Gar-ran was deadly serious. He at least believed what he was saying.

'How does it work, this dimension bomb thing?'

Gar-ran pressed more buttons on the console and a new picture appeared on the screen – an exploded view of the orb, the four segments split apart to reveal what looked like a crystal encased in silver mesh.

'The golden outer case is highly conductive. It protects the power stone within. When activated, if it detonates within a close radius of the demon, it will create a counter-portal and Mephango will be sucked through and back into his own dimension, hopefully forever this time.'

Tim nodded slowly. It was worse than he thought. He was stuck in a nightmare. The key question still nagged at him though.

'But, why do you need me? You've got Nerissa, and this ship and everything.' Surely Gar-ran didn't *really* need his help?

Gar-ran held out the relic, which Tim took. Again, he felt the faint tremor running through the metal as if it was a living thing.

'Since you found it, have you had any strange dreams or visions?'

Tim shook his head but then remembered the recurring dream of the last few nights.

'Well yeah, but it was nothing to do with the relic.' He wasn't keen on where the conversation was going.

'Tell me what happened,' Gar-ran said, leaning forward.

'Well ... the last few nights I've had this dream where I was running through a desert, towards something, but I can never see what it is. Then I wake up. It's just a stupid dream.'

The marshal didn't reply at first. He closed his eyes, nodding to himself.

'I think it might be more than that, Tim. After Mephango was defeated the dimension project was wound down and eventually the surviving bombs were decommissioned in case they ended up in the wrong hands. However, there was a persistent rumour that a few prototypes still existed, and were either sold to private collectors for enormous sums, or dismantled and the parts hidden at secret locations. Over the years though they fell out of the historical record and nobody is certain where they are.'

'But what's that go to do with my dream?' *Get to the point,* Tim wanted to shout. He could feel the anger building in him again, a burning throb that made his chest feel tight. What right had this old guy to kidnap him and bring him here and interrogate him like this? He squeezed the armrests of his chair until his hands ached, and forced himself to listen.

'I'm coming to that now,' Gar-ran continued, and Tim detected a touch of irritation. 'It was also rumoured that the engineers who designed the bomb built into it a special nanotechnology, a program that could imbed itself in whoever found a missing segment. This technology contained an imprint or virtual map of the location of the other pieces. This information could be revealed under hypnosis, through a dream, or in a vision. Ridiculous as it may seem, the culture that produced this bomb was highly advanced.'

Tim dropped the relic. The clang as it hit the floor sounded loud in the hushed room. He waggled his tingling fingers as the awful thought bloomed in his head. Was he poisoned? The idea of something imbedded in him sounded horrible.

'I don't think it's harmful. It's meant to assist whoever needs to find the other pieces,' Gar-ran said briskly.

Realisation thudded into Tim and he felt dizzy, as if something heavy had whacked him around the head. 'So … you want me to help you find the other pieces? This is why you've brought me here then?'

'Yes.'

'I can't do this.' He went to stand up but his legs were wobbling again, so he sat down quickly.

Gar-ran opened his mouth to speak but Nerissa got in first, her face filling the viewing screen again.

'Tim, I know this is hard to take in, but one way or another the remaining pieces must be found before it's too late. The demon can't be allowed to come again, and whoever wants to summon him must be stopped too. We believe you're the only one who can really help us.'

She sounded so earnest and appealing that Tim hated what he had to say. 'Nerissa, I don't know what you think I can do, but I'm just a kid; I'm not old enough to drive yet, let alone try and save the world. I can't do this.'

'You're more capable than you know, but we're not asking you to decide now, this instant. We know this is hard.'

'Yes, you don't have to decide tonight,' Gar-ran chimed in. 'This has been overwhelming, of course. I'll take you back home now, but please, say nothing of this. I'll be on the beach at 3 p.m. on Sunday afternoon and you can give me your answer then, and if it's no, we'll come up with another plan.'

An enormous flood of relief surged through Tim, but as he jumped up, another thought pounced into his brain.

'Hang on a minute. You said there's a time limit to deal with this thing, but to find other the other pieces could take ages, months even.'

'We don't have that sort of time. We must be back before the full moon,' Gar-ran said, plucking the relic from the floor. He offered it to Tim.

'No, you keep it.'

'I believe a lot of the answers we'll need are in there,' Gar-ran said, gently tapping Tim's head. 'I've also done some research and I've a theory of where we can start. It won't be easy, but important things never are.' He smiled and moved to the pilot's chair.

'Now, I'll take us down.' He pressed a sequence of buttons on the command console and the viewing screen showed the outside world again. Tim saw they were descending fast.

'What if someone sees us?'

'They can't. Nerissa has engaged the cloaking shield.'

Tim gawked at the viewing screen. *I'm on an invisible spaceship.* He wondered if he would see Nerissa again before he left.

As they touched down, he thought of something else.

'What about my parents? I couldn't just disappear on them.' He felt guilty for even starting to believe in this mad scheme. All he had to do was get back in his house and not go near the beach for a few days.

'I have a plan for that.' Gar-ran spun his chair round to face him. 'You're about to go away to the sports camp, aren't you?'

'Hey, how did you know that?'

'I made some investigations. I had to.' Gar-ran stood and gestured towards the door.

Now that it was time to go, Tim's head was bursting with questions and ideas. Could this still be a fantastic trick? What really happened to the missing people in Snowdonia? And how would he ever go to sleep again?

'You've got a lot to think about, I know.' From one of the pockets on his belt Gar-ran produced a small, pale, pebble-sized stone. It had a hole in one end which was threaded through with a leather cord.

'Take this amulet; you might find it useful.'

Tim waved it away. 'Necklaces are for girls.'

Gar-ran laughed and offered it again. 'Amulets are different.'

Tim took it reluctantly and gasped as the stone glowed bright blue.

'Blue when you're with friends, red for danger,' Gar-ran explained.

'I can keep this?'

'Yes, it's yours.'

Tim grinned and nodded his thanks. He had a great idea of how he could test it.

'Now I'm hoping you'll never need it, but take this too.' Gar-ran held out a white, disc-shaped object and passed it to Tim.

It was heavier than it looked and felt like if it was made of hardened resin. In the centre was a small, recessed button.

'Press the button twice and it will send a signal to me and I'll come immediately. You probably won't need it, but just in case.'

Tim stared at the device, unimpressed.

'Goodbye Tim. Nice to meet you.' Nerissa's smiling face appeared once more.

'Bye,' Tim replied, feeling his cheeks redden. Gar-ran escorted him back to the cream-coloured room and clasped him on the shoulder.

'You're free to go. Just walk back through the wall of light. It's quite safe, I promise.'

Feeling dazed, Tim turned towards the shining wall. Before stepping through, he looked back at Gar-ran, who was calmly watching. Then, closing his eyes, he walked forward into the light. Within a moment he felt the damp grass beneath his feet and stood before his wide-open bedroom window. He spun round but the garden was empty.

Shivering, he quickly climbed up into his room and, after stowing the amulet and disc in the drawer of his bedside table, he dived into bed and cocooned himself in the duvet. Sleep seemed impossible; there was too much racing through his mind. He tossed and turned trying to make sense of it all until at last he drifted off. His last conscious thought was of Nerissa.

***

The designer sat patiently in his workshop waiting for his spy to arrive. Presently, there was the faint tell-tale buzz and the hornet shot through the open window and gracefully landed on his open palm. He pressed the midsection of the creature's thorax and a tiny SD card ejected itself. The hornet immediately took off and flew to its charging station on the wall above.

The designer smiled as he watched its flight. Even with his limited resources he could still create something beautiful *and* functional.

He turned his attention back to the SD card. The previous footage of the boy had been useless. Hopefully this latest film would be better. If not, he might have to make a personal visit.

Four
Slothra

Tim woke early. He'd had a restless night and, for a moment or two after waking, he wondered if the whole time on Gar-ran's ship had been just a nightmare. He heard footsteps in the hall, probably his mum getting up, and remembered the amulet. Yanking open the drawer of his bedside cabinet, he saw the stone was glowing bright blue.

It still worked! He held it up to the light but couldn't see any mechanism or inner workings. Where could he keep it safely? Maybe, if he kept it on him, in his jeans' pocket or somewhere. There was no way he could wear it round his neck. For now, he hid it in a sock and pushed it to the back of the drawer.

Yawning heavily, he opened his curtains and stared at himself in the wall mirror. He frowned. As far as he could see, he didn't look any different to the day before. Definitely not like someone who had gone through a life-changing experience just hours before. His thick, dark, curly hair was getting long, his lower arms and neck were still more tanned than the rest of his body and his face had the same alert expression.

Inside, though, it was quite different: he could feel himself veering between excitement and unease.

If only he could tell someone about what had happened. His dad, Josh, anyone. Would Gar-ran let him keep the amulet afterwards, he wondered. Afterwards? He hadn't properly decided whether he would go, or could go, yet. The whole idea scared him. What if he did decide to go and something happened to Gar-ran? Or the ship itself? What if Nerissa had some kind of meltdown and they were stranded?

On the other hand, this was a chance to do something amazing, something no one had ever done before. He could help stop that demon thing appearing. He shivered as he remembered the thing's awful, blackened face. *Don't think about it. Think about something else, breakfast, anything.* He didn't really feel hungry but being in the kitchen with his mum was better than staying up here worrying.

***

The designer sat alone in his secure office. No one knew about this place and that suited him. What he was about to do was risky. If the broadcast was intercepted, they'd be able to track him down, but it was a risk worth taking. The footage from his spy hornet was incomplete but that had only heightened his curiosity. Something highly unusual was happening and it was all to do with that artefact the boy had found. There was something familiar about it, something he couldn't quite put his finger on.

He'd decided against a personal visit. Much better to keep his distance and send a specialist. The light above his monitor glowed white and he leant forward to adjust the signal. The screen shimmered before clearing. The resolution wasn't perfect but, considering the distance it was being transmitted from, it was good enough.

He concentrated on not showing his distaste as the creature moved forward and bowed his head. It was a token show of humility, of course; the creature hadn't become the most feared bounty hunter in three sectors by kowtowing. Still, it showed a certain respect; they hadn't forgotten who he was, or what he was capable of.

So, this was the infamous Slothra. On first acquaintance the designer was glad there was a long distance separating them. Slothra oozed malevolence, and he was as hideous as he'd been described. Bigger too. At least seven and a half feet tall. The thick brown pelt that covered his body looked damp and ragged and infested with something. The designer peered closer at the screen but still couldn't tell what the tiny, scurrying creatures were. Moths perhaps. He wondered how many more were trapped under the thick chest armour the beast wore.

The creature scratched its neck lazily, displaying a good view of its savagely sharp claws, but to the designer's eye the bounty hunter's most chilling feature was its face. Those huge, oval opaque eyes which lacked irises and appeared blank, but subtly changed colour, giving them a mesmeric quality. That, combined with the tiny snout and that huge slit-like mouth with its chipped, yellowing fangs, was more than enough to scare the life out of the toughest cases. He was perfect for the job.

The designer smiled, and then spoke out in the Galadrian language which apparently the creature would understand.

'So, we are agreed then? You will apprehend the boy and the item I mentioned and bring them to me. There is no time to waste. And of course, you must not be seen.'

The creature nodded his assent and made an excited rasping sound. A few drops of black spittle tricked down the fur of its chin and the designer repressed a grimace.

'For this you will receive a double payment in the usual manner.'

The creature bowed its head. The designer leant over and switched off the screen. He slumped back into his leather chair, surprised at the relief he felt. His plan was so close to fruition. Nothing must stop it. Nothing would stop it. He poured himself a generous measure from the decanter on his desk. He would soon have his answers.

***

Tim was looking forward to the evening ahead. He would think about his big decision in the morning. Right now he needed a few worry-free hours. He was going to hang out with his best mate, Josh. They'd fire up the X-box and play *Destiny* and later watch the horror film that Josh's brother Shane had downloaded: *Dead Meat 2*. Tim hadn't seen the first one but Josh said it wouldn't matter.

The Saturday night ritual involved a trip to the local shop to get coke, juice, biscuits and crisps. It was just starting to drizzle as they came out of the shop. Tim put the bag containing the huge bottle of coke down for a moment while he zipped his jacket up.

'Let's cut across the field; it's going to bucket down,' Josh said as he pulled the hood of his jacket up. The field was at the end of the road and if they cut through it would save them several minutes' walk. Tim hesitated for a moment; he didn't know why, but tonight he didn't feel like taking the quicker router, even though it was raining.

'It'll be muddy. I don't want to mess up my trainers,' he said.

'Don't be a wuss, it's only a bit of drizzle.' Josh stalked on ahead. Tim tutted to himself and followed. They sped up as the rain increased, crossed the road and the field was ahead of them. Further away from the street lights, it seemed a lot darker, and Tim slowed down.

'Come on, keep up.' Josh strode ahead.

'Maybe we should stick to the road.'

'I'm not going all the way back there.' Josh was already twenty feet further along.

Tim was feeling more and more nervous with each step. It didn't make sense as he'd lost count of the times he and Josh had taken this shortcut. He kept thinking about what the marshal had said about him being in danger. He'd never asked him why. Why would he be in danger?

By now they were in the middle of the field. Josh had stopped and was looking at something ahead. A gust of wind blew rain into Tim's face and he shivered. On impulse he pulled the amulet out of his pocket. *Oh no, not now.* It was glowing a fierce red. There was a cry and Josh was knocked backwards. Fear seized Tim and he wanted to run away, but he stopped himself, and ran towards his friend. Something massive struck him and sent him tumbling sideways.

He tried to sit up but couldn't. A shadow fell across him and, trembling, he looked up. For a second he thought he had been attacked by a huge bear, and felt more surprise than fear. *What would a bear be doing here anyway?* But the thing that looked down on him was much worse. Every sense screamed at him to run, but he couldn't seem to move his legs. Then the creature opened his mouth.

Five
Hunted

T he sight of the beast's fangs galvanised Tim.
He scrabbled backwards, frantically digging
into his pockets for the disc Gar-ran had given
him. Behind the beast he saw Josh was up and
staggering towards him.

'No, stay back!'

The creature made an odd rasping sound and
Tim had the crazy idea that it was laughing.

He watched, horrified, as Josh lurched towards
the beast and clumsily swung his bag in a wide arc
towards its head. The creature parried the blow easily,
his claws shredding the flimsy plastic and sending
crisps and biscuits flying everywhere. Seeing a
chance, Tim snatched the big coke bottle and
smashed it into the beast's face just as it turned
towards him. The bottle exploded as it connected,
covering them both in the fizzy liquid.

Tim darted towards Josh, bracing himself for the
retaliation which must surely come any second now;
once the beast got its claws into him, it would be all

over. But the attack didn't come. He looked back and the thing was on its hands and knees, spluttering and clutching its throat.

Josh was frozen to the spot; Tim grabbed his arm.

'Come on! We've got to go. Move it!'

They hurtled across the field, but where could they go? Not home. What if the thing tracked them? Panic welled in Tim's chest. He looked back; it was still down. The beach! Yes, that would be better. He knew all the nearby coastline. There were even caves where they could hide. He turned to Josh.

'We can't go home, that thing will follow us. We can hide on the beach.'

Josh nodded dumbly. Together they ran on, nearly slipping in the mud at the edge of the field. There was a gap in the hedge. It wasn't big but they could get through it one at a time. Tim pushed Josh through and quickly followed. A bramble scratched his neck and he winced but didn't stop.

Ahead was Pelham Lane and at the far end was a footpath down to the beach. They sprinted towards it. As they began to descend the slope there was a roar from behind them, the sound of a huge, wounded beast bellowing with rage and pain. The boys bolted down the path, nearly tripping over one another in the mud and darkness. The path became so overgrown they couldn't see where they were going and were forced to stop. A couple of wrong steps and they'd be tumbling down the embankment onto the rocks below.

Josh was frantic. 'Come on! We can't stay here!'

'We need to see where we're going,' Tim replied, thinking hard.

The moon was still hidden behind cloud and it was darker than ever. Josh pulled out his phone. The illuminated screen lit a little of the area ahead of them.

'Yes, that's it!' Tim said.

He turned on his phone's torch app and they could see the path now. They raced on. As they reached the beach, they heard the beast roar again. It sounded closer.

'The cave by the sailing club,' Tim said, his voice ragged and high-pitched. 'Come on.'

The beach was a mixture of pebbles and sand, and the clatter of their steps and their rough, ragged breathing sounded deafening to Tim as they pounded along. The cave was in sight now, but then Josh went down hard. He tried to stand but his leg wouldn't support him. They had been so close! Tim felt he could cry with the frustration. He tried not to show it as he helped his friend up.

'I'm sorry, I was trying …'

'It's OK.' Tim helped him up. Josh tried to take a couple of steps but stumbled, yelling with the pain.

The cave was out of the question. Tim scanned the surrounding area; it was desolate apart from a couple of upturned rowing boats. The nearest one was about twelve feet long.

'That boat. We could hide underneath,' he whispered to Josh.

Josh looked doubtful. 'Do you think it's still coming?'

Tim felt terrible that he'd gotten his friend into this situation. If only he hadn't climbed down the cliff that day, none of this would have happened. Where was Gar-ran? Would he come? He forced himself to stay calm. They were wasting time just standing there. He stole a quick look at the amulet, which still glowed blood red.

'What's that?' Josh asked.

'We have to hide, quick. And keep your voice down.' Tim helped Josh over to the boat then squatted down and took hold of the gunwale. The boat was chained at one end to an iron peg but if he could lift the bow, they could slide underneath. He tensed and lifted but it was lighter than expected and came up easily.

'In there?' Josh asked.

'There's nowhere else.'

Josh looked back along the beach then slowly eased himself down and slipped beneath the boat.

Tim waited for a moment, listening, then ducked under. They huddled together. Tim listened intently but could hear nothing except the soft thrash of the waves breaking on the shore. He wondered how long they'd have to crouch there in the darkness.

The minutes dragged by and Tim felt sick with tension. Josh had gone very quiet. Where the hell was Gar-ran? He pressed the alarm signaller again. Beside him he could feel Josh tense and prayed his friend would be able to keep quiet. Another minute crawled by and the sweat began to trickle down Tim's neck, making it itch.

Something smashed down through the hull, narrowly missing Josh's leg, and they both yelled out. Two huge paws ripped the damaged planking apart and the beast towered over them. Josh was screaming and Tim reached out to him while never taking his eyes off the thing.

Then a brilliant white light covered them, the beasts head snapped up and it leapt over the boat. Tim watched, astonished at how quickly it covered the ground.

It was nearly out of view when the beach ahead erupted and Tim clamped his hands over his ears against the ear-splitting boom. The beast was thrown high into the air, before crashing down against the cliff face. Bits of shell and pebble fragments rained down on it as Tim stared in awe. Patches of the thing's fur were burnt and smouldering but it was still alive. It dragged itself up and threw a small canister down. Immediately, thick grey smoke engulfed it, billowing out like a cloud that had fallen to earth.

'Tim!' The voice rang out, making him jump and he turned to see Gar-ran running towards him carrying what looked like a big gun.

'Gar-ran! Where is it? Where's the thing?'

'He's gone. You're safe now. Are you hurt?'

'No, but my friend …'

'Look!' Josh pointed upward. Forty feet above them Gar-ran's ship hung in the air. No longer disguised, it resembled an enormous silver beetle: sleek, powerful, and deadly.

'Is that how it really looks?' Tim asked. It was nothing like he imagined it would be, but it was still amazing.

'Yes. I'm sorry I took so long; I was far away when I got the signal. Are you all right?' Gar-ran looked pale and worried.

'I think so, but my friend is hurt.'

'I can treat him on board. Let's go.' Gar-ran raised his hand and the Scarab swiftly descended.

'Wait. Who are you?' Josh said.

'I'll explain later, but for now we need to get you treated. I have good medical facilities on board.'

50

Already the ship was touching down. A doorway opened and a wide ramp slid out, scraping against the wet shingle.

'What is this? Tim, what's going on?'

Tim could hear the panic rising in his friend and went over to him.

'It's all right, I'll explain when we get on board.' Tim wanted to get as far away from the beach as possible; the thing, whatever it was, might come back, and other people must have heard the explosions. Probably the police and coastguard were already on their way.

'I'm not going on there.' Josh sat back down, nursing his injured leg.

'It's OK, really. I know this guy. He's all right, he'll help us. I'll explain but we have to go, now,' Tim urged.

Josh opened his mouth to protest but there was a shout from the clifftop, making them all jump. Josh held out his hand and Tim pulled him up. Gar-ran led the way and they shuffled up the ramp and into the Scarab.

Tim followed Gar-ran into a room he hadn't seen before. It was set up like a laboratory. Gar-ran helped Josh into a reclining lounge chair made from white leather, then opened the cabinets above and took out an oblong foil packet the size of a paperback book and a small silver jar. He tore the packet open and wiped the blood and sand from Josh's face. Then, from the jar, he applied a clear paste to Josh's head cut. He flinched at first, but then relaxed.

'This will help it heal.'

'It's gonna mess up my hair.'

Gar-ran and Tim both laughed at this, Tim as much from relief than anything.

'It's not that bad at all. Looks worse than it is. You were lucky; not many people escape Slothra,' Gar-ran said, wiping his hands on a small towel.

Tim and Josh exchanged glances. Tim spoke first.

'Is that what it's called? The thing that attacked us? Who is he?'

'He's a bounty hunter.'

The boys looked at each other again. Tim wished he hadn't asked. Gar-ran looked grim.

'Now tell me what happened.'

Tim related the whole story of the attack to Gar-ran, with Josh chipping in as well.

'I'm glad I got to you in time. I wish though I could have finished him off. Nerissa's trying to track him, but nothing so far. It was clever of you to use that bottle as a weapon. He must have had an allergic reaction to the liquid, that's why he collapsed. That was lucky, but you're both very brave to even think about taking him on.' Gar-ran smiled.

'What now?' Tim said. He didn't feel brave at all.

'Now it's time we got you both home. Your parents will be wondering what's happened to you.'

'Oh, but can't we have a look around your ship? Could you fire one of the cannons again? And why was that thing ...'

Gar-ran cut Josh off.

'Sit down a moment, you've been injured. You can't jump around.' Reluctantly, Josh sat down again.

'There's one more thing I need to check. Because you were hit on the head, I need to check your vision.'

'I can see fine.'

'Nonetheless, I need to make sure. Now stand in front of this screen, and in a moment, I want you to tell me what symbols you can see. Tim, do you remember the way back to the command hub? Good. Please ask Nerissa if she's making any progress.'

Tim dashed out.

Gar-ran led Josh to the viewing screen at the end of the room.

'Now keep watching the screen and in a moment tell me what symbols you can see.'

Gar-ran moved to the table in the centre of the room and activated the control panel. The screen in front of Josh lit up and a series of small symbols began to appear.

'Now Josh, tell me what you see.'

'There's a cross, a squiggle thing, a hexagon.' Josh paused; it was hard to concentrate. The symbols flickered and pulsed before him. He began to feel very calm and relaxed and forgot to describe what he was seeing, but it was all right because the old man didn't seem to mind.

Tim darted back into the lab. Josh was back on the lounge chair.

'She said she tracked him for half a mile then he completely vanished.' He realised Josh was still staring into space with a dreamy expression on his face.

'Josh? Hey, what's going on? What's happened?' Tim glared at Gar-ran.

'He's in a hypnotic trance. I had no choice; he's seen too much. When I take you back, he won't remember what happened tonight.'

'You can't just do that!' Tim was appalled.

'Tim, think! It would be dangerous for both of you, and your families, if people knew the truth. They might not believe you, but it's not worth taking the risk.

Others may come. Do you understand? It's far better if just you and I know what really happened tonight.'

'But … but what are we going to say.'

'Listen.' Gar-ran sat down next to Josh. 'Josh, this is what happened tonight. As you took the shortcut across the field you met a group of older boys. They wanted to see what was in your bags. You refused to show them. One boy pushed you over and the others turned on Tim. You went to help him. Tim swung the bottle at the biggest boy, knocking him over. In the confusion you and Tim ran off. The boys chased after you. You took the footpath to the beach to try to hide, but you slipped and fell down, banging your head and twisting your ankle. You hid on the beach. Afterwards, Tim helped you home. You were never here and you never met me. This ship doesn't exist. Now, you will tell this story in your own words to your parents or, and this is very important, to anyone else who asks. Do you understand?'

'Sure.' Josh smiled. He looked calm and relaxed, which was more than Tim was feeling.

'Good boy. Now lie down and rest. Soon you'll be home.'

Gar-ran stood up. 'It has to be this way, Tim.'

'I wish I could tell him. I wish he could be part of this.'

'I know.'

A new thought crossed Tim's mind. 'That bounty hunter thing, was he after me or you?'

'Both of us. Someone must have been watching us.'

Tim's stomach flipped over. 'Do you know who?'

'Not yet. Not for sure. It's a long story Tim; I'll tell you another time perhaps. We need to get you and Josh home now.'

Tim wanted to ask more but he could see Gar-ran wasn't in the mood for further discussion.

'Is Josh going to be all right?

'Yes, he'll be fine. Come with me to the command hub.' Gar-ran walked quickly out of the lab. Tim lingered for a moment. He felt guilty his friend had been hurt.

Things were happening so fast. When he got to the command hub, Gar-ran was sat in the far chair. Tim took the chair next to him.

'Brace yourself.' Gar-ran said as he pressed various coloured buttons on the panel.

Restraining belts wrapped across Tim's chest made him yelp. Nerissa's face appeared on the viewing screen.

'I'm glad you're OK Tim,' she said, giving him a little smile.

'Uh, thanks,' Tim mumbled, feeling himself blush again.

They soared upwards. The G-force squashed Tim further and further into his chair as if some enormous hand was pressing him down. He was sure he would rip out through the other side, but the chair held together and gradually the pressure began to ease. He looked across at Gar-ran and saw the belts around him disappear back into the chair. A moment later, Tim's belts dissolved too. Gar-ran leant forward and pressed more buttons on the control panel.

'If people see the ship as it really is, they'll freak out. They'll think it's a UFO,' Tim said.

'They won't. I've engaged the cloaking shield. They'll only see what I want them to,' Gar-ran replied.

'Now I'll drop you by Pelham Lane. Do you have your phone?' Tim nodded. 'Call Josh's parents, and explain what's happened and ask them to pick you up. I'll wait until they come.'

'All right.'

They touched down and Tim sighed with relief. Gar-ran turned to him.

'Now go and get Josh and meet me in the first room.'

Josh was still calm and relaxed. *Too relaxed*, Tim thought as he helped him along. He glared at Gar-ran as they moved into the first chamber.

'Don't worry; once you're outside he'll be fine. Tim, don't feel you have to make any decision tonight about coming with me. The important thing tonight is to get you both back safely,' Gar-ran said.

'Do you think Slothra will come back?' Tim voiced the question that had been gnawing away at him.

'Not while I'm around,' Gar-ran replied, looking stern.

The door opened with a soft clunk and Tim's chest tightened. Even though he knew Gar-ran would have disguised the ship, he still felt anxious. It was all too weird: spaceships, alien monsters, cloaking devices. The door closed behind and as Tim turned, he gave a little gasp of amazement. The Scarab was now disguised as an old camper van.

'Let's phone my parents. I can't go any further,' Josh piped up, making Tim jump.

'OK, good idea.' *Just as Gar-ran said,* Tim thought.

Josh pulled out his phone and dialled. It had mostly stopped raining but a few light drops spattered the screen.

'Mum, it's me. We … got into some trouble on the way back. Tim's with me. Can you pick us up?'

Josh's dad arrived a few minutes later. Tim was so pleased to see him, he felt like crying. He looked back as they drove off. The camper van was still there.

Six
Decision

Tim lay awake in his bed. It was long past midnight but sleep was far away again. Josh's mum had called just as he got into bed. The local hospital was keeping him in overnight as a precaution but he should be able to go home tomorrow. Tim felt horribly guilty. Of course, he couldn't have known the attack was going to happen and they'd been able to get away, but that was mainly down to luck, he felt. *If Gar-ran hadn't arrived ...*

He leant over to check the time on his phone. It was still hours away from the morning and tomorrow he'd have to tell Gar-ran his decision. There was no way he was going to go. The marshal would have to find someone else, some orphan kid with no friends or family. Someone older, braver. He got out of bed and drew back the curtain. Outside it was still raining and the cloud meant few stars were visible. He stood there gazing up though for some time before getting back into bed. In the morning he'd go to see Josh. He turned over, pulled the duvet tight around him and lay still until he drifted off.

'Tim, Tim!' Dimly, he became aware of some distant banging. For a moment he couldn't think where he was, what day or time it was, or where the banging was coming from. He staggered out of bed and opened the bedroom door. His mum called from downstairs.

'Tim, Yvonne just called. They just got back from the hospital with Josh.'

'What time is it?' he shouted back as adrenaline surged through him, driving the sleepy-headed feeling away.

'Oh, I don't know, after ten.'

'Ten?' He looked at the landing window. Broad daylight was streaming in. It didn't seem five minutes since he closed his eyes. He lurched back into his room to get dressed.

Twenty minutes later he was out the door and on his way to Josh's house. He usually rode his bike but today he wanted more time to collect his thoughts, so decided to walk. Just before he stepped out, his mum had collared him and made him promise never to take another shortcut. Tim had been taken back by the force of his mum's concern. He hated having to lie to her but he could hardly explain the truth about last night; his parents would never let him out again, even if they believed him, of course.

The closer he got to Josh's house the more nervous Tim felt. What if Josh had remembered what really happened? What if he blamed him? He stood outside the front door and took a deep breath. The door swung open before he could knock.

'Hi Tim, I saw you coming up the path. Come in. Mum, Tim's here!' Josh called out.

Yvonne, Josh's mum, came out of the living room. She was a tall, slim lady with shoulder-length brown hair. She was always friendly but today looked pale and fretful. Tim tensed up. What did she know?

'Hello Tim. How are you doing?'

'Oh, I'm OK thanks. A bit tired.'

'I bet. I don't think any of us got much sleep last night. Still, things are all right now. Would you like a cup of tea or squash?'

'Oh, I'm fine thanks; just had breakfast.'

'OK.' She smiled and headed back into the front room.

That wasn't too bad, Tim thought as he watched her go.

'Let's go up to my room,' Josh said.

Josh's room was on the first floor and he leant heavily on the banister as he hobbled up the stairs. He flopped down on the bed and Tim sat in the computer chair.

'What did the doctor say?'

'Not much. I had to have a couple of stiches and they said they wanted to keep me in overnight to check everything's OK in here,' Josh said, tapping his head.

'You should have told them it's too late for that,' Tim quipped. They both laughed and Tim relaxed a little.

'My knee hurts a bit but it's not as swollen.'

'What was the hospital like?'

'Depressing. I didn't like it. One of the nurses was fit though, but I didn't get to see much of her. Anyway, thanks for helping me. Did you know any of those boys?'

For a second, Tim couldn't think what his friend meant. Then he remembered the cover story Gar-ran had suggested. 'No, no, I'd never seen them before.'

'My brother reckons we were lucky not to get our heads kicked in.' Josh winced as he straightened his leg.

'He's probably right.' Josh's older brother, Shane, considered himself an authority on most things.

'We'll have to watch the film when you get back from camp. Dad wants us to have a family night.'

'Yeah, sure.' Josh seemed as normal as ever and Tim felt he could actually breathe again. Some of his guilt began to dissipate, although a darker thought crept in: would Gar-ran have to brainwash him too at some point?

They played *Portal 2* and chatted for a bit before Tim headed back home. He thought everything out on the walk back home. Seeing Josh had made things easier.

Later, he clipped Frankie's lead on and headed out towards the beach. He saw Gar-ran from some way off, although he looked totally different in regular clothes, instead of his flight suit. Despite his mounting anxiety, Tim couldn't help smiling. Gar-ran wore chinos, deck shoes and smart, dark blue polo shirt. He looked like any paid-up member of the sailing club. Tim wondered where the Scarab was now. Gar-ran was staring out to sea, but turned as he approached. Frankie pulled at the lead and wagged his tail as he sniffed Gar-ran's shoe, something that Tim took to be a good sign.

'You live in a beautiful part of the world,' Gar-ran said, patting Frankie's head.

Tim nodded. He'd planned what to say, but now the time had come, his carefully rehearsed excuses seemed weak and childish. He did have one big question though.

'Did you really mean everything you said the other night about what could happen if this demon thing comes through? Where does he come from anyway?'

'Yes I meant it,' Gar-ran said sharply. 'Mephango thrives on chaos, and death and destruction; human sufferings would mean nothing to him. He would enjoy it. He draws his power from the life energy around him, and every death he causes only increases his power. Where he truly comes from no one knows, but just as there are many different worlds in our system, the Milky Way, there's some evidence there are other dimensions, perhaps alternative worlds that co-exist alongside us, places that we're never meant to see. I believe he comes from such a place.'

Tim shivered and kicked at a pebble. He hated talk like this, which seemed so wrong on such a warm, sunny day.

'But why do we really need the bomb? You've got weapons on your ship. It's powerful. If something bad comes through the portal you mentioned, can't you just fire on it, like you did to Slothra?'

Gar-ran shook his head. 'I wish it could be that simple. Mephango is a primeval force. He can't truly be destroyed; ordinary weapons won't work against him. He can absorb their power. The assembled bomb is the only thing proven to work. If it's charged and strikes him cleanly, the energy released will trigger another portal which will force him back to whatever dimension he comes from. Hopefully forever this time. I wish none of this was necessary, but it is.' He gave Tim a bleak smile.

'You never told me what happened to the boy, that apprentice Terry or whatever you called him. What happened to him?' Tim was half afraid to hear the answer. What if it was something really bad?

'Terius. He survived. He was a hero to his people. He lived a good life. So all the old accounts say.'

Tim looked out over the sea. He wished Nerissa were here too. A few gulls had come down onto the water and the small yachts moored farther out rolled lightly in the tide swell.

'I made up my mind last night not to come. I was scared after what happened. But today I've been thinking a lot. If I don't come with you, if I did nothing, it could be worse. That bounty hunter or someone like him would come again, wouldn't they? We were lucky last night he didn't get both of us. That could have been my sister, or my mum and dad. So, I've decided I'm coming with you. If you really think I can help?'

Gar-ran didn't reply at first; he just looked at Tim as if making an assessment. It wasn't the reaction Tim had been expecting and he shuffled his feet and fidgeted under the older man's steady gaze.

'I do. Having you on board is going to make all the difference, and I'd be very glad to have you with me. But are you sure, Tim?'

'Yes, I think … it just feels right. I can't really explain it, but it feels like the right thing to do. But what do we do about my parents? I can't just take off.'

'I have a plan for that.'

Tim expected Gar-ran to elaborate, but he remained silent.

'So what happens now?' Tim prompted.

'You'd be due to leave for the sports camp on Tuesday, correct? Well that will give me some time to make a few arrangements. There's quite a bit to discuss. Do you have time now?

'Yes.'

'Good.'

They walked further along the beach and Tim's eyes widened as Gar-ran outlined his plan. It seemed incredible, but the way Gar-ran explained things, it might just work.

***

Typical. Just when he'd sat down. David Traylor sighed as he stared at the scrambled picture on the TV. He'd been looking forward to a quiet hour with his wife watching *Countryfile* but, just as they'd gotten comfortable, the set decided to go haywire.

'I'll check the aerial,' David said with a sigh, but as he went to stand up, he found he couldn't move. He was transfixed by the screen that now glowed blue and the strange, wondrous symbols that appeared on it. Then the voice spoke to him and Beth: a man's voice, rich and deep. David smiled. It was a nice, soothing voice, and he found he wanted to hear what it was saying. The voice introduced himself as Gar-ran and explained he had something important to say.

Sometime later the TV flickered and resumed its original broadcast. David woke with a start and stared bleary-eyed at the screen. He checked his watch and turned to his wife, who was dozing next to him.

'Beth, wake up, we're missing it.'

Beth's eyes blinked open and, smiling, she sat up.

'Sorry, have we missed much?'

***

Tim lay on his bed wondering if Gar-ran's plan had worked. It seemed crazy, but then the last few days had been mad. What would tomorrow bring? One day to go.

Seven
Into Space

Monday was a funny day. Some of it went by really quickly while other parts of the day seemed to drag on and on. He spent some time at the beach and hung out with Josh, who was definitely on the mend, and in the evening his dad took them all out to dinner at The Starfish, a restaurant by the harbour. Tim wasn't really hungry but ate anyway. He slept better than he thought he would and awoke early.

After a family breakfast he hugged his mum and sister and headed off with his dad to the train station. Driving along in the car next to his dad, he had an almost overwhelming urge to tell him what was really going on. His father sensed his mood.

'Are you OK, Tim? You're very quiet.'

Tim knew this was his chance to explain what was really going on but, as he started to speak, he found himself stalling. What could he say, really? It would sound nuts. He didn't want his dad to think he was going weird.

'Ah … I … I'm just going to miss being at home, that's all.' He looked out of the window, not able to meet his dad's eye.

'I know son; we're going to miss you too. I'll know you're going to be too busy to contact us much, but your mum and I will be thinking about you all the time. And Cate too, of course.' He patted Tim's leg reassuringly.

Tim couldn't speak at first. Gar-ran's plan must have worked. His parents had been conditioned to believe what Gar-ran wanted. His dad truly thought it was perfectly fine that he wouldn't be hearing from his son for a while. Part of Tim was relieved the plan had worked, but a bigger part of him was concerned about how easily it had been accomplished. What if Gar-ran had brainwashed him too, but he just didn't realise it? No, that couldn't be; he was sure he was making all his own decisions.

'Uh … sure, I'll be thinking of you as well,' Tim mumbled.

***

Before the train pulled out, his dad slipped him a few extra quid and told him to enjoy himself at the camp. He stayed and waved at Tim through the window as the train left the station. When he was out of sight, Tim slumped back in his seat feeling sick with apprehension. He stared out of the window, lost in his thoughts.

Three stops later he got off. Gar-ran was there to meet him and they dodged past other commuters and holidaymakers and out into the high street before turning off into a quiet side road. The Scarab was parked a little way down, still disguised as a camper van.

Once inside, they went straight to the command hub. Nerissa's face popped up on the viewing screen and she flashed Tim a brilliant smile as she welcomed him. Tim's stomach gave a flutter and he had to remind himself she wasn't actually a real girl.

'How are we going to take off with all these people around?' he asked.

'Don't worry. They won't see a thing.' Gar-ran turned a dial on the control console and the viewing screen instantly displayed what was going on outside.

'We can get a view from all directions,' Gar-ran said, smiling. He pressed a few other buttons. 'OK, we're now invisible to any observers. I'm going to start the ignition sequence. Brace yourself.'

Tim sat down quickly. The automatic seat belts emerged again, pinning him down, and for a second he felt he couldn't breathe. The whole ship began to faintly vibrate and they shot up. The viewing screen was a blur of images as the G-force pushed him deep into his chair. Gradually the pressure eased and he felt the ship slowing. Tim was about to ask what had happened when he looked at the viewing screen and was rendered speechless. Ahead was an endless vast black carpet of space punctuated with more stars than he would ever have thought possible.

He realised the blue curve he could see at the lower edge of the screen was Earth below him.

'Beautiful, isn't it?' Gar-ran said, breaking Tim's reverie.

'We're, we're in space!' Tim said. It seemed utterly incredible, despite the evidence of his own eyes. He jumped up and pressed his face against the viewing screen.

'It's been years since my first flight, but I still love it. No matter what's going on down there, it will always look beautiful from above.' Gar-ran sounded wistful and Tim turned to face him.

'I'm sorry I couldn't prepare you better, but time's against us. Now, we'll stay in orbit for an hour while I show you your quarters and the rest of the ship. Follow me.'

Gar-ran strode out and Tim reluctantly tore himself away from the viewing screen and hurried to catch up. A thought hit him.

'Wait a minute, how come we're not floating around? I thought space was zero gravity.'

'Our ships have had Anti-grav tech for a long time, Tim,' Gar-ran replied casually.

Tim felt a bit cheated; he'd been looking forward to floating about. Gar-ran paused by a large door.

'Place your hand on that square panel next to the door,' he said.

Tim did so and the door whisked open. He stepped into a large room furnished with a round table in the centre framed by four smaller stools and a large cream sofa against the far wall. On the left was a single bed with a small control panel above the pillow end. On the far side of the room, an open door led off to a smaller room.

'If you press the blue button on the panel above the bed, you'll be able to communicate with me, should you wish. The room beyond is your bathroom. The facilities operate automatically.'

'I've got my own room?' Tim was amazed. He hadn't given a lot of thought to his accommodation but had half expected to be crammed into a tiny bunk somewhere.

'Of course; you're a marshal cadet now.' Gar-ran was smiling and Tim wasn't sure if he was joking or not.

'Do I get a badge like yours?'

'One step at a time. Let's continue. My quarters are in the first section before the command hub, but I spend a lot of time in the lab where we treated your friend Josh.'

Where you brainwashed him, Tim thought. He could understand that Gar-ran felt he had no choice, but he hated the idea of someone wiping his own memories. It made him wonder if all this was real or just some memory implanted by Gar-ran. He ran his hands along the smooth wall; it was cool to the touch and felt solid enough. Ahead, Gar-ran slowed.

'Take a look at this,' he said, sliding open a large compartment on the wall to reveal a cache of unusual-looking weapons. There was a fantastic array of high-tech guns, spears and rifles fixed to various shelves.

'Our arsenal. And no, you can't have a pistol yet. The Scarab has its own weapons and defences, of course.'

'Of course,' Tim echoed, convinced at any moment he was going to wake up in his bed at home. It was all too fantastic, and he'd barely been on board an hour yet.

'With all those weapons, you need somewhere to practise, so there's a shooting range on board where you can learn each weapon's characteristics, but that's for another day,' Gar-ran said from over his shoulder as he continued down the corridor.

The final stop was a small, recessed room with complicated-looking circuit boards and diagrams with symbols in strange, scrawling script.

'This is the heart of the ship, so to speak, and elaborate engine room of sorts,' Gar-ran said. 'Right, let's have a little break and then I have a surprise or two for you. Think of today as an orientation day. Tomorrow is when we'll begin the real work.'

They made their way back to what Gar-ran called the galley, and Tim knew now was the time to ask about something which had been on his mind for a while.

'What's your home like, Gar-ran?'

'Big. Three times the size of Earth. Our sun is a yellow dwarf, like your sun, and there are many similarities between our worlds, but it's been a while since I was back there – over eleven years now. The life of a marshal takes you far and wide.'

'Sounds a bit lonely.' Tim wondered how long Gar-ran had been travelling through space, and if he ever had companions. Surely he was getting close to retirement age? Did marshals retire? He wanted to know, but it seemed rude to ask.

'It can be. It's not a life for everyone,' Gar-ran replied, as they turned the corner.

'There's another thing I've been meaning to ask.' Tim paused; he wasn't sure if he really wanted to hear the answer to his next question.

'Why aren't we travelling with other marshals if the stakes are so high and it's a race against time? Surely the more people looking would be better?'

'Yes, it would be, but I've been unable to convince the marshal hierarchy that the threat is genuine, which I'm certain it is. There's a view in some quarters that my being posted to a remote part of the galaxy, away from the more advanced civilisations, has skewed my judgement, and without being able to offer definitive proof, we're on our own for the time being.'

Tim nodded as he mulled over Gar-ran's answer. *They think he's past it, in other words.* Maybe though it was a good thing that it was just them and Nerissa. He wasn't sure if he wanted to keep meeting different aliens. Especially aliens who carried big guns.

'So, who controls the marshals? Do you have to report back to someone?'

'Usually yes, but we often operate autonomously. Ultimately, we're all responsible to the chief marshal, who's responsible to the council of the United Alignment. The way to think of the alignment is as a federation of planets, just like on Earth the United Nations is a federation of nations. It all started over

2,000 years ago. A collective of planets formed to promote trade, exploration and development. Also, peace-keeping, which was the start of the marshal service. The headquarters is actually on Cathrox, my home planet.' Gar-ran smiled as if this was the most natural thing to discuss.

Tim was hanging on to every word. This now was encouraging. It meant that Gar-ran was really part of a bigger agency; he wasn't just some lone wolf rogue agent.

'So how many planets in the alignment? Have you been to them all?'

'No, not all. There's forty-three planets across sixteen systems which are part of the alignment, but there are also lots of other planets who aren't part of the UA, who have their own ideas, a bit like on Earth.' Gar-ran spoke with enthusiasm and Tim could tell he was glad that he was taking an interest.

They stepped into the galley and Tim was astounded to see food he recognised. Packets of cereal, dried fruits, drinking chocolate, crisps, bottles of water and, amazingly, fresh bread.

Gar-ran laughed at his stunned expression.

'I thought I'd get some familiar foods for you so that things will seem less strange and not so overwhelming. I thought we could have some chicken soup and crusty bread?'

'Uh … yeah, great.' Tim took a seat, feeling dazed. Gar-ran had thought of everything. Right then, Tim wanted nothing more than to call his mates and tell them where he was, but then he remembered he was already hundreds of miles away, and there was no way they could share this with him. He felt a pang of loneliness, just like the first time he first went away from home to sports camp. He clenched his fists. He wasn't a little kid any more; he had to deal with this. He had to do what he'd agreed to do, so he could get back home again.

'Have you got a mug with my name on?'

'That could be arranged, but you might have to wait a while,' Gar-ran said with a chuckle.

Tim sipped his soup. It tasted great. At least the food here would be good.

As they ate, Gar-ran outlined his plan for the day.

'While it's important you have a period of acclimatisation, I am going to drop you in the deep end, but only because I think you can handle it.' He paused as he watched Tim's reaction. 'Today we're visiting the moon and Mars.'

Tim spat his soup out, but his smile faded as he realised Gar-ran was serious.

'You are joking, right?'

'Nope. We'll have to go all over in our quest, and we'll end up in some strange places. It's important you get used to it as soon as possible.'

'But what about space suits, and oxygen and all that?'

'We're fully equipped. Come on, I'll show you.'

Tim's legs felt wobbly again as he walked back to the command hub. Things were moving so quickly, there was no time to think. Maybe that was the idea. Perhaps Gar-ran wanted to keep him busy in case he changed his mind and asked to go back. He hesitated in the doorway of the hub. Nerissa's face appeared on the viewing screen smiling at him. Wanting to seem confident, he strutted in and sat down in the co-pilot seat.

Gar-ran hit a button on the console and Earth's moon completely filled the screen. Tim gasped; it was incredible. He'd never seen it in such detail. Some of the craters looked huge, and it looked near enough to touch.

'How close are we?'

'We'll touch down in half an hour. Let's suit up.'

Twenty-five minutes later, they stood in the airlock. Tim wore a bulky white flight suit that just fitted him. He couldn't tell what material it was made of, but he felt very warm. The belt around his waist had numerous pockets. His hands were covered in thick gloves and his heavy boots made walking awkward. The suit had an integrated helmet with a dark blue visor and there was a radio mike clipped behind his ear. A lightweight oxygen pack was fitted to his back. Gar-ran wore an adult version of the same suit.

'OK, ready?' Gar-ran's voice sounded tinny though the microphone.

'Ready,' Tim lied, giving a thumbs up. He didn't know if he could go through with this. The bulkiness of his suit masked the trembling that was running through his whole body but he was sure that when they airlock opened, he'd collapse. He was sweating already and beginning to feel claustrophobic.

'We'll be visiting an area that none of the Apollo missions ever reached,' Gar-ran said, sounding very chipper.

'Really?' Tim mumbled.

The floor tilted slightly as they touched down. Gar-ran disengaged the airlock and carefully they made their way down a ramp onto the surface of the moon. It was darker than Tim had expected and it took a little while for his eyes to adjust. The lunar landscape was eerie when experienced up close. The ship threw long, distorted shadows and the landscape was totally devoid of any colour. It was like living in a black and white film, he thought.

'Where exactly are we?' he asked as he scanned the surrounding area.

'This area of the moon is called The Sea of Vapours, or Mare Vaporum to give its correct name.'

'Is that Latin?' Tim asked.

'Yes. The early astronomers thought there were actually seas on the moon,' Gar-ran answered.

'What? That's stupid,' Tim scoffed. He was beginning to feel better; it was nowhere near as bad as he'd imagined. Looking around at the expanse of flat, rocky terrain, he realised it did actually resemble the sea bed of some enormous ocean. Maybe those old astronomers weren't so crazy after all. He knew it was years since anyone had landed on the moon. The last astronauts had left way before he was born.

He bent down and brushed his hand along the ground. The surface was covered with a light grey powder. He was tempted to write his name, like he used to do in the wet sand of the beach back home, but then his mike crackled again and he realised Gar-ran was watching him.

'How are you doing?'

'Good, I'm good, this is amazing.' He picked up a small rock. It was just the right size to fit into one of his pockets.

'Are you up for little jaunt to that hill?'

Tim turned to where Gar-ran was pointing. A small hill rose up about seventy feet away.

'Sure, let's go.'

With the lower gravity, Tim found it was easier to move in small jumps and hops, and he cracked up when he saw Gar-ran was doing the same. They reached the brow of the hill and Tim saw below was a huge crater, at least 100 feet wide and much deeper than anything he had seen before. He suddenly felt very small and fragile.

'What happened to the meteorite that made this?'

'Vaporised on impact, I expect,' Gar-ran answered. 'This is just a little one.'

'Little?' Tim turned to Gar-ran, but he couldn't see his face behind the visor. How could anyone think this was small?

'The Tyco crater in the southern lunar highlands is fifty miles wide and 15,000 feet deep.' Gar-ran spoke as if he'd read Tim's mind.

Fifty miles wide. Tim could hardly imagine it. He shuddered.

'They think something like that killed the dinosaurs. The dust and debris blotted out the sun. I saw a programme about it at school.'

'Yes, it would kill anything,' Gar-ran replied as he peered down. His matter-of-fact tone made Tim shiver despite his suit's warmth.

'Time to go back, I think.' Gar-ran turned away from the edge and Tim breathed a sigh of relief. He was glad they were going back. It was incredible being there but the whole experience was giving him the creeps. It was too grey, too desolate, *too dead.*

***

'How was that?' Gar-ran asked when they got back into the airlock.

Tim thought for a moment before replying. 'It was amazing, but a bit scary. I kept thinking about what would happen if we fell into that crater, and the whole place is, well, like a big desert.'

Gar-ran nodded. 'Yes, but if we had got in trouble, I would have called Nerissa to get us out.'

'Yeah, I suppose. Are we really going to Mars as well?' Tim could hardly believe what he was asking.

'Yes, that's our next stop. I think you'll enjoy it more.' Gar-ran gave a faint smile.

'But isn't Mars millions of miles away? Won't it take ages to reach there?'

'Not in my ship. We'll be there in three hours.' He turned and calmly strolled ahead. Tim remained behind for a few minutes until he could no longer hear his heart pounding away in his chest, then followed.

***

'So how fast can the Scarab go?' Tim asked. They were back in the command hub, having changed back into their normal clothes.

'Incredibly fast, but we won't be flying there; we'll be making a rift jump. It's much quicker.'

A rift jump? What is he talking about now? Maybe it was something like in *Star Wars* when they make the jump to light speed. That would be fantastic.

Gar-ran cut into his thoughts.

'Sorry, I'm not explaining properly. A rift is a naturally occurring hole, a tear in spacetime. Some are very small, others are huge. These rifts connect two areas of space which are a long way apart. You enter in one side and come out in a totally different area. But only if you have a craft which is capable of navigating the jump and withstanding the forces involved.'

Tim nodded. He understood – just about.

'The rifts were created when the universe first formed billions of years ago. Since then other races have developed a technology which can replicate these rifts so you can travel much further. The one we're using today is a natural one though. Sit down and I'll show you.'

Tim sat down, feeling dazed again. Every time he thought he was getting a handle on things, Gar-ran would come out with some new fact or revelation and the ground would shift beneath him again, as he was forced to reassess everything about the world around him, which until then he'd taken for granted. He wanted to understand, but there was so much to take in.

'But how come NASA or someone hasn't detected this already?'

'It's too small, and I doubt they have anything refined enough to detect it, and even if they did, it would likely be dismissed as an incorrect reading.'

That made sense, Tim thought. He could hardly believe it himself.

'I have the coordinates pre-set already. Now bear with me a moment.' Gar-ran typed a series of commands into the control panel and an image of the solar system appeared on the viewing screen. Tim was about to speak when he felt the straps of his chair enfold him again and he stalled his question.

Gar-ran hit a sequence of buttons then sat back as his chair straps secured him. 'Ready Tim?'

'No, not really. What's actually going to happen?

'We're going to cross a big distance very quickly; this is a natural rift jump, so very little can go wrong. You'll see.'

Tim opened his mouth to object but the cockpit and the whole ship began to tremble and he stopped.

Gar-ran's attention was focused on the viewing screen. Tim looked up at the solar system image; it was distorting then became intensely bright before dimming and fading to black. Tim blinked rapidly to try to clear the spots that floated in front of his eyes. The straps around him released and he relaxed. He'd been holding his breath without realising it.

'Now for the rest of the journey we will fly normally. Nerissa will plot the course and I will have control. There's a lot of space debris here, many fragments of asteroids, meteorites and so on, so I like to see myself what's coming up,' Gar-ran explained.

'Uh, OK, whatever you think is best.' Tim wasn't keen on the idea of crashing into a meteorite, but clearly Gar-ran knew what he was doing, so there wasn't much choice except to sit tight and ride things out.

Three long, tense hours later they entered Mars's orbit. The ship slowed and then came to a halt and they slowly descended the last few metres until, with a gentle bump, they touched down. Gar-ran switched display on the viewing screen and the Martian landscape appeared before them. It was quite dark, but Tim could still make out the famous red hue of the surface.

'Ready?' Gar-ran asked. Tim nodded and jumped up. His nerves had been building for the last hour, and now that they were there, he just wanted to get on with it. He stalked ahead to the airlock. Gar-ran carefully checked both their suits were functioning and, as before, they descended the small ramp to the surface. On the way down, Tim had wondered if he should say something before taking that first step, like Neil Armstrong had done when the Apollo mission first landed on the moon, but in the end he was so apprehensive he just jumped out and nearly fell over as he landed. He gazed around for a minute or two before shuffling along to where Gar-ran waited.

Through his visor the landscape appeared as a rich shade of terracotta. The terrain was rocky and desolate, although in the distance he could make out the outline of a massive mountain range. Mars! He was on Mars! The most famous planet outside of Earth.

Looking up at the intense blackness of space, Tim felt his worries fade away and be replaced by a deep sense of peace. Gar-ran was a little way ahead of him and examining some large rocks embedded in a small crater. His voice sounded in Tim's ear piece.

'Asteroids.'

Tim instinctively looked up, half fearing to see a huge rock plummeting towards them.

'Don't worry; these impacts are hundreds of years old,' Gar-ran said.

Tim bent down and selected a few fragments and stashed them in his utility belt. He then withdrew a tiny phial made of a toughened plastic and scooped a little of the fine red topsoil into it before securing the tube with a metal bung. He stored this in another pocket. Souvenirs safely collected, he gazed out across the landscape.

Seeing the terrain as he did now, it was hard to imagine that for decades people wondered if the planet could hold similar life to ours. Everything around him seemed to be part of a vast, eternal desert. Still, it was beyond any of his wildest dreams to even be there.

After a few minutes he began to feel cold. He tensed, fearing that his suit was malfunctioning before remembering that Gar-ran had told him the temperature on Mars can plummet to incredible lows at night-time. He slowly walked over to where Gar-ran was sitting on a large boulder.

'I keep expecting to see that robot NASA sent up.'

Gar-ran laughed for a moment before replying. 'That would certainly cause some excitement for the scientists back on Earth. Better I think we remain undetected.'

'What about our footprints?'

'Oh they'll soon go; Mars has seasons just like Earth. Just more extreme.'

'It's getting cold,' said Tim.

'Yes. Let's go back.'

'That was amazing!' Tim said as they went through the Scarab's airlock. He hurried back to his room to change back into his regular clothes and then rejoined Gar-ran in the command hub.

***

On the near side of Earth's moon, Slothra's ship homed in on the strange signal. There was no sign of anything unusual now, but the scan indicated recent surface activity which was confined to a small area. It had to be them.

The pain racked him again and he hunched over in his pilot's chair waiting for it to pass. He shouldn't be flying, as the vison hadn't fully returned in his right eye. Large sections of fur had been burnt away on his arm and upper back, leaving the dark skin raw and tender despite the balms and poultices he'd applied. He wondered if it would ever grow back. There was more at stake than money now: it was personal.

The designer had been furious when he reported back, and had dared to cast aspersions on his hunting prowess. He'd snapped back with the fact that he hadn't been briefed on the presence of another alien with a powerful ship that had appeared at the crucial moment. After some haggling, the designer had agreed to triple his fee, and even paid half in advance. He now wanted the boy, the alien, and his ship. Slothra had wondered if the alien was also a bounty hunter. Surely, he couldn't be law enforcement? Would the marshals be monitoring a backward planet like this, which was so far from civilisation? It seemed unlikely, but on the other hand if the marshals were involved, it could mean more money.

He typed in a command and the ship quickly rose and began to speed upwards until, after a few minutes, he was clear of the moon's orbit. Earth rose before him, blue and beguiling after the monochrome of the moon and space. He entered more commands into the control panel, which was scratched and pitted from his claws. Wherever the fugitives had gone, he could follow. He would have them; it was just a matter of time.

Eight
A New World

———————◇———————

'So, where are we off to first?' Tim asked, hoping he sounded casual. Inside, he was beginning to feel anxious; from today they were moving into uncharted territory. Of course, Mars yesterday was unbelievable, but it was still in his own star system. *Everyone* knew of Mars, after all. Today though they were venturing into the real unknown. Well, unknown for him, anyway; there was no telling what exotic worlds Gar-ran knew about.

'Tell me more about that dream you keep having.' Gar-ran leant forward.

'It's always the same. I'm in some kind of desert and the wind is blowing. I'm running towards something, don't know what. There're other people with me, two others, I think. But I can't see who they are. I'm scared and excited but when I look up, the dream ends and I'm awake. You think it's a clue to where we have to go, don't you?'

'It could be, yes. I have an idea I want to try. Will you come with me to the lab?' Gar-ran stood up abruptly.

'Uh, yeah sure.' Tim slid his chair back, wondering what Gar-ran had planned.

As they walked through the door to the lab a thought occurred to Tim, halting him in his tracks.

'Hey, you're not going to brainwash me, are you? Like you did to Josh?'

Gar-ran turned around, looking astonished.

'Of course not. Why would you think that?'

'I just don't want my memories messed up, or erased or whatever it was you did.' Tim knew he was sounding stroppy, but he couldn't help it. He lingered in the doorway, hands jammed into his pockets.

'I have something different in mind,' Gar-ran said, perching on a high stool. 'Remember what I told you before? The theory that the engineers who designed the dimension bomb built in a nanotechnology, a program that imbeds itself in whoever finds a missing segment, this program contains an imprint or map of the location of the other pieces ...'

He paused and it dawned on Tim where the conversation was heading. In their first meeting, Gar-ran had mentioned that the info they needed might only be revealed in a dream, a vision, or through hypnosis.

'You want to hypnotise me?'

'I do. I think it's the quickest way to find out more.'

Tim nodded but didn't reply. He didn't really know how hypnosis worked. He hoped that Gar-ran wouldn't ask him to do any funny stuff. He'd already thought there was more to his dream than he could remember.

'It's very straightforward and you'll be conscious the whole time.'

'How long does it take?'

'That would depend on how detailed your memory of the dream becomes.'

'But it won't last for hours?' He didn't want to be trapped in a zombie state all day.

'No, not at all. It's not like you may have seen on TV.' Gar-ran smiled.

Tim leant against the doorframe as he thought things out. It was another step into unknown territory with someone he barely knew. But it might help them. It could make all the difference.

'OK, how does it work?'

'Just sit down here.' Gar-ran gestured to the metal tubular chair against the wall.

Tim slowly walked over and sat down. Gar-ran positioned his stool so he sat directly opposite.

'Now just breathe easy, close your eyes and try to relax. Focus only on my voice.'

Tim did as instructed. After a little while, Gar-ran began to speak in a low voice.

'Imagine you're at the top of a staircase, a staircase with twenty steps. See the steps clearly in your mind, feel the stairs under your feet. As I count, you'll take a step down, and with each step you will become more and more relaxed. Ready?'

Tim nodded, eyes closed.

'Twenty … nineteen … eighteen … deeper and deeper into a relaxed state. Seventeen …'

***

The wind shrieked and the whipped-up sand stung his neck as he ran. He stumbled on the hard, stone-strewn ground, but regained his balance. Gar-ran urged him on and he was surprised to see the old man was outpacing him. Immediately to the right was a massive, golden orange stone building that looked as if it had been hewn directly from the cliff face. Further ahead, above a gaping doorway, were four enormous carved faces, but they were smashed, and distorted. He edged closer but Gar-ran yanked him down and handed him a black metal ball.

They surged off again, staying close against the rough stone wall, but then the sound of the wind began to fall away and everything around him faded to white and Tim found that he was on the staircase again.

Looking up, he could see a doorway with warm sunlight streaming through. A few more steps and he'd be outside again. The sun's warmth on his face felt lovely, and he blinked his eyes open to find himself back in his chair in the lab with Gar-ran peering anxiously at him.

'Tim, are you OK?'

'Uh, yeah, I think so.' He touched his face, expecting it to feel warm from the sun.

'Did it work? Did you learn anything?' he asked.

'Yes, I have an idea, but I'm not certain. We need Nerissa's input. Back to the command hub.'

***

'Now Tim, tell Nerissa in as much detail as you can remember, what you saw, and heard.'

Tim sat forward in the co-pilot chair and went through the whole scene.

'The carved faces, above the door, what were they like?' Gar-ran urged.

Tim screwed his eyes tight as he concentrated. More and more details were coming back. 'There were three in a row, and a fourth, a bigger one on top. They were smashed up, distorted, and they looked ancient.'

'Nerissa?' Gar-ran looked up to the viewing screen.

'I'll start scanning but it will take a while. Tim, if you remember any more let me know.' She winked at him, then the screen went blank.

Tim smiled as he sat back. He was beginning to enjoy himself now. The hypnosis must have relaxed him, he decided.

Nothing happened for a while, then the screen blinked on and Nerissa appeared.

'I have something.'

'Go on,' Gar-ran said.

'The place Tim described matches descriptions of Malabat in the Moloco system.'

Gar-ran slumped back in his chair. 'Moloco,' he whispered.

Tim glanced between Nerissa, who was now looking solemn, and Gar-ran, who looked as if someone had punched him.

'What are you two talking about?'

Gar-ran roused himself. 'Sorry Tim, I was just surprised. I was in Moloco once, a long time ago. I was looking for someone, but I never found them. That was a long time ago though. I never went to Malabat, but that's where we'll start our search. Nerissa, set a course.'

'But where is it? This Molo, whatever you call it?' Tim was feeling left out. His school work never covered astronomy.

'Look at this.' Gar-ran tapped a button and a giant image of the Milky Way appeared.

'Wow. That's cool.' Tim gazed at the screen. He'd never seen a picture of the galaxy before, and to think it was just one of billions in the universe, and even in Gar-ran's ship you could never, ever see it all.

Gar-ran stood and touched a small yellow dot on the screen. 'That's Earth's sun. Now you see here, this whole band of stars that curves around below?'

'Yes.'

That's the Perseus arm, and we need to go here. He tapped the screen further to the left.

Tim frowned as he looked closer. 'But that's miles away.'

'Light years away,' Gar-ran chuckled. 'It'll take us three days.'

Tim shook his head; it didn't seem remotely possible. He remembered something. 'Which bit are you from?'

Gar-ran pointed to the other end of the Perseus arm. 'About there. And the Vothrun system, where Terius lived and the dimension bomb was created, is here.' He pointed to another cluster of stars behind the Orion spur.

'This is mad,' Tim muttered. Another thought pulled at him. 'How come I didn't see more when I was under the hypnosis? Shouldn't I have seen where the other pieces of the bomb are?'

Gar-ran frowned. 'Not necessarily, it might be that the other locations are revealed later. Maybe in another session?'

He doesn't know either, Tim thought. 'If we do find all the other pieces, will they work again, after so long?'

'I think so, but I'm not going to think about that yet, and neither should you. There's a long road ahead of us.'

Tim nodded. That was for sure. 'Can you tell me more about where we're going?'

'Of course.' Gar-ran sat again. 'Moloco is largely a desert world, one of only two habitable planets in the Moloco system. So, it's hot. Hot and dry.'

'Are there people there then?' Tim cut in.

'People? Yes, but it's sparsely populated; the climate can be harsh. The people there are not the kind you'll have met before. I'll tell you more on that when we get nearer. We'll land in Ter-ran. It's the capital of the northern territories. It's a strange place, not very civilised and a bit of a backwater. There's no marshal presence there, so we'll be on our own. We'll need to find a guide there to take us further in.'

'Sounds like the Wild West,' Tim said, imagining himself as a cowboy. 'I guess when we get there,

there'll be a new sheriff in town.' He laughed at his own joke.

Gar-ran gave a faint smile. 'I'm planning on us keeping a low profile. In the meantime, there's a part of the ship you haven't seen yet. Follow me.'

***

A few minutes later they stood before an open door that led into a long room. On a table nearby were two white metallic pistols, identical in all but size. Gar-ran plucked up the smaller one and handed it to Tim.

It was lighter than he expected. The grip was silver with a light grain, and was comfortable. At the far end of the room various glowing geometric shapes hung suspended in the air at different heights.

Gar-ran tied back his long, wavy hair and picked up the larger pistol.

'We won't be able to take these with us into Terran, but I want you to get used to the feel and handle of these guns; they could save our lives one day. Now, observe.'

He aimed at a triangular target about twenty metres away. He squeezed the trigger and a white beam of light shot out, instantly disintegrating the target as it struck it. Tim gaped in astonishment.

'Now watch this.' Gar-ran adjusted the dial on the barrel of the pistol and fired again. This time a wider beam of light blasted out, obliterating four targets.

'Hey, this is good. Can I have a go?' A shooting range was the last thing Tim had expected to find on board, and he wondered what other secret areas the Scarab contained.

'Pass me your pistol for a moment please,' Gar-ran requested.

'Now I just need to make a couple of adjustments.' He pressed a series of buttons above the handle and the gun beeped quietly for a few seconds.

'Right, I've calibrated your pistol so that it if you accidentally shoot me, nothing will happen.' He handed it back to Tim.

'Don't worry, I'm not going to do *anything* that'll stop me from getting home.'

Tim brought the pistol up and took aim.

'Don't close your eyes. Keep them both open and just squeeze the trigger; don't snatch at it,' Gar-ran instructed.

Tim squeezed hard, the gun reared up, his shot exploded against the celling and, for a horrible second, he thought he'd wrecked the room, but there was no damage except for a faint scorch mark. He turned sheepishly to Gar-ran.

'Try again. Hold it with both hands and just squeeze the trigger gently.'

Tim took aim again and this time clipped the target.

'Well done. Keep practising and then we'll try some wide-angle shots.'

For the next half an hour Tim shot various targets with both the narrow and wide-beam settings until Gar-ran pronounced himself satisfied. Tim placed his pistol back on the table and rubbed his shoulders. Shooting stuff was surprisingly hard work and his arms were beginning to ache.

'Right. You seem to have the hang of it. Let's take a short break, then we'll do another fifteen minutes. I want you to practise every day from now on.'

'Sure.' It sounded like a good deal to Tim. If he continued to improve, maybe Gar-ran would let him handle some of the bigger weapons. They made their way back to the galley.

***

'Gar-ran, I've been thinking about something.' Tim was sipping from a bottle of water as he sat at the table.

'Yes?'

'You said before that you had an idea of who was behind the disappearances back home. Who are they? Why is it happening now?' Tim watched Gar-ran carefully. His expression darkened for a moment, and he saw real anger there, then a more guarded expression as he looked Tim in the eye.

'I don't know for sure. I just have a theory. A long time ago, I tracked a wanted criminal called Karron-Dell from the Canbeela system in the outer arm of the galaxy, all the way to Earth. Earth was out of my jurisdiction in those days, but Karron-Dell was so dangerous, there was no way I was going to let him escape. There were three of us tracking him, me and two other marshals, but Dell found a way to hack into their ships' navigation system and they both crashed, and were killed.'

'Oh, I'm sorry.' Tim didn't really know what to say. He suddenly felt embarrassed.

'It's all right. He tried to hack into my ship too, but Zania stopped him fortunately.'

'Zania?' In Tim's mind was the image of a glamorous lady marshal: tall, blonde, deadly.

'Zania was Nerissa's predecessor. This was before I had the Scarab.'

'Oh, right.' *Not quite the same thing.* 'So, who is this Karron-Dell character?'

Gar-ran pulled out a chair and sat down. 'He was a Canbeelan engineer. The Canbeellans are technologically minded people, but their relentless pursuit of knowledge and disdain for other races they feel are inferior has led to a lot of conflict and upheaval. Dell was particularly brilliant. He started out as a military engineer specialising in weapons systems. However, he felt his talents weren't properly appreciated so started secretly selling his designs to the highest bidder. Eventually he was caught and sent to a military prison.'

'And then he escaped?' *It's like something from a film,* Tim thought. He wished Gar-ran would tell him more stories like this.

'Yes. I don't know what happened to him in prison; the details are still classified, but he went insane. He was actually broken out from the jail by a big arms manufacturer, who obviously wanted his expertise. After that he vanished for about a year. When he next surfaced, he'd taken over the arms dealer's business and it was discovered he'd sold a new weapons system to the Dengardins. They're an alien race that in the past have gone to war against the Canbeellans. This was treason, so a death sentence was pronounced, but he escaped in a stolen ship, and that's when the marshals were called in.'

'So, you followed him all the way here? Then what?'

'I'm coming to that now.' Tim noted another flare of irritation.

'My ship was better equipped; I was able to score two direct hits on him and I saw his ship crash and burn.'

'Where was this?'

'In New Mexico, years ago now.' Gar-ran went silent for a while, lost in his own thoughts. After a while he looked at Tim.

'Time to get back to the range.' He stood up abruptly.

'But what happened then? He was dead, surely?'

'My colleagues always thought so, but we could never find the body. There was little chance he could have lived, but then he always had a talent for survival. I went back a few times, but I never found him. I have to say, I became a bit obsessed. One of the reasons I requested my jurisdiction to be extended to include Earth.'

'That's the most amazing thing I've ever heard. So you think he's alive? He opened the portal?' Tim gabbled his words out as he hurried to keep pace with Gar-ran.

'Well, you remember I told you that the disappearances in Snowdonia always coincided with the full moon?'

'Yeah, I remember.'

'The next full moon is a supermoon, and comes almost exactly forty years to the day that Karron-Dell fell to Earth. That's too much of a coincidence for me.'

'Wow.' Tim couldn't think of anything else to say; he was still trying to process Gar-ran's theory. It sounded frighteningly plausible though.

***

Later, Tim recorded the day's events in his journal. He didn't usually keep one, but he wanted a record of all the places they'd go and the things they'd see. Journal entry complete, he stifled a big yawn. Bed soon. His watch said half ten, although he was beginning to wonder if a watch that displayed Earth time was going to be much use in outer space. He got up and wished Gar-ran goodnight via the intercom and, after a shower, lay on his bed. The light in the room started to dim automatically, which took a bit of getting used to. There were no covers but it felt very comfortable. After a few moments his eyes began to close and he could feel himself drifting into sleep.

He woke suddenly and sat up. The room was totally dark. He'd been dreaming he was back at home in his house, but his parents and sister couldn't see or hear him at all. No matter what he did, they just carried on as if he wasn't there at all. He reached over to the table and picked up his watch. 7.15 a.m. Time to get up.

They were still two days out from the Moloco system but the time passed quickly as Tim learnt more about the ship and how it functioned. More time was spent on the practice range and he found himself adjusting to life on board. He still got pangs of homesickness, but every day brought something new and different to look forward to.

He woke early on arrival day and, after a quick breakfast, dashed along to join Gar-ran in the command hub.

'We're nearly within radio contact with Ter-ran. I'll negotiate our entry. We should touch down within the hour,' Gar-ran said.

'OK, I'll get changed in a minute.' He was beginning to feel apprehensive. He recalled Gar-ran's briefing from the night before. Moloco was a small planet with large areas of wilderness and desert. Once it had been home to a powerful religious cult which had been violently suppressed centuries ago. They'd be travelling under the guise of scholars and pilgrims. 'Pilgrims to where?' he'd asked as they sat in the galley.

'Malabat, and maybe another temple on the way. The cult worshipped the elements, and most of all the god of the winds, Mathran, who they considered the most powerful. The cult started in the city but because of persecution it moved further and further out into the wilderness, where they built a temple. Over time they gained more and more recruits. Ter-ran's principal ruler became jealous of them, and scared too of their influence. So, he decided to eradicate them. He led an army to their temple. And the Mathranians, as they now called themselves, were destroyed. Some survived and escaped though, and to this day they still have some followers and believers in Ter-ran and other worlds.'

Gar-ran paused and broke off a chunk of what looked like liquorice from a long strip and popped it in his mouth, something he only seemed to do in the evening. He'd explained that Tim wouldn't like it, so he never shared his stash, but that had only made Tim more curious.

'So, isn't it going to be dangerous, to pretend to be disciples, or pilgrims to this cult thing?'

'No. In the centuries since the suppression, much greater tolerance has developed and now their views and beliefs are studied quite widely. Today most people who follow or are interested in the Mathranians are dismissed as eccentrics, and largely ignored.'

'But what we're looking for really is that place I saw in my dream, their old temple you said?' Tim wondered how far into the wilderness the place was, and if they couldn't take weapons, how would they protect themselves from whatever was out there?

'Yes, the old temple, Malabat. It would be an ideal place to hide a segment of the bomb. But, as I mentioned, I don't have any authority here as a marshal; it's out of jurisdiction, so we'll need to disguise ourselves.' He looked serious and Tim spent the rest of the evening pondering what they were heading into.

***

'Twenty minutes to landing,' Nerissa's clear voice announced through the speaker in Tim's room. He slipped the black tunic Gar-ran had provided over his head and carefully wrapped the dark brown scarf around most of his head until only his eyes were visible. Next came the elaborate metal necklace, which reminded him of a mayor's chains. Regarding himself in the mirror, he had to laugh. The scarf muffled his voice. He looked like some kind of desert hobo.

'Perfect. Every inch the humble pilgrim! Let's go to the lab. There are a couple of things we need,' Gar-ran said as he came in.

Lying on the table in the lab were two wooden staffs, one longer than the other. Both were made of a light-coloured wood and elaborately designed with strange glyphs and markings.

'Pilgrims' staffs. Although these come with something extra. The smaller one is yours. We'll go to the practice room,' said Gar-ran as he selected the longest staff.

***

Tim was surprised to see how different the shooting range looked. In place of the holographic targets stood several mannequins of various shapes and sizes. The mannequins were human in shape but devoid of any distinguishing features.

'Now watch.' Gar-ran held his staff out and twisted the lower end anti-clockwise. The staff extended six inches to reveal a stainless steel core and what looked like a switch. Gar-ran pointed the staff at the nearest figure and pushed the switch up. There was a loud POP! and the mannequin flew violently backwards, colliding with other figures and toppling them.

'Wow, that's great!'

'Weapons are confiscated on arrival in Ter-ran but we'll be allowed to carry a pilgrim's staff. You try.'

Tim stepped forward, lowered his staff and firmly twisted the bottom section. He pressed the switch up and the figure he was aiming at hurtled back, but the recoil from the blast jerked him off balance.

'You need to hold on firmly,' Gar-ran instructed. Tim tried a few more times until there were no more figures left to knock over.

'This is good. Can we set them up again?' The staff was much easier to aim than the pistol and Tim found he preferred it.

'We need to move on, but one thing first. It'll be handy if you can understand the language. This device will make that possible.' Gar-ran held up a metallic band which looked similar to a watch, but instead of the clock face was a silver disc with indented horizontal lines. Gar-ran fitted it around Tim's neck.

'The strap's adjustable, so make sure it's comfortable. Now this receiver will detect the spoken language and translate to English.' Gar-ran held up a small round device slightly bigger than a coffee bean. Tim took it and pushed it into his ear.

'Not too far in. Good. Now it's probably best in this situation if you leave the talking to me, but if you have to speak, the throat processor will translate into Ter-rainian.

'Are you going to wear one?' Tim asked.

'I speak the language already.'

'Of course you do,' Tim muttered to himself.

*∗∗∗

Ten minutes later they touched down on Moloco. Gar-ran was dressed like Tim. The descent had been rapid and Tim hadn't been able to see much detail on the viewing screen, just glimpses of a vast, flat, desert landscape.

'Now the inhabitants of Ter-ran are going to be different from anything you've ever seen. But it's important that you don't react. This is an alien world, but as scholars and pilgrims we're meant to know what we're heading into. No matter what you see, try to remain calm.'

'OK,' Tim said, although his heart was racing. *'Going to be different.'* That was likely to be an understatement. He was beginning to feel ridiculous in his costume. Why all this gear when it was going to be so hot?

They docked in a small vehicle hangar, descending into it vertically through the roof which had unfolded like a huge metallic flower. The airlock opened and they stepped out onto the exit ramp. Immediately the heat hit Tim and he took a step back. It was an intense, dry heat and he began to worry how he would handle it.

In front of them was a tall metal booth and, despite Gar-ran's warning, Tim gasped as he saw the figure standing waiting for them. He hadn't known really what to expect but it certainly wasn't this. An enormous lizard stood upright, garbed in a flowing white tunic. The creature's tail was mottled orange and black and extended several feet across the floor.

As they got closer the lizard appeared to speak, although at first all Tim could hear was a series of differently pitched hisses and he felt a surge of alarm that his translator wasn't working. Then, miraculously, he could understand. Gar-ran was explaining that they planned to visit the shrines and settlements of the Mathranians. The lizard took the papers Gar-ran held, inspected them for a few moments and handed them back, waving them through. Tim kept his eyes on the ground as he passed.

Other ships had docked and two in particular caught Tim's attention. He couldn't believe how small they were. No more than two feet in length and shaped like the paper darts he and Josh made at school to fling out of the windows at lunch time. The strange craft was suspended in mid-air and was formed from a sleek black metal which gleamed like polished ebony. He would like to have spent more time looking but Gar-ran was already by the exit, which was flanked by two more giant lizards who were armed with long blaster rifles similar to the ones in Gar-ran's armoury.

One of the guards stepped forward. 'You will be searched for weapons,' he rasped. The creature patted Gar-ran all over and, satisfied he was weapons-free, moved to Tim. The lizard's touch was quick and nimble and, although nervous, Tim was fascinated to see the details and markings on the guard's skin, with the black-blue mottled shading, and the thick folds of leathery skin on the creature's powerful neck. The reptilian eyes fixed on him for a moment and then the lizard quickly sprang back, making Tim jump.

'Pass through,' it said, its long tongue flicking in and out.

The door of the hangar opened and he and Gar-ran stepped out into sunshine so bright he had to shield his eyes until they adjusted to the glare.

'We'll need supplies, a map and a guide,' Gar-ran said, adjusting his scarf.

'A guide? Rahhsan will be happy to assist you?' A little figure stepped up to them. He was four feet tall and wore a loose, flowing top and wide, cream-coloured trousers. He looked tough despite the elegant clothes. Wrapped around his head was a faded white scarf. Tim suppressed a shudder though, as the face that looked up at them was the face of a hyena. Gar-ran sidestepped and tugged Tim's sleeve to hurry him along. The little figure darted in front of them, still entreating them to follow him, but Gar-ran waved him aside and eventually Rahhsan skulked off.

'A typical hustler. If we'd followed him he would have led us into a back street where his friends would have robbed us. There are no proper guides in this part of town,' Gar-ran said confidently. Tim stole a glance behind but the street was empty.

I'm on an alien planet with talking lizards, and hyenas, Tim thought. The whole thing was too weird for words, but one thing in particular that bothered him was that the wide streets were surprisingly empty. Where was everyone? What did they know that he didn't? Gar-ran seemed unfazed though, which was reassuring.

As he began to relax, Tim was able to take more note of the surroundings. Most buildings were low-level and none were taller than two floors. All were round or oval and covered with either a smooth cream or terracotta plaster. Gar-ran explained they were approaching the hottest part of the day when a lot of the inhabitants took a siesta.

So that's where everyone is, Tim thought. *Just like in Spain.* After ten minutes they came to a large house which was built from pitted, tan-coloured stone. A sign hung above the door, but it was written in a script that Tim had never seen before.

'This is the place,' Gar-ran announced. He swung the door open but as they stepped inside a voice halted them.

'We're closing now for two hours.'

'We seek assistance and will pay well for your help,' Gar-ran said.

There was a sustained hissing sound which sounded like an exasperated sigh, then the voice said, 'You may enter.'

The store interior was dark after the brilliance of the sunshine and wonderfully cool with the door closed. Tim blinked as his eyes adjusted. He slowly realised they were in some kind of camping store. There were headscarves and flowing robes arranged on different mannequins, a rack of what looked like sunglasses, or in this case goggles, various rugged pairs of boots, and what looked like a giant insect cocoon hung on one of the walls. The room was lit by four standing lamps in the corners casting a diffused glow, and gave Tim the impression he was in a well-stocked cave.

'I am Ker-nan,' the voice said. 'What do you need?' Tim suppressed a yelp as he turned to look at him. The Ternanian's skin, pale green and massively wrinkled, hung down in folds beneath his neck and pulsed slightly as he moved. His bright yellow eyes did not waver as he gazed at Tim before turning his attention to Gar-ran. His head was bare and a crest of spines ran down his head and neck, and as he spoke

Tim caught of glimpse of the needle-like teeth. He was a little shorter than Gar-ran but lithe and alert.

'We seek to walk the path to the old places and pay homage, and to learn. We need maps and advice on choosing a guide,' Gar-ran said.

Ker-nan sighed impatiently. 'More cultists. Others of your sort came not so long ago. They walked the path too. Didn't come back though. Don't you have enough superstitions to explore on your own planet?'

Tim was taken back by Ker-nan's brusque manner but Gar-ran didn't miss a beat.

'The way of the pilgrim was never meant to be easy. How else one can reach truth and enlightenment without overcoming obstacles?'

Ker-nan stared impassively at them for a few moments before responding. 'Well it's your life. Is that your boy you're dragging along with you?'

Tim was about to answer but Gar-ran got in first.

'He's my student.'

'Hmm.' Ker-nan regarded Tim for a moment. 'Well I'll sell you what maps I have. They're incomplete of course. So many of the older places have been swallowed by the desert, but you should find them of some use.'

He ducked beneath the shop counter and rummaged through different layers of maps and charts before selecting two, which Gar-ran took and opened out.

'Excellent,' he said after a few moments of scrutiny.

'Fifty Moloco dollars for the pair of them.' Ker-nan's pink tongue darted in and out.

'Fifty? We're poor pilgrims my friend. Surely we can come to a more suitable arrangement.'

They began to haggle. Tim listened for a moment but quickly lost interest and began to wander the store. He went over to the rack of sun goggles. He tried on a pair with orange lenses. They fitted well but he couldn't see much. Maybe they only worked in bright sunlight.

Gar-ran and Ker-nan had finally agreed on a price, and Tim waved to get Gar-ran's attention.

'Could we get these too? To protect our eyes.' His voice translated into Ternanian sounded incredibly alien to him.

'Good thinking. Grab me the black pair, please.'

For a second Tim thought the haggling was about to begin all over again, but Ker-nan seemed more than happy with the coins Gar-ran produced.

'Now as for a guide. Head to the Western district. You know it?'

Gar-ran nodded.

'Malar or Sharvar are the ones you want. They're both Caracali.'

Gar-ran thanked him and they headed out.

'Good luck,' Ker-nan hissed as the door closed.

'It's this way,' Gar-ran said. 'You're doing very well so far, by the way.'

I haven't done anything really, Tim thought. He was wondering why he was there. He didn't have a clue what to do, where they were going, or what he was supposed to do when he got there. Maybe he'd be able to help more when they got to the Malabat shrine. Gar-ran seemed happy to have him tagging along, at least.

'What are Carakelly?' Tim stumbled over the pronunciation.

'*Caracali.* They're another native species. They'll look cat-like to you. Excellent trackers.' Gar-ran winked.

He loves this, Tim thought as he tried his sun goggles again.

They tried to keep to the shaded areas of the street as much as possible. Tim found he could see more easily now. 'So, when did you come here before?'

Gar-ran didn't reply immediately. 'It was some years ago. I was looking for a friend, but I never found her. A place like this, a fringe world in an outer system, it's easy to disappear.'

'Ker-nan said other pilgrims were here too, not long ago. What do you think happened to them? Tim knew from Gar-ran's briefing that in town they were likely to be OK, as long as they kept their wits about them. The desert though was lawless; anything could happen out there, and their weapons were pretty basic.

'I've been wondering. They may not have actually been pilgrims. I don't think Ker-nan makes too much distinction between scholars, pilgrims or other, let's say, fanatics who pass through here. Moloco can be useful for people looking to escape something or someone, or who think they may find an answer to their problems in the wilds and wilderness,' Gar-ran mused.

Tim wasn't sure what to make of that, so said nothing. They were coming to the edge of the settlement and ahead of them the path widened out. The wind was beginning to freshen and Tim squinted at the figures ahead.

'This will be it.' Gar-ran halted.

Tim stared at the three figures ahead, relieved that his scarf masked his face. Two were Ternanians. The nearest was tall and similar to the customs official they met earlier. His long tail flicked lazily to the side as he chatted to the other two. He appeared to be telling a joke as his companions were laughing, although they stopped and turned to watch as he and Gar-ran approached. The other one was shorter and stockier with a very wide back and short spines protruding from his head. Tim took note too of the thick, serrated tail. The third was totally different and Tim blinked in astonishment.

Lynx! The word shot into his mind. Definitely some kind of wild cat, but standing upright and dressed in long, white, baggy trousers and a loose, sleeveless white top that revealed powerful shoulders and strong, lean arms.

Gar-ran stepped forward, bowed respectfully and addressed him.

'I seek the ones called Malar and Sharvar.'

'I am Sharvar. Malar is away.' The Caracali's voice was a soft, low growl and Tim felt a shiver of alarm despite the baking heat.

'We need a guide to help us on our pilgrimage to the old places where we wish to study and pay homage. You've been recommended to us.'

'Pilgrims,' Sharvar spat. 'Let us talk a little.' He turned and nodded towards his companions and moved further away. When they were out of earshot, Sharvar turned to Gar-ran.

'In my experience, Pilgrims are poor clients to have. No money,' he said, his voice now more of a growl. Tim tightened his grip on his staff.

'We are scholars too. Our organisation has provided us with funding for our endeavours. You'll be well paid. If you do a good job,' Gar-ran countered.

Sharvar's lips curled back a little, revealing frighteningly large fangs, but Gar-ran seemed unconcerned. When he spoke, Tim could detect a hint of amusement in Sharvar's voice.

'Pilgrims with money? Show me.'

Gar-ran opened his hand to reveal a few large coins. The sun glittered off them and Sharvar licked his lips.

'How far do you wish to go?'

Gar-ran drew out one of the maps and pointed to a place name. Sharvar glanced briefly and shook his head.

'This map is terrible. I do not know how Ker-nan gets away with selling such rubbish. I can take you to the Markat Shrine. It is half a day's journey. Anywhere else?

'Perhaps Malabat.'

Sharvar looked up from the map. His orange eyes seemed to burn. 'Malabat is cursed. Only the fools and the mad venture there.'

'We're not afraid of the dangers. The old Gods are with us.'

Sharvar chuckled softly.

'Fools and mad men. Well, I will take your money then. What about the boy? Is he up to such a journey?'

'Yes I am. I … am ready to walk the path.' Tim amazed himself by speaking up. He could feel Gar-ran's eyes on him.

Sharvar looked doubtful but turned to Gar-ran and nodded. 'Very well. We will leave in an hour and a half when the sun's heat is not so fierce. I suggest you use the time to buy water and supplies; the traders will open again soon. And remember the nights here are cold. Before you go though, I need to provision three beasts, and I require a small retainer to ensure my services.'

Gar-ran took out two coins which Sharvar took, inspected briefly and tucked away in a deep pocket.

'In one and a half hours then,' Gar-ran said, turning back towards the town. Tim stared out across the desert scrubland for a few moments. The heat made the horizon ahead of him shimmer and dance. There was no sign of life. He took a deep breath and headed after Gar-ran.

Nine
The Three Travellers

T hey spent the next hour stocking up. Gar-ran
found a nearby trader who ran a general store
selling a little of everything. The owner
resembled Ker-nan and Tim wondered if they were
related. Gar-ran haggled again for the best prices. In
the end they came out with as many water pouches
as they could carry.

'We can fill them from the well in the centre of
town,' Gar-ran explained.

Tim had been tasked with tallying what they
acquired and he was particularly curious about the
cactus fruit that was meant to be very sweet, and the
strips of a strange, dark meat which Gar-ran assured
him was close to beef. They also had some energy
bars from the Scarab, stashed in their belt pockets.
Last but not least were two light but warm sleeping
bags which were sand-coloured and folded up easily.

Sharvar was waiting for them when they got
back, and he wasn't alone. Next to him were three
strange animals that looked like a cross between a

camel and a giraffe. One of the beasts was a third smaller than the others and looked at Tim with a curious expression.

'The smaller one will be yours, Tim,' Gar-ran said.

'But, but how do I control it?' Tim's heart began to bang again. The beast looked placid enough, but he'd never ridden a donkey before, let alone whatever this was.

'Don't worry, there's only three basic commands. I'll teach you them on the way,' Sharvar said casually.

'Ready?' He addressed Gar-ran, who nodded.

'We'll make a start then. It'll be dark in around three and a half hours. I want us to be halfway there by then.' Sharvar swung himself up into the saddle. He hissed a word that Tim didn't catch and Tim's beast knelt down and allowed him to climb up. The saddle was worn but comfortable and resembled a giant chamois leather. The beast quickly stood up and, for a horrible second, Tim thought he was going to fall but managed to regain his balance, gripping hard on the reins with both hands. Sharvar called out something else and Tim's beast surged forward at a canter. Within moments they were clear of the town and into the wilderness. Tim felt a surge of excitement; this wasn't so bad after all.

***

Two hours into their journey, Tim's enthusiasm was waning. He'd learnt the beasts they rode were called drongos, and were a popular pack animal, but after the novelty of the first half-hour, nothing much had happened. Ahead of them was a small range of hills that didn't seem to be getting any closer and, once or twice, he'd lost his balance and nearly toppled off. As they travelled, Gar-ran passed around some of the desert fruit he'd bought. Tim regarded it dubiously. It looked like a large satsuma without the skin but when he bit into it his mouth flooded with thick, sweet juice which tasted faintly of peach.

Tim studied the surrounding landscape. It was almost entirely flat except for the hills ahead, but the desert floor was littered with small, loose rocks which slowed their progress. The earth was scorched to a golden brown and occasionally small lizards darted from cracks in the ground. Other than a few stunted trees, there was very little vegetation. The wind blowing from the west began to pick up and Tim tightened his scarf. It was difficult to keep any accurate sense of time. Finally though, they approached the hills.

Sharvar waited for them to catch up but continued looking past them into the distance.

'What is it?' Gar-ran asked.

'It is nothing,' Sharvar purred. 'Let's move into the hills.'

The hills marked a beginning of a change in the terrain. The land ahead was much hillier and you couldn't see so far ahead. They reached the top of the highest hill and Sharvar called a halt.

'We'll camp here tonight,' he said, surprising them both.

'Trouble?' Gar-ran asked.

Sharvar looked at Tim and then back at Gar-ran.

'Speak up,' Gar-ran said. 'We're all in this together.'

Tim tensed. His staff was strapped to his back and not easy to reach.

Sharvar scratched his neck before continuing. 'We're being followed. They will come when it's dark. At least here we have the advantage of the high ground. And the only way up is the way we came.'

'Any idea who it is?' Gar-ran asked.

Sharvar shook his head. 'They're too far away to be certain, but we'll need to be ready.'

Tim wondered if it was anything to do with the little hustler who'd hassled them when they first arrived. He hoped not. Maybe there was an innocent explanation, although that didn't seem likely. He felt more annoyed than afraid. He'd been starting to enjoy himself and now it was spoiled, plus they weren't going to cover as much ground as they wanted, so the whole thing was going to take longer. He kicked a loose rock down the slope.

'My bet is a desert gang. Out here there are few laws and the scum who roam these wilds will rob and steal from whoever crosses their path. The desert is a hard place to survive and people take what they can.' Sharvar's voice was harsh and Tim felt the hairs on the back of his neck rise.

'Do you have any ideas of their numbers?'

'Difficult to be sure. Four or five perhaps. They're unlikely to send more against a couple of mere pilgrims and a guide. One thing's for sure: they do not fear us,' Sharvar said, baring his teeth again.

'Then we'll have to give them cause to respect us,' Gar-ran said.

'We'll need more then belief in the old Gods to get out of this,' Sharvar hissed.

'Oh, we're prepared,' Gar-ran said, brandishing his staff. 'Do you have any weapons?'

Sharvar regarded the staff suspiciously before holding up his paw. His five claws extended, each of them over an inch long.

'They're even sharper than they look,' he growled. 'Once this is over, I think you and I will renegotiate my fee.'

Gar-ran smiled. 'I look forward to a spirited discussion. For now though, I have one or two suggestions to make.'

***

Tim inched forward and peered over the edge of the hill. It was about seventy feet to the bottom. Too far to jump. Half an hour had passed since last light. A brilliant canopy of stars twinkled above, so many that Tim felt very small and alone despite the presence of Gar-ran and Sharvar. It was also cold. He'd wanted to light a fire but Gar-ran had pointed out that would just make it easier for the raiders to pinpoint their location.

Gar-ran sat on the ground a few feet away and facing towards the path leading down. His staff rested across his legs. The beasts had been hobbled and now lay on their haunches side by side. Sharvar was nowhere to be seen but Tim knew he must be close by as he'd moved ahead to cover anyone approaching. The stillness of the night was broken by a low, faint whistle just loud enough to be heard. Tim's stomach clenched. This was the prearranged signal and meant that the gang was approaching. Gar-ran turned to him and Tim nodded to confirm he'd heard the sign. Suddenly, two glowing lamps appeared.

Gar-ran passed Tim some of the dried meat and desert fruit. They had agreed to maintain the illusion they were just simple travellers resting after a long day's journey. It wasn't long until they heard footsteps on the path, and slowly out of the darkness four figures loomed. One was a native Teranian, tall and slim with a long neck and whip-like tail. He carried a long rifle, bigger than any Tim had seen so far. The other three were much shorter and stockier and had hyena-like features. They were armed with shorter, bulkier laser rifles and carried a melon-sized, round glow lamp.

Gar-ran stood up.

'You are welcome friends. Our meal is humble but you're welcome to share with us.'

Two of the hyenas broke into a high-pitched, yelping laughter which set Tim's nerves further on edge. The third one, who was slightly bigger, stepped forward.

'Share, he says! How noble.'

The tall lizard spoke next.

'We'll take what food you have, those clothes you're wearing, your packs, and any money or valuables you may be carrying.' The lizard's voice was soft and pleasant sounding, but his black eyes were bright and defiant.

'But friend, we're just poor pilgrims. Would you leave us with nothing?' Gar-ran said.

'You may keep your lives.' The hyenas broke into fresh laughter.

'My companions think me far too generous. Where is the cat?' The Teranian's forked tongue darted in and out.

'Our guide, do you mean? He ran off; he wants no trouble,' Gar-ran said.

'How unfortunate, but also how like a Caracali,' said the lizard.

'He can't be too far away, boss. I can smell him,' the second hyena said. The Teranian nodded and turned to Gar-ran again.

'Now tip out the contents of your pouches please.'

Slowly Tim and Gar-ran stood up.

'I'm afraid we're unable to comply with your request,' Gar-ran said. Tim darted to the side and Gar-ran lowered his staff and fired. There was a loud POP! which sounded deafening in the still of the desert night and the three hyenas were thrown violently backwards. One of the hyenas hit his head against an outcrop of rock and fell heavily, face forward.

'Grab the rifle!' Gar-ran shouted. Tim moved towards it but, at that instant, Sharvar came bounding out of the darkness. He had almost reached it when the Teranian's tail whipped out and knocked the rifle further back. Fluidly changing direction, Sharvar flung himself on the still-groggy giant lizard. There was a flash of claws and a plume of blood sprayed up and the Teranian lay still.

That left only the two hyenas who were still struggling to get up. Tim lowered his staff and began to unscrew the bottom section, but his hands shook so much he couldn't get a grip. Snarling, the nearest hyena leapt at him. Frantically, Tim swung the staff at the beast's head, but it ducked underneath and the wild swing threw him off balance. Then, as if caught by a monstrous gust of wind, the hyena was blown up into the air and over the hillside, howling piteously as he fell out of sight.

'Got him,' Gar-ran said triumphantly. Tim whirled around as Sharvar dispatched the last assailant.

'Well that takes care of that,' he growled. The blood down his front was a glossy black in the moonlight.

Tim stood there shaking. It had all happened so fast. Gar-ran came up to him when suddenly Sharvar leapt over both their heads, making them flinch. He piled into the big lizard, who'd been sneaking up behind them. The lizard tottered back clutching its throat, lost its footing and tumbled back down the hill.

'I knew there had to be another one somewhere,' Sharvar said, retracting his claws.

Tim shivered. If Gar-ran hadn't saved him, he would have been the one lying dead and broken on the hillside, instead of their assailants.

'We can't stay here. Can you find the trail in the darkness?' Gar-ran asked.

'I can. We'll be safer when we reach the shrine,' Sharvar replied.

***

They gathered up their belongings and, as quickly as they could, headed down. Sharvar led them along the foot of the hills. After twenty minutes, a gap emerged between the rock face, and they were able to walk through single file until once again they were on the flat plain. They continued onwards into the night.

Occasionally Tim glanced behind but there was nothing to be seen. After some time, Sharvar fell in beside them.

'You two are like no pilgrims I've ever seen before. You don't fight like a scholar either.'

Gar-ran smiled. 'We're no use to our order if we're weak.'

'Hmm. It's not far to the shrine now. An hour or so more.' Sharvar slinked off again.

'Do you think we'll get in trouble for what happened back there?' Tim asked.

'No. There are no laws out here. And they were bandits. No one will care.'

'I mean with the other gangs.'

'Ah, well there are few allegiances out here. I doubt they'll be missed.'

The night wore on and the cold bit further into Tim, who huddled against his beast as it plodded inexorably onwards. They came over a small hillock where Sharvar waited for them.

'The Markat Shrine.' The Caracali pointed eastwards.

Tim squinted. He could just make out a large, ruined structure some way to the side. Some of his tiredness fell away and he felt impatient to get there. Even so, they all approached the shrine warily. They walked beneath a towering, lopsided sandstone arch and into a large courtyard. Many of the flagstones were broken, as if struck by a giant hammer, and they had to pick their way carefully through the debris.

***

'There should be an entrance to a chamber somewhere where we can shelter,' Gar-ran said.

'Yes I know it, but it was sealed up some time ago,' Sharvar answered.

'Then we must unseal it.'

'You would desecrate a temple you profess to venerate?' Sharvar's voice was an amused purr.

132

'We must be thorough in our research. It's also bloody freezing.'

Tim laughed; it was funny to hear Gar-ran swear.

They found steps in the north-west corner of the courtyard which descended downwards in a clockwise direction. At the bottom was a wide doorway filled up with piles of rough, broken stones. Gar-ran pressed firmly but the rocks held fast.

'Maybe we could blast our way inside?' Tim said.

'I think that's an excellent idea. We must be careful though. Use your staff on its lowest settings.'

Tim nodded and made the necessary adjustments. Sharvar and Gar-ran moved back. He pushed the switch on the staff up and there was a series of quiet popping sounds and gradually the stones filling the doorway began to crumble backwards. After a moment a whole section of rocks fell back. Hot dust and air rushed out of the gap and forced them to cover their faces until the cloud dissipated. Now there was enough space to step through. Sharvar went first.

'It's clear,' he said.

Carefully, Tim and Gar-ran made their way over the small remaining pile of rocks and into the chamber. Although still quite dark, they could discern they were in a medium-sized chamber.

'We should be safe here. After we feed and water the beasts, you two should sleep. I'll keep watch.' Sharvar raised a paw to still Gar-ran's protest.

Tim and Gar-ran unfolded their sleeping bags and laid them out on the dusty floor. Tim's bag felt incredibly warm and surprisingly comfortable. He stretched his whole body out and was asleep in minutes.

Ten
The Old Gods

Tim woke early the next morning to discover Gar-ran was already up and filling in for Sharvar on sentry duty while the Caracali got some rest. Later they shared a meagre breakfast of dried meat and desert fruit and Tim pondered what today would bring. Already the temperature was rising and, as he gazed out through the giant arch and across the plains, the horizon shimmered in the distance.

'We should press on,' Sharvar purred.

'How long to Malabat from here?' Gar-ran asked as he rolled up his sleeping bag.

'Two days if we really push it. That is if you still want to go?'

'We do.' Gar-ran answered for both of them. Sharvar let out a long hissing sound.

'Very well.'

They mounted their beasts and headed out. Tim's mount seemed reluctant to move and it took several minutes of cajoling and then shouting to get it to stand up. Once they set off though, it seemed more contented. The morning sped by quickly despite the monotony of the trail. They rested at midday from the worst of the heat in the partial shade of a patch of thin, withered desert trees before breaking camp and continuing until night fell.

After the small fire was built, Gar-ran boiled some water to which he added some pungent, small, green leaves he'd bought in the store in Ter-ran. It gave the water a faint minty taste which was said to be restorative. They ate a simple meal of dried meat and some pale, soft beans, and a feeling of contentment spread through Tim as he gazed at the flickering flames.

He was itching to know more about Malabat but, as a pilgrim, he should of course have the knowledge, so he could hardly ask Gar-ran to elaborate with Sharvar so close by. Instead he sprawled out full-length and gazed up at the numberless stars and listened to the crackle of the firewood and slowly drifted off into a deep, dreamless sleep.

They rose with the dawn and by mid-morning passed through an area where the thin trees and low-lying shrubs were pink with flowers and grew in more abundance. Suddenly they were startled by a small flock of plump, cream-coloured birds that erupted out of a bush, squawking in alarm. Sharvar explained they were a type of game bird, but one which was seldom hunted at this time of year.

'There will be water nearby,' he added. Sure enough, they soon came across two small ponds fringed by short-cropped grass. As they approached the nearest pool, a rabbit-like creature darted away.

'Pity, some fresh meat would be nice,' Sharvar said, licking his lips. 'They say, thousands of years ago, there were rivers here. Now all that remains are a few oases fed by underground springs. Hard to believe, isn't it?'

Tim nodded. Looking around, you'd think it'd been desert forever.

They tested the water. It was fresh and sweet although, as a precaution, Gar-ran crumbled a small pink tablet into his and Tim's water canister, which he said would destroy any harmful bacteria. A little before midday they entered a small range of low hills and rested in the shade until the sun lost some of its ferocity. In contrast to the day before, the rest of the afternoon dragged by and the stifling heat sapped any desire for prolonged conversation. They stopped to make camp in the half-hour before the light faded. Tim prepared the feed for the beasts while Gar-ran got the fire going.

'I'm going to have a scout around for a little while,' Sharvar announced, and loped off into the darkness.

Once the beasts had been fed, Tim sidled up to Gar-ran.

'Tell me some more about Malabat. Is it really cursed?' He kept his voice low because, although he couldn't see Sharvar, that didn't mean he wasn't around.

Gar-ran frowned as he eased himself down by the fire.

'It's just superstition, Tim. Don't take any notice of what Sharvar said.' He turned his attention back to the fire, which was starting to burn nicely.

'I'd still like to know.' Tim sat down close by.

Gar-ran sighed and glanced around before speaking.

Malabat is where the Mathranians made their last stand. It was their chief temple but it fell to the army of the principal ruler over 400 years ago. There were a few survivors who escaped into the desert, but as a religious order they were finished. And the beliefs they had, and the influence they wielded, died with them. It's only relatively recently that people have begun to revere them again, but it's still very much a fringe religion. Of course, people in less advanced civilisations are prone to superstition, and because of what happened, all sorts of stories and myths have sprung up about Malabat over the years. But that's all they are: stories.'

'What sort of myths?' He didn't want Gar-ran to stop. It was a good story.

'People began to say it was cursed, and that the souls of the dead Terranians still walk there, calling out to the Gods of the Wind and Earth to avenge them. Some people say that the desert storms are the rage of the Wind God as he scours the land looking for the ones who destroyed his followers.' He paused and scratched his neck.

'Depends what you believe, of course. In more modern times, the reputation of Malabat has attracted, ah, eccentric characters, as well as genuine pilgrims,' Gar-ran added.

'Mad men or fools,' Tim said.

Gar-ran was about to reply when they heard a soft footfall nearby. Tim reached for his staff but relaxed a moment later as Sharvar appeared. Over his shoulder he was carrying a dead creature that resembled a hare.

'We will dine well tonight, my friends.'

'What is it?' Tim asked, wondering how much of their conversation Sharvar had heard.

'A springer. Not easy to catch, but extremely tasty.' He patted the springer's thick hind leg. 'I

suppose you prefer the meat cooked?' Tim winced
and Sharvar laughed, his voice a throaty growl. The
springer took an hour to cook and, despite his
reservations, the smell of the meat as it roasted made
Tim's mouth water and he was ravenous by the time it
was ready. The meat was surprisingly tender and
tasted like rabbit, but stronger. With some beans and
dry bread, it made for a satisfying meal.

Later, Tim curled up in his sleeping bag facing
the fire. He put all thoughts of Malabat and desert
gangs out of his mind and just stared at the flickering
fire casting shadows on the ground until he could no
longer keep his eyes open.

Eleven
Malabat

M alabat loomed into view at mid-afternoon the following day. Even from several hundred feet away, Tim felt the first prickles of fear tingling through him and had to remind himself to breathe. Under the pretence of rearranging his scarf, he consulted the amulet. It glowed a reassuring blue. He tucked it away quickly as Sharvar turned to him.

'We should be on our guard from now on inwards.'

The wind had begun to pick up again, whipping small bits of gravel and sand around them. Tim pulled the scarf tighter around his face as he tried not to think about what Sharvar had said about the God of the Wind and his eternal search for vengeance. The terrain was fairly level as they approached Malabat and he could pick out more and more details. The stronghold appeared to have been cut directly from the huge, golden-orange sandstone cliff, and was composed of two levels.

The entrance was a big arch on the lower-left side, flanked by two columns that seemed more decorative than supportive. To the right of the door there was a long platform and, above that, a series of arched windows. Tim counted six in total. Above, four smaller arch windows marked the second level of temple stronghold. Gar-ran tapped his shoulder and pointed off to the right.

Around 200 feet away were the remains of a shrine, similar to the Markat Shrine but on a bigger scale and more ruined.

'Malabat's main shrine,' Gar-ran said.

Tim nodded and they trudged onwards. After a few minutes, Sharvar stopped abruptly. He turned to them and raised his paw. It was clenched over, a sign for them to wait. Alert now, they watched as Sharvar dismounted his beast and stalked forward. There was something lying on the ground ahead. Sharvar masked their view, although Tim caught a glimpse of what appeared to be a ragged cloak.

With painstaking slowness, Sharvar approached the tattered object, sniffed the air a few times and, after a few tense moments, gave the signal for Tim and Gar-ran to approach.

Tim's stomach heaved as he saw the battered figure lying there. The body of the native Terranian lay face downwards. The creature's black robe was largely intact but badly ripped, allowing sun-bleached bones to poke through. Most of the Terranian's olive-green skin had gone, although a few withered pieces remained attached to the head and fluttered as they were buffeted by the wind. The skull had been smashed at the back and the spine was also broken. From the position of the body, it appeared the attack had happened as the creature had been running away from Malabat.

'One of the lost pilgrims?' Gar-ran asked.

'Yes, I believe so,' Sharvar replied. He was silent for a few moments.

'Do you really need to visit this foul place so much? Is what you seek so vital?' He seemed weary for the first time.

'It is. More than I can say,' Gar-ran replied.

'How long do you wish to remain here?'

'Our studies may take a day or they make take three or four. It depends on what we can learn. Can you stay that long? I'll increase your fee.'

Sharvar frowned, looked at Gar-ran and then at Tim.

'Safety in numbers as they say. Besides, I have my reputation as a guide to think of; can't have my clients getting themselves killed. Bad for business. I will stay, and accept your generous offer of doubling my fee.'

Gar-ran smiled. 'All right. Lead the way.'

They walked in single file with Sharvar leading, Gar-ran in the middle and Tim at the back. Both Tim and Gar-ran had their staffs lowered and ready. Above the entrance were four large carvings, badly damaged and vandalised, the faces on them barely discernible. There were three in a row and a large carving directly above. Tim shuddered as he gazed up at them. They were almost exactly like the ones he'd seen in his dream and he could see now that this ancient, despoiled place, so lonely and desolate, could give rise to any number of fears and superstitions. He swallowed nervously; his mouth was as dry as a stone. He reached for his water when Sharvar made the halt sign.

Slowly, the Caracali stalked forwards into the doorway, paused to sniff the air and then slipped inside.

Three, then four minutes staggered by. The wind increased to a shriek and Tim huddled down, eyes fixed to the entrance. He became aware of an ache in his hands and realised he was gripping his staff which such force that he'd be too tense to use it effectively. With an effort, he forced himself to take some deep breaths and began to relax a little. The chamber beyond the doorway seemed brighter now. Then Sharvar finally reappeared and signalled for them to approach. Out of the corner of his eye, Tim saw Gar-ran visibly relax and realised he, too, was feeling the strain.

'It took a moment for me to light the wall torches,' Sharvar said as they caught up.

They hobbled the beasts again, but as they stepped forward, Sharvar blocked the doorway.

'There is another body inside. A second pilgrim.'

'May he rest in peace,' Gar-ran said.

Tim's gut tensed as he wondered how bad it would be. Tentatively, he stepped inside. Wind-blown sand covered the entire floor ankle-deep, which made movement awkward. Despite the mess, the interior immediately reminded Tim of a church as he slipped his goggles off. In the centre of the floor were four rows of long stone benches and, further beyond, stood a battered and wrecked podium which was now half its original height. Tim stopped dead. In front of the podium, a robed figure knelt, bent over and slumped forward as if in devoted prayer.

As he got nearer, it became obvious that the pilgrim's prayers had not been answered, and never would be. The spear which had impaled him had snapped off, but several inches still protruded. Dried blood had congealed around the wound, leaving an ugly, dark stain on the rich blue fabric. Mercifully, this time the Terranin's head was covered by the hood of his robe.

'Why did they do this? Why kill them?' Tim's voice sounded loud in the stillness around them.

'Gangs like the ones we encountered ourselves show no mercy to the defenceless,' Gar-ran replied.

'It could also be that one gang has claimed Malabat as their own and they don't welcome visitors. This one may have been left here as a warning,' Sharvar added.

'Yes, I was thinking of that too,' Gar-ran said.

It made sense to Tim too, but the matter-of-fact way the others discussed it unsettled him. They didn't really seem that concerned.

To the right was an open doorway which Gar-ran peered through.

'The entrance to the crypt. Where the chief priests were buried. What d'you think, Tim?'

'Ah … yeah, I suppose so.' He swallowed nervously. He didn't like the sound of the crypt much. He'd thought that once they reached Malabat he'd know what to do, or gain some insight as to where the next segment of the relic would be, but instead he just felt more confused and uncertain. He was beginning to feel like a dead weight on this trip.

Gar-ran took up the lead, Tim followed and Sharvar guarded the rear as they descended into a large chamber. The single torch wasn't enough to illuminate the entire room, but Tim could still make out the remains of various extravagantly carved ornate tombs, many badly damaged and thick with dust. It didn't appear as if anyone had been down there for a very long time, which was a good thing, he decided.

Gar-ran lit the other wall torches and gradually the room began to reveal itself. There were seven tombs, laid out in a diamond pattern. A tomb to the right of the stairs was empty.

'This place makes my fur crawl,' Sharvar growled.

'We may need to study these tombs for a while; perhaps you would be more comfortable upstairs?' Gar-ran said, giving Tim the distinct impression he wanted the tracker out of the way.

'An excellent idea. Someone needs to keep watch anyway.' Sharvar slinked back up the stairs.

Gar-ran walked over to the empty tomb.

'This one would have been for Yorkath, last of the high priests. Malabat was overrun before it was completed,' Gar-ran said.

'What happened to him?'

'He was martyred. Legend has it the principal ruler had his head stuffed and mounted in his dining hall as a warning to other rebellious factions.'

'Yuck, that's gross.' Why did Gar-ran have to tell him that? To distract himself, he bent down to look at the side of the tomb, where a repeating pattern of circles and half-moon shapes were carved.

'That's odd,' Gar-ran said.

'What is?'

'Does anything strike you as unusual about the interior of this tomb?'

Tim looked closely for a few moments. It was just plain, hollowed-out stone and smooth to the touch. He shrugged.

'It's not decorated at all.'

'Something else. Compared to the outside.'

'If you know what it is, why don't you just say?' Why did Gar-ran have to make *everything* into a test?

'I want your opinion. That's why,' Gar-ran replied, unruffled.

Tim tutted, but walked slowly around the tomb comparing the outside with the blank exterior. He had nearly completed a full circuit when one particular thing struck him.

'Well, it seems a bit weird that it's not deeper inside. Where the body will lie is only at half the height of the depth of the tomb.'

'Yes, good. What could be the reason for that?'

Tim thought for a few seconds.

'Perhaps they wanted the body higher up so that people who wanted to see the high priest lying in state wouldn't have to peer right in?'

'That's good reasoning, but there's no evidence the Mathranians ever adopted such practices. No, what struck me is that perhaps it's a false bottom, concealing something underneath.'

Tim leant right into the tomb. The bottom was entirely flat and perfectly joined to the sides all the way around.

'So, there could be a segment stored underneath?' Tim's irritation dissipated as his heart began to thump with excitement.

'Possibly. Although I doubt it'll be that easy.'

'So, we smash our way through?'

'I'm hoping that won't be necessary. If it's as I suspect, there should be a mechanism to uncover what lies beneath.'

Tim smiled to himself; Gar-ran's enthusiasm always made him seem younger.

Gar-ran squatted down and took out a small multi-tool from his belt pouch. He unfolded a narrow-pointed blade and began working it around the carving of a round, embossed shape the size of an apple.

Tim was surprised at how soft the white stone was, almost like chalk. Gripping the disc shape, Gar-ran pulled it out from the main body of the sarcophagus, but only an inch or so.

'How did you know that?' Tim asked.

'Lucky guess. I have heard of similar devices before, but never come across one.' He moved around to Tim's side and repeated the procedure.

'Now, we'll need to do the next part together. Grab hold of the disc on the other side and when I say, turn it to your left.'

Tim dropped down and took position.

'Ready? Now.'

Tim turned the disc as directed and Gar-ran on the other side turned his to the right at the same time. Nothing happened. They sat there for a few moments in silence.

'Shall we give it another go?' Tim ventured.

'Yes. This time turn back to the original position.'

Still nothing. Tim had to stifle a laugh as the whole thing suddenly struck him as funny. Gar-ran though was looking puzzled.

'OK. Once again turn to the left. Now.'

For a second or two everything was still, then the sides of the tomb began to vibrate slightly. Tim jumped back. Slowly the bottom of the tomb was dropping away at the far end as if on a giant hinge, revealing what was clearly a descending passageway.

Gar-ran grabbed one of the wall torches and brought it over to improve their view.

'Well done! That was great!' Tim said.

'We're not there yet,' Gar-ran cautioned.

Sharvar bounded down the stairs to the crypt.

'Is everything all right?' he asked as he skidded to a halt before them.

'Yes my friend. We're making good progress.' Gar-ran sounded delighted.

He can't wait to get down there, Tim thought.

Sharvar approached the tomb dubiously and peered inside before looking at Gar-ran and then to Tim.

'You're not going down there, surely?' The Caracali's face was creased with concern and Tim felt a spasm of anxiety. Could Sharvar sense something bad down there, or was he just claustrophobic?

'We must,' Gar-ran said.

'It could be a trap.' Sharvar paced the length of the tomb and looked far from happy.

'I know, but we've come this far, and it's very important to us.'

'Hmm. Are you both going?'

'Yes,' Tim answered. He didn't like the idea of climbing into what was essentially an open grave, but he couldn't let Gar-ran go on alone. And Gar-ran was right: they'd come that far, and earned the right to be there. Better just to get it out the way and move on.

'Hopefully it won't take too long and then we can all leave this place,' Gar-ran said briskly.

Sharvar peered into the tomb again before replying.

'Very well. I will remain above where there is sunlight and where you can see where you're going.' He turned elegantly and stalked away to the steps.

Gar-ran smiled and looked to Tim.

'Shall we?'

Tim nodded slowly. 'It's like Indiana Jones.'

'Indiana who?' Gar-ran asked as he climbed into the tomb and slipped down into the tunnel.

'Never mind.' Tim swung his leg and dropped inside.

Twelve
In at The Deep End

Tim found himself in a crudely-hacked-out tunnel. It was tall enough to stand, but only wide enough to allow single file movement. Gar-ran took the lead, torch in hand. Tim lowered his staff and kept his finger on the fire switch. He was glad Gar-ran was in front. The path veered down sharply and they had to grip the walls to brace themselves as they descended. After a few minutes the slope began to lessen and level out. Gar-ran lit the other wall-mounted torches as they passed. Not all of them caught, but gradually the tunnel became brighter. The smell of the burning dust was repulsive in the confined space, but they did their best to ignore it.

It's not too bad, Tim told himself, then cursed silently. He didn't want to tempt fate; perhaps even down here the wind god might hear him.

The path was level and widening with every step. Suddenly Gar-ran halted and he nearly bumped into him.

'What is it?' he whispered, then saw for himself as he squeezed alongside. Ahead of them was a gulf of space, easily twenty feet across. The roof of the tunnel sloped higher on the other side and Tim could just make out that the walls were decorated with many different pictograms, similar to the ones they'd seen at the first shrine.

'The next test,' Gar-ran said, his voice low.

'Looks deep,' Tim mused aloud as he peered over the edge into the void.

'Deep enough. Let's hope we don't find out.' He moved to the wall and crouched down.

'Have a look at this.'

Tim came over and knelt down.

'What do you see?' Gar-ran asked.

Tim looked hard at the stones Gar-ran indicated. They were a set of three – two lower ones and one on top, all of them oblong and the size of a small loaf of bread. Tim saw that the mortar around these particular stones looked newer, fresher.

'They look like they were placed more recently than the others.' He smiled to himself; he was getting better at this.

'Yes, you've got it. Gar-ran took out his multi-tool again and unfolded the long blade. As in the crypt, the mortar around the stones was easy to cut though and Tim realised it was more like dried resin. Carefully,

Gar-ran cut around all three stones. He handed Tim the blade.

'Cut around the same section on the other side and then place your hands like me,' Gar-ran instructed, passing him the tool.

Tim shuffled into position and quickly cut around the three stones. He slid the tool back to Gar-ran and placed his hands on the two lower stones.

'Now push.'

Tim did so and slowly the stones gave way, barely yielding at first but then gradually easing back.

'Now the one above,' Gar-ran said.

The top stone moved back more easily and, almost immediately, they became aware of a growing grating sound. Tim stood up quickly, afraid that the sounds meant that the walls were closing in on them, but instead he saw a line of stones on each side extending to form a set of stepping stones which would take them safely over the chasm. He grinned with relief.

'Wow. Shall we take a side each?'

'I think it will be safer if we stay on one side. I'll go first,' Gar-ran said.

Slowly they stepped out onto the first step. There was just enough room for both of them. They faced inwards towards the wall and side-stepped, crab-like. Half way across, Tim couldn't resist looking down. The void below him was indelibly black and everlasting. As he stared down it seemed to be expanding, rising up to slowly surround him, but it wasn't scary. If anything, the darkness was comforting. He closed his eyes. Gar-ran's hand on his shoulder snapped him back to his senses. He wobbled for a second and Gar-ran held him hard; the unexpected strength of his grip made him gasp.

'Don't look down. Keep moving.' Gar-ran sounded worried, spooking Tim even more.

'OK, OK.' Disturbed, Tim struggled to focus his attention on the last few steps. The urge to look down into the void was almost overwhelming. Somehow, though, he knew at all costs he must keep moving. Finally, after what seemed an age, he reached the other side.

'Are you all right?' Gar-ran asked as he caught his breath.

'Yeah, I'm fine. But it was weird. It felt as if I could just step off the ledge … and it would be OK to just fall down into the darkness, to … become a part of it.' It seemed ridiculous to voice that thought, but it was what he truly felt.

'I know. I felt it too. Best we keep moving.' Gar-ran patted him on the back.

Tim nodded. The sooner they got through this the better.

They walked for several minutes in silence. It was stifling in the tunnel and Tim suddenly had a longing for the clean, fresh, salt air of his home town. Home seemed further away than ever now. He pushed those thoughts away for now and fell into step with Gar-ran.

The tunnel broadened and they made swifter progress, although they took care not to rush into another trap. Soon they came to a tiled oblong chamber. The walls on each side were smooth and the stone finely dressed. Many had holes bored into them and Tim knew that this would be their next test.

'Has to be a trap,' Gar-ran said, echoing Tim's thoughts. 'We'll have to be very careful.' Gar-ran lowered his torch to illuminate the flagstone floor and they crouched down to look more closely. Tim noticed something. Some tiles had a faint red smear in their centre. These tiles formed a pattern which led diagonally outward and then diagonally back in toward the far doorway.

'Look at the tiles with the red paint. It's like they form a path.'

'Yes. Excellent. But can we trust them?' Gar-ran replied.

That possibility hadn't occurred to Tim, but it was a good point, he conceded. 'How can we tell?'

Gar-ran stood thinking for a few moments.

'I'm going to try something. Let's move back a little.' Gar-ran lowered his staff into the fire position and turned the power output down a few degrees. He fired at the first marked stone. Nothing changed. He continued to fire at each marked stone that led across the chamber.

Tim flinched at each shot, but did his best to conceal his reaction from Gar-ran, who stared ahead intently.

'So far so good,' he said. The next shot hit a marked stone just past the middle and instantly there was a sound like a wire snapping and a series of wickedly sharp, needle-like bolts shot out from the holes in the sides of the wall. They were released with such velocity that some embedded themselves in the opposing wall. Tim goggled at the sight; at least twenty bolts had pierced the far wall, and if they could do that to stone … He shivered despite the mugginess in the tunnel.

'Nasty. Let's see if there are any others.' Gar-ran continued to fire at the other marked stones all the way to the far door, but no more bolts fired. Just to be sure, Gar-ran repeated the process in reverse, but nothing else was triggered.

'Now, slowly walk exactly where I do.' Gar-ran stepped to the first tile and then out to the marked one. He looked around to Tim. Tim moved carefully, feeling constricted in his long robe and still unsettled from the previous trap. Gingerly, he placed his foot down and slowly transferred his weight and then stepped fully onto the tile.

'Good, just take it easy and watch me.' Gar-ran took the next two steps and Tim followed. He felt as if he would explode with tension. The simple act of walking had never seemed so hard. The chamber appeared much bigger than before, and the sweat now dripped from his face onto the other potentially lethal tiles. How sensitive were they? How much pressure was needed to spring the trap? The phrase walking on eggshells came to mind and he would have laughed at the absurdity of it, if his mouth hadn't been so dry.

He paused as they came to the trigger stone. Gar-ran turned and pointed to the flagstone immediately left.

'This one only.'

Tim nodded. As he stepped out, his eyes flicked to the spikes embedded in the far wall.

'Don't look,' Gar-ran commanded sternly and Tim shifted his focus back to where he needed to step. Moments later they were safely across.

'Phew, how much further do you think?' Tim mopped his brow as he sagged against the tunnel wall. That was enough adventure for one day.

'Can't be much further,' Gar-ran said, sounding far from certain. 'There'll probably be one more test though.'

Tim took a long drink from his water bottle. He screwed the top on quickly so Gar-ran wouldn't see his hand shaking.

'Let's get it over with.'

Outside, near the main entrance, Sharvar shielded his eyes as he stared into the distance. He thought he'd seen movement on the horizon, but now as he looked carefully, nothing stirred except the sand and loose bits of desert detritus blown along. He watched for a few minutes more before settling down again. Relaxation was of course impossible with the incessant wind and the ever-present sense of malice that Malabat exuded. The sooner they were away the better it would be. Moving further back into the shade and shadows, he resumed his watch.

Deep below, Tim and Gar-ran stared at the three doorways which confronted them.

'So only one is the right one?' Tim asked.

'Yes, the others will lead to … something unexpected.'

Tim peered ahead. The three doorways were identical. Nor were there any carvings or pictograms on the walls which gave any kind of clue. He hoped

Gar-ran wouldn't ask his opinion, as he could only guess.

'It seems we'll have to call on the assistance of technology rather than reason and deduction, which is a pity, but will save time.' Gar-ran swung the small satchel off his shoulder and took out a narrow, black, oblong box. Inside were three metallic balls which were covered with various tiny switches and sensors.

'What are they?' Tim had no idea, but they looked cool. Gar-ran must have loads of great stuff that he hadn't yet shared. Maybe he'd get to see more as time went on. Assuming they'd made it back to the Scarab, of course.

'Image sensor drones. We'll send one through each door to map the path ahead. Shouldn't take too long.' He pressed a sequence of tiny buttons on each of the drones and they came to life, hanging suspended in the air before each heading into a separate doorway.

'Hey that's great!' Tim was enjoying himself now he'd calmed down. He'd love to have a gadget like that. He had a GoPro back home which he used on his mountain bike and at the beach, but those little drones looked much better. He could send them anywhere.

Within a few minutes each drone came back. Gar-ran selected one, pressed a few more buttons and a detailed image was beamed onto the wall which they both studied.

'That's amazing. So it can build up a picture by scanning what's around it?'

'Yes, exactly, and as you can see, this way would be no good. See all these passageways and tunnels?' Gar-ran said, pointing at the lower end of the image which showed a warren of various routes.

'Go down there and we'd never find our way out.' Tim nodded. It reminded him of the ant farm cross section he'd seen once at the science museum.

Gar-ran tried the second drone and they peered at the new projected image.

'No. Not this one either. See that huge hollow area. Most likely it's a concealed, artificial lake, probably filled with mercury or other deadly substance. Just waiting for someone to fall in.'

Tim stared hard at the image. He didn't know how Gar-ran could possibly guess that, but he wasn't about to argue.

The drone which had gone through the far right-hand door was the one they needed. The image projected from it showed a clear passageway ahead to a medium-sized chamber with what appeared to be a staircase leading up.

'That's what we're after.' Gar-ran sounded excited again and Tim smiled too.

They set off ahead but, within minutes, the path was blocked by what appeared to be a solid stone wall.

'That shouldn't be there should it?' Tim asked. He rapped the wall with his knuckles. It was solid all right.

Gar-ran frowned and knelt down.

'Somewhere there'll be a handle or switch to open up access to the next chamber.' Tim squatted down too and spotted a small round hole about the size of his fist at the bottom of the wall.

'Here, what about that?'

'Yes, that's it. The switch is hidden inside a recess. Clever. It's too big for my hand.'

Tim moved closer. 'Is it safe?'

'Yes, it should be, but let's make sure.' Gar-ran shoved his staff in the recess and waggled it about. Nothing happened. He lowered his torch and Tim peered into the hole. He spied an oblong handle nearly a foot in. Stretching out, he took hold of it and tried to twist clockwise, but it wouldn't budge. He tried the other way and slowly it began to turn. Miraculously, the wall ahead slid down with a low rumble. A dust cloud gushed from the now open doorway, making them cough and cover their eyes with their headscarves. It was a full minute before they could see the way ahead.

Inside the doorway of the chamber were two wall torches which Gar-ran quickly lit. The chamber had a deep, musty smell which felt oppressive in the confined space, but it was stocked full of treasures and artefacts. Tim gazed in awe as he realised he was the first person to see any of it for hundreds of years. Headless mannequins garbed in richly decorated robes adorned the sides of the room, elaborate crowns and headdresses hung from the walls and various golden statues of the Gods of The Elements were everywhere, their brilliance masked somewhat by a fine sheen of dust. Close to the far wall stood a mannequin draped in a deep red robe with finely embroidered silver sleeves. What caught Tim's eye though was the magnificent golden medallion necklace which contained in its centre a bright pink crystal covered with a fine silver mesh.

'Gar-ran, look. Is it?'

Gar-ran moved over and leant close in.

'Yes, yes, that's the power stone all right. Incredible. Well done, Tim. You should be the one to lift it.'

Tim suddenly felt nervous. He hesitated, feeling the weight of Gar-ran's stare. Taking a deep breath, he plucked the medallion up. He saw straight away he could slide the stone out by grasping the enclosing mesh and lifting it straight up. He replaced the necklace and gasped as he felt his whole hand begin to tingle, but as quickly as the sensation began, it faded away.

'Did you feel something?'

'Yeah, but only for a second.'

Gar-ran nodded. 'Right, we should get back to Sharvar and get out of here.'

'Great, let's go.' That was the best idea Tim had heard in days. He carefully tucked the stone inside his satchel.

'I wonder where that goes?' Tim gestured to the stone steps at the far end of the chamber.

'Probably up to the shrine we saw on the way in. We know some of the Mathranians escaped. It's quite likely they came this way,' Gar-ran replied, sounding pensive.

'I'm glad some of them got away.' Tim felt buoyant. They had a key component: the vital crystal that, when charged, would power the dimension bomb. Now they just had to get back, and that journey should be quicker.

Hurriedly they retraced their path. Tim was picturing the brilliant smile on Nerissa's face as he walked triumphantly back into the command hub, when there was movement up ahead and they froze. Gar-ran lowered his staff.

'Stay behind me,' he mouthed to Tim.

'It's OK. It's me,' a familiar voice called out.

'Sharvar!' Tim exclaimed as the Caracali came into sight.

'We've got trouble.'

Tim's smile dropped instantly. *What now?*

'There's a gang of bandits on their way in, about a dozen or so. All armed. Whatever you two are looking for, it's going to have to wait. We need to get out of here.'

'We've got what we came for, and back there we found a staircase which I think will lead up into the shrine,' Gar-ran said without missing a beat.

Nothing phases him. Tim thought, before remembering something. 'What about the beasts and our supplies?'

Gar-ran looked at Sharvar.

'Too risky. They'll be here soon.'

'The shrine it is then.' Gar-ran turned and led the way.

Thirteen
Outnumbered

Q uickly they headed back to the treasure
chamber and climbed the narrow staircase. The
stairs led to another dead end and a flat
sandstone ceiling. On closer inspection, Tim saw
there was a square block above them which was
slightly recessed.

'There must be a switch somewhere,' Gar-ran
said, but a study of the surrounding wall and steps
revealed nothing.

Tim's heart thudded. They had to get out of
there; the bandits must be close by now. 'I'll check
below.' He bolted downwards. The lower wall was
clear, but then he noticed on the side of the lowest
step there was an embossed, raised disc like the one
which triggered the opening of the high priest's tomb.

'Gar-ran, pass me your knife.' Gar-ran tossed the
multi-tool down and, using the sharp blade, Tim sliced
around the disc. He took hold and twisted hard
towards the right. Nothing happened, so he twisted
left and then back again. Immediately, Gar-ran and
Sharvar called out in excitement.

'That's it!'

Tim raced up the steps to join them. A trapdoor had opened above them and weak sunlight filtered in. Best of all was the sweet smell of fresh air.

They climbed up into a small room with more steps leading up to the right. Gar-ran reset the trapdoor and Sharver dragged a heavy rock on top.

'That's to stop anyone sneaking up,' he purred.

The steps led them into the main square of Malabat's ruined shrine. The wind blew as fiercely as ever, and it was very warm.

Stealthily, Sharvar climbed some battered steps to a small platform and peeked over the wall. After watching for a few moments, he gestured for them to join him. Tim looked out but what he saw wasn't encouraging.

He counted eleven desert bandits gathered in front of the huge stronghold. Most were native Terranians, but at least four were the stocky, hyena-like predators. Tim spotted the small, stout figure of Rahhsan among them. He pointed him out to Gar-ran, who nodded. All the bandits were armed. The hyenas carried laser rifles, while the Terranians had smaller pistols and long, wickedly-pointed spears. One also carried what looked like a huge crossbow. The group split apart and a detachment of six headed through Malabat's main entrance, while the remaining five took up guard positions outside. Tim looked over the whole area, but there was no way to reach their transport without being seen.

'They know we're here now. But after what happened to their companions, they'll be wary.' Sharvar's voice was a whispered growl.

Tim thought for a moment.

'If only we could somehow trap them inside.' Sharvar's ears pricked up at Tim's comment.

'Yes, that would work nicely, but how?'

'It won't be long before they find the open tomb.' Gar-ran said. Tim's stomach was churning and he wished that the three of them were somewhere far away from there. Even with their own weapons, they were massively outgunned.

'My guess is they'll send a few down to investigate, leave a few more guarding the entrance and send the rest over to check the shrine out. That might be our chance. If we can take those ones out, we'll have more weapons and better odds.' Gar-ran had to raise his voice over the growing wind.

As if on cue, three of the bandits, two hyenas and a Terranian started to head towards the shrine, weapons at the ready.

'You two hide; we don't want them to pick up your scent. But make sure you can see me,' Sharvar hissed urgently.

'What about you?' Tim asked, alarmed at the prospect of his new friend facing three deadly bandits alone.

'I can take one, or maybe two of them, but the lizard will be the most dangerous. You two concentrate on him.'

'Agreed,' Gar-ran said, answering for them both.

Tim and Gar-ran ran to the other side of the courtyard, and concealed themselves behind the remnants of a small building. Tim made sure his staff was ready this time, and kept his finger on the fire switch. The howl of the wind made the ruins feel lonely and isolated. Sand blew everywhere and his face felt gritty. He watched Sharvar slink along the parapet before settling on a ledge several feet above and to the side of the entrance.

A moment later the two hyenas appeared within the arch of the entrance, and Tim was surprised at the jolt of hatred and fear he felt as he looked at their snarling features. They paused for a few moments, sniffing the air, then headed through. The Terranian followed behind. He was enormous, easily over seven feet, and towered over his two companions. Tim stole a look at Gar-ran. His face was grim.

With blinding speed, Sharvar flung himself down onto the hyenas, sending them sprawling, their rifles clattering across the hard flagstones. At the same moment Gar-ran lurched forward, staff lowered. Tim saw where he was aiming and concentrated his fire on the same area. His shot clipped the lizard's shoulder, spinning him round, but Gar-ran's shot hit him dead centre, knocking him flat. Then with a yell that made Tim flinch, Gar-ran raced ahead. He fired again but missed as the giant lizard twisted away. Still rolling, he grabbed his spear and flung it hard, straight at Gar-ran.

In one instinctive movement, Tim flicked his staff to the wide-beam setting and fired, blowing the spear aside. The lizard crouched as if preparing to leap but, at that moment, there was a searing flash and he reeled backwards. A gaping, blackened hole appeared in his chest. Tim whirred round to see Sharvar wielding a laser rifle. The motionless bodies of the two hyenas lay at his feet.

'That was a close one!' Sharvar's fangs gleamed in the sun. Tim caught up with Gar-ran and leant on him as he let out a huge sigh of relief.

'You saved me, Tim. Great shooting.' Gar-ran clapped him on the back and Tim nodded; he couldn't trust himself to speak right now.

Sharvar bounded up to the parapet again and looked out. Tim was about to climb up when Sharvar leapt down, landing gracefully.

'There are three guarding the entrance. I think I can get two of them with the rifle from here. Do you think you can deal with the other one?' This question was addressed to Gar-ran.

'Yes, I'll take a run in if you cover me,' Gar-ran said, retrieving a fallen rifle.

'Hey I'm coming too,' Tim said. Gar-ran opened his mouth to protest but Tim stalled him.

'I've saved you once already.' Gar-ran exchanged a look with Sharvar and nodded.

'All right, but stay behind me.'

Tim grinned. He was nervous but felt he could do this. The success in the skirmish and the relief at finding the vital power stone had given him confidence and he wanted to keep the momentum going.

After a short discussion it was agreed Sharvar would attempt to take out the three guards with the laser rifle while Gar-ran and Tim would make a run into Malabat and grab the beasts and their supplies. Sharvar would then high-tail it to them while providing cover.

Tim and Gar-ran started out keeping low. From their position they wouldn't be seen until they came over the brow of a small dune. Tim had taken the dead Terranian's pistol and its weight in his hand felt comforting. They stopped just before the crest of the dune.

'Ready?' Gar-ran asked, his rifle in the aim position.

Tim nodded. He felt a little sick now, but there was no turning back.

'Go!' Gar-ran raced over the top of the dune and Tim followed close behind. From his peripheral vision he saw the flash from Sharvar's rifle. The wind was behind him, pushing him on, but already Gar-ran was outpacing him. He wouldn't have believed the old man could move so fast.

Tim saw that two of the guards were down, but where was the third? The main entrance was only forty feet away and he realised it was exactly like his dream. He slowed and then came to a halt as an intense feeling of déjà vu swept over him.

'Come on!' Gar-ran yelled, snapping him to attention. He ran on to where the marshal was crouched against the wall of Malabat, twenty feet from the main entrance. They hugged the wall tightly. Tim turned and saw Sharvar bounding towards them and in a moment the Caracali was beside them.

'The other one escaped inside,' he panted.

Gar-ran nodded and drew something from his satchel. He opened his hand to reveal three small, matt-black metal balls, the size of a large plum and with a thin red line around the centre.

'Impact grenades. Throw them hard and they explode on whatever they hit. Don't drop them. We're going to have to bring the roof down.'

Gar-ran handed Tim a grenade. It was heavy, like a steel ball-bearing, but so small, Tim found it hard to believe even three of them could bring down hundreds of tons of stone that had withstood the elements and scores of raiders over the years. Sharvar, too, looked doubtful.

'Trust me. We'll aim at the ceiling. I'll throw mine through the main entrance. You two take a window each, but stay low.'

Gar-ran turned and moved off before Tim could reply, and he felt a stab of alarm. What if they got caught in the backdraft of the explosion? What if they didn't all detonate? There was no time to worry though; Gar-ran was almost at the main entrance. Keeping low, Tim moved to the middle window.

Gar-ran halted on the threshold of the entrance. He turned and nodded and then jumped up and flung his grenade. Tim launched himself up and hurled his too, and then flung himself down, grazing his chin on the hard, gritty ground.

A huge boom ruptured the air and an immense rumbling shook the earth.

'Run!' Gar-ran bellowed and Tim leapt up. He saw Gar-ran was heading to their tethered animals

174

when a huge dust cloud bloomed out of the doorway, coating him in fine powder. He tugged his goggles on and ran hard, not daring to take a breath. The visibility gradually improved and, coughing and spluttering, he made it to his beast, who was bleating pitifully, its eyes wild and staring. All the drongos were making a terrible racket and Tim longed to be far away from this crazy, cursed place and safely back on the Scarab.

It seemed to take Sharvar ages to calm the drongos, and Tim thought he would go mad with the tension, although he did his best not to show it. Gar-ran untethered the raiders' beasts and they bolted off in all directions. Eventually, Sharvar got the animals settled and they climbed on and galloped hard towards the east. After two hours of hard riding, they changed tack and, following Sharvar's lead, cut to the south and the long trail back to Ter-ran. Tim had been checking every few minutes, but no one appeared to be following them, and the wind soon obliterated their trail. He felt an enormous sense of relief, which was probably misplaced, he realised. There was a long way to go yet.

***

Three hours later, the light was fading rapidly and they stopped to make camp. Tim's stomach had been rumbling for a while and Gar-ran quipped it was becoming louder than the constant wind. Tim laughed, even though the joke was bad. Everything seemed so much better the further they got from Malabat.

'I think it best not to light a fire,' Sharvar purred.

'Yes, of course,' Gar-ran agreed as he rubbed his neck and shoulders.

He's tired too, Tim realised. Gar-ran often seemed tireless, but now he looked beat. Dinner was a shared meal of dried meat washed down with water and the last of the desert fruit.

Tim thought sleep would be impossible but, after only a few minutes curled up in his sleeping bag, he realised he was already nodding off. Mercifully, the night was uneventful and they were up and away a few minutes before the first streaks of light heralding a new dawn appeared in the sky. The wind had now dropped to a pleasant breeze. The journey back to Ter-ran seemed much quicker than their outward trek, but still they waited until nightfall before entering the city.

While still in the wasteland, Gar-ran paid off Sharvar, handing him a heavy purse which, judging by the Caracali's expression, was more than he'd anticipated.

'What will you do know?' Gar-ran asked.

'I've been thinking about that. I will head east. Six days' journey from here will take me back to the lands of my birth, which I have not seen for many years. It will be a fine thing to be among my people again.'

'I wish you well. You've been an enormous help to us, and a good friend.' Gar-ran offered his hand, which Sharvar took. Tim hugged Sharvar and they said their goodbyes.

The walk through Ter-ran's darkened street was nerve-racking. They were so close to getting clean away, Tim was afraid something would happen at the last moment. It seemed a very long twenty minutes until they reached the spaceport. The Terranian on duty gave a cursory glance at their papers before waving them through.

Once on board the ship, they hurried into the control room, with Tim taking his usual seat while Gar-ran started the ignition sequence. Within moments they soared up through the opening roof and tore through the clouds and on into space.

'I'm glad that's over,' Tim sighed as he sprawled back in his seat.

'The next piece may not be so easy to obtain,' Gar-ran said, looking stern. Tim's eyes widened and it was a second before he realised the marshal was joking with him.

'I'll think about that tomorrow.'

Fourteen
An Old Friend

'No, that's all I can remember,' Tim said through a mouthful of cornflakes. It was breakfast time in the galley and Gar-ran was frowning at him as he nursed a cup of coffee.

'Tell me again,' he said.

Tim rolled his eyes and sighed theatrically. He'd had another dream last night, but this was the fourth time they'd gone over it. 'I was standing in this big circle and opposite was this giant man. He looked like he was made of stone. Behind him was this mountain. Then it seemed like the mountain was moving, then I woke up. That's all.'

Gar-ran nodded but didn't reply.

'Are you going to hypnotise me again?' Tim said, realising too late he was sounding aggressive.

'No, I don't think so. The mountain you described, was it also grey, or brown?'

Tim blinked in surprise. The question was unexpected and he struggled to remember. He closed his eyes. 'Grey, with white streaks. Does that help?'

'Yes, I think I know where we have to go next, but I'll need to make some preparations.' Tim studied Gar-ran's face; he saw anxiety in his eyes for a moment but then it was gone as he stood up abruptly.

'Well, where is it?'

'The place you describe sounds like Dimantia, home of the stone giants, or stone guardians as they call themselves. It's a long way from here and we'll have to make a stop on the way. Finish your breakfast and then meet me in the command hub.'

He stalked out and Tim stared after him, then got up and tipped the rest of his cereal into the bin. He wasn't hungry any more.

***

'Continuous transmission through all usual relays.' Gar-ran was issuing instructions to Nerissa as Tim sidled into the command hub. She gave him a brief smile as he sat down.

'Notify me when you get a response,' Gar-ran said, swinging round to face Tim.

'I've put out a call to an old friend. He might be able to get hold of something which will come in handy if we're going to Dimantia. If I haven't heard anything by tomorrow, we're going to have to proceed anyway.'

'OK. Who is this friend? Another marshal?' Tim hoped it would be; they'd been seriously outnumbered in Ter-ran.

'Definitely not a marshal. He's a colleague from way back. Runs a shipping business. If I can reach him, we can meet at TX-1450.'

'That's a funny name for a planet.'

Gar-ran smiled faintly. 'It's not a planet, it's more of, ah, what you would call a service station.'

'What, out here in space?' He had a memory of the roadside service stations he used to stop in with his parents on the long trip to visit grandparents. They always had a shop with cool toys or games that were different to the ones he could find in his home town, but the idea of a galactic Roadchef seemed ridiculous.

'Of course here in space. Where else?' Gar-ran sounded testy and Tim wondered what was bothering him.

'So, we just wait to hear then?'

'Yes.' Gar-ran turned his attention to a readout on the viewing screen and Tim, feeling snubbed, wandered back to his quarters.

He spent the rest of the morning writing up a journal he was keeping as a record of their quest. He paused for a while after recording their escape from Malabat. What was Sharvar doing now? he wondered. Later on, he practised with his staff and pistol on the weapons range. Sometime after lunch he was lying on his bed reading a magazine when Gar-ran's voice came through on the intercom.

'I've made contact with my colleague Zarox. We'll meet him at TX-1450 in five hours.'

'OK.' Tim was dying to know more about this mysterious colleague but he was still feeling aggrieved after Gar-ran's earlier dismissal. He tried to read some more but his mind kept darting ahead to the upcoming rendezvous, so he gave up and wandered down to the galley to get a bag of crisps. The time dragged on and he was debating whether to swallow his pride and wander up to the command hub when Gar-ran's voice came through on the intercom again.

'Tim, I have the station on the viewing screen.'

Tim dashed out of his room without replying but forced himself to slow down as he got to the command hub. He gasped though as he saw the magnified image on the screen. TX-1450 appeared as a ginormous halo standing boldly out in the darkness of space, like a silver ring in a black velvet box.

'It's massive!' he said, remembering too late he was meant to be playing it cool.

'Yes, six and a half miles in diameter. Eighteen floors. It's the perfect place for a discreet meeting as you could spend years on board and not see half of it.'

Gar-ran seemed more upbeat and Tim's own mood thawed a little.

'Why is it so big?' It didn't seem possible any building could be that size. The construction alone would take years and years.

'Well there are some pretty big ships out here that need to dock and sometimes get repaired. So, they need space for workshops and parts storage. They also have a range of refurbished ships, which is very handy. There are stories of some of the workers spending their entire lives there without ever leaving. Although nowadays a lot of the labour is automated, of course.'

Automated, that could mean robots. I'm going on board a galactic service station run by robots. This is going to be great, Tim thought as he slid into the co-pilot chair.

'How long until we dock?'

'Forty minutes.'

The descent was routine, and shortly they both stood in the exit bay waiting for the door to unlock. Tim had changed into another deep-blue flight suit with a marshal's badge pinned to his chest. Gar-ran was similarly attired. Weapons were prohibited, so neither of them was armed.

'Now you get all sorts at places like this, so keep a cool head. Our cover story is that you're a marshal cadet in training and I'm your instructor. We're here on an orientation exercise,' Gar-ran whispered.

'All right, sounds simple.' *At least on here nobody's trying to kill us*, he thought as the airlock swished open.

Tim stared up at the iceberg-white, cavernous spacecraft hangar. The place was almost deserted and he wondered if Gar-ran had picked this time especially. There was a faint rumbling sound and he turned and got an eyeful of a truly strange sight.

'Docking official,' Gar-ran whispered. Tim nodded dumbly. He'd been warned not to stare but that was, frankly, impossible.

The robot was a gun metal grey and his lower section resembled a tank complete with wide, continuous track tread. His upper half was humanoid, although primitive looking. The skull-shaped head had a small grill for a mouth and its eyes were two small silver discs the size of a ten-pence piece. The robot spoke English, much to Tim's amazement until he remembered his was still wearing his universal translator.

Gar-ran explained they were looking for recreation section 3 and the refreshment quarter. The robot duly directed them to a large door some distance away. Gar-ran nodded and they set off. At the back of the hangar a large wedge-shaped ship was surrounded by several tall, athletic-looking robots holding laser rifles, while two more had climbed on board and were peering into the craft.

'Checking for stolen equipment,' said Gar-ran in reply to Tim's questioning look. The captain will be undergoing an interview on level 4. That's one place we won't be visiting, I hope.'

The door, which was marked with strange symbols in red paint, slid silently open as they approached. Another robot official was waiting for them on the other side and directed them to a small lift in the opposite wall. They went inside and Tim marvelled at the lift's control panel, which was a confusing array of glowing buttons, switches and dials.

'The lifts here can go sideways as well as up. Saves time,' Gar-ran said.

For a moment Tim was totally disorientated and he stumbled against the side of the wall. Gar-ran gave him a knowing smile. It was impossible to tell which direction they were heading in. He'd imagined it would be a short ride, but the minutes ticked away and they were still stuck inside. He began to feel unsettled and more than a little claustrophobic. Where were they? Finally, the door whisked open and they stood in a grey corridor.

'Takes some getting used to, doesn't it?' Gar-ran said sympathetically.

'You can say that again.'

On the wall in front of them were yellow painted symbols which Tim took for some kind of directions. Gar-ran studied them for a second before striding off to the right. Ahead of them the corridor curved around.

Tim quickened his pace to keep up with Gar-ran. Another door opened and three men came out. Tim goggled at them. They were very similar to earth men except that they were just over a foot tall and incredibly slender, as if they'd been stretched on a rack to reed-like thinness. They wore deep-blue coveralls and their voices sounded like highly pitched whistles.

'Craneians. They'll be here to do precise work on engines and drive systems. Don't stare. They can be quite volatile,' Gar-ran cautioned.

Tim quickly averted his gaze as they continued on. The wide double door at the end of the corridor was open, revealing what was clearly some kind of canteen. There was row after row of white metal tables, with some closely bunched, others spread out. What struck Tim was that many of them were at different heights. Some tables were only a few inches off the floor while others reached way up into the air.

'They have to cater for everyone,' Gar-ran said, answering Tim's unspoken question. Tim wondered if whatever ate at the giant's table ever accidentally stepped on the smaller dinner guests.

It must have been a quiet period as the canteen had few customers. They passed near to a table occupied by two enormous, insect-like beings that resembled giant locusts. They turned to look at the two new arrivals as they passed. Tim kept his eyes firmly forward this time.

Further along, at a low table, sat three figures that were carved from what looked like black glass. Tim racked his brain for the precise word to describe them, something he had once heard in geography class ... Obsidian! The dark glass formed by the intense heat of a volcano. The trio were entirely motionless until one moved forward, making Tim jump. He glanced at Gar-ran, who had raised his hand to wave at someone.

Near the end of the canteen and seated at a regular-sized table was a youth of about sixteen or seventeen years old. As Tim got closer, though, he had the distinct impression that the boy must somehow be older. While his face was very youthful and the rich brown skin was smooth and unmarked, the closely cropped curly hair was greying and there was something ancient and knowing in the boy's eyes. Smiling, he gestured for him and Gar-ran to sit.

It took a moment for the universal translator to kick in and Tim adjusted his earpiece to be able to hear more clearly.

'Tim, this is my old friend Zarox. Tim's a cadet.'

'They get younger and younger!' Zarox leant over and clasped Tim's hand in both of his own. His grip was strong – stronger than would be expected in a teenager. Zarox gestured and a serving robot came over. He said something in another language which was so quick Tim didn't catch it, although Gar-ran nodded. The robot zoomed away.

'He's ordered drinks,' Gar-ran said.

The two men politely enquired after each other's health and journeys for a few minutes before Zarox asked how he could help. At that moment the drinks arrived. Tim relaxed as he saw they were being served in glass beakers which looked reasonably familiar. His drink was as dark and shiny as black treacle and he peered at it apprehensively.

'Try it. It's a bit like chocolate,' Gar-ran said.

Tim took a tentative sip. It was cool and sweet and did taste like chocolate. There was another subtle flavour too, but he couldn't make out what it was. He didn't think he'd be able to drink it all.

'I need a Xeon-class weapon. Something small though. Portable,' Gar-ran said as he lowered his glass.

Zarox looked incredulous for a moment before replying.

'What you hunting out there?'

'It's just precautionary.'

'When?'

'Today.'

Zarox sat back in his chair and remained silent for a few moments. Then he broke into a broad grin.

'And I don't suppose you're able to tell your old pal what you're up to?'

Gar-ran shrugged, then smiled. Zarox scratched his chin and looked thoughtful.

'I may have something, but you'll need to install it.'

'That's OK.'

'Take me about half an hour,' Zarox said.

'Agreed. So, when will your new ship be ready?'

'Less than a week now and I can't wait. She's a beauty. Gonna be able to go further and for longer than ever before. Plenty of firepower too. You still flying the Scarab?'

'Yes, she suits me well. You'd never catch her.'

'Ha, well perhaps. We'll see about that some time. Maybe a little wager?'

'Perhaps.'

'Well I'm gonna head down to B deck, check those Craneians have their eye on the ball. See you in thirty.' He stood and moved out from the table. Tim noticed his leg for the first time. It was a meld of various metals which joined directly onto the flesh of his thigh and continued down his calf.

'Bet you've never seen anything like it before, huh? Had a smash a little while back; they had to do a cybernetic fusion to save my leg. It's not pretty but it sure works. It's even better than before. I could have it covered in Nu-Flesh, of course, but I like how the metal looks. Actually, I've been thinking of getting the other leg done too. Just kidding. See you soon.'

Tim watched him walk away. He liked the way Zarox had accepted him, and hadn't made him feel like a kid totally out of his depth, but most of the conversation had gone over his head. Why would Gar-ran need another weapon? What was Xeon class? And there was something else about Zarox that was undefinable. It bothered him. Could they trust him?

'What was that all about?' he asked.

'I'll tell you when we're back on board. How's your drink?'

'It's OK. He looks young, but he seems old somehow?'

'He's Estruthian. They have a different concept of age, and they mature late. So, yes, he's far older than he looks.'

'How old?'

'I don't know his exact age, but by now, he must be over 300 years.'

Tim choked on his drink, which amused Gar-ran.

'Seriously?'

'Yes.'

Tim knew it was rude to ask, but he couldn't help himself. 'Gar-ran, how old are you?'

'Old.' He smiled, and Tim knew that was all he was going to get. He was glad the rec area was quiet; he didn't think he could handle a canteen full of aliens. He sipped his drink, and they waited.

Presently Zarox returned carrying a small silver case. It reminded Tim of a portable toolkit. He slid it across the table to Gar-ran.

'It's not top line, but it should do. Now, wanna tell me what this is all about?' He grinned broadly.

'Some other time.' Gar-ran smiled as well and passed something across the table. Tim only got a brief glance at what looked like an oversized credit card before Zarox smoothly pocketed it.

'Classy.' Zarox said as he stood up. 'Be seeing you again sometime. Stay safe out there.'

'You too,' Gar-ran replied. Zarox clapped Tim on the shoulder as he sidled out.

'So, what now?' Tim asked.

'Now we get back on board and get out of here,' Gar-ran replied.

***

They took a different route back to the elevators and were back on the Scarab in fifteen minutes and headed straight to the lab.

'It'll need to be assembled,' Gar-ran said as he flipped open the silver case and unpacked the stored components, which looked to be constituent parts of a big lantern. Several pieces were covered in rust.

'Doesn't look like much. What exactly is it?' Tim asked.

'This is a Xeon-class laser lantern. At least that's the easiest translation to English. It's a prohibited weapon, very powerful. Or it will be when I've restored it. Possession of such a weapon is illegal in many sectors, which is why it's always stored in a dissembled state. Technically, you can only carry them if you have a special licence.'

Tim peered at the lantern with more interest. It didn't look powerful; it looked like something that'd been lying around in his dad's shed for years.

'Do you have a special licence?'

'No, and I'm not going to get one either. Officially we were never in possession of said laser lantern,' Gar-ran said brightly. He was in his element now and Tim smiled at his contagious enthusiasm.

'We will test it on the range later?'

'Oh, no, it's much too powerful for that. I'm hoping we never have to use it, but all the same ...'. His voice trailed off as he inspected a small piece of machinery that was particularly corroded. Tim looked at the spread-out components; there were at least twenty different parts, some in very bad shape. Gar-ran was going to have his work cut out.

'Well I'll leave you to it. I'm gonna hang out with Nerissa.'

'By all means,' Gar-ran replied without looking up.

Fifteen
The Stone Guardians

---◆---◎---◆---

'No more, please, no more.' The Terranian's words were a hoarse rasp as he struggled for breath. There was something broken inside him, he was sure. He raised his head to look up at the huge, implacable figure that stood over him. The sheer size of it was terrifying, but worst of all were his eyes: opaque and utterly alien.

'I've told you everything I know. They were heading to the shrines. Malabat too, I think.'

The creature said something he didn't understand but, from the tone, he had the idea that the thing believed him. Thank the Gods. Maybe now it would leave? He wiped away some of the blood which was running into his eyes and, as his vison cleared, he saw the creature was pointing a plasma pistol at him. He didn't even have time to scream before the brilliant flash illuminated the dimly lit store.

***

'So how giant are these giants?' Tim asked, lounging back in his chair in the command hub. It was the following morning and they were heading to the Dimantian system.

'The older they are, the bigger they get.' Gar-ran was standing up looking at a star chart displayed on the viewing screen.

'Some of them are thousands of years old and as big as a small mountain. The younger ones who are only a few hundred years are twenty-five to thirty feet tall.'

Tim mulled this information over for a while. The giant that confronted him in his dream wasn't that big, and what was the significance of the big circle he'd been standing in? He mentioned twice now that he would be OK with another hypnosis session, but Gar-ran had brushed the idea aside. Why? What was he afraid of? He must have spent most of the night working on the laser lantern because, when Tim had been down to the lab, he was amazed to see it nearly fully restored and freshly painted a bright orange.

'And what do they do? What's their purpose?'

'The same as any living creature, I suppose: to keep on living. They're a solitary race. Not much is known about them. Occasionally if you travel a great deal you may encounter some of the young ones. They tend to show up as bodyguards, or enforcers.'

'So, they're tough guys then?'

'The toughest, and from what I've heard, they aren't keen on visitors. It may be difficult to gain their trust.' Gar-ran zoomed in on a particular section of the chart.

That's why he wanted the special weapon, Tim thought. Dimantia didn't sound much fun as a place to visit. Maybe Gar-ran could negotiate with them from on board the Scarab and then they wouldn't even have to go outside.

'Do you speak their language?'

'Only a few words. We'll have to rely on the translators.'

Probably have to go out and meet them then. 'And how long till we get there?'

'By tonight. We're two rift jumps away, but there's a lot of rock debris in the Dimantian system. We'll have to fly manually for the last stages.'

Tim sat up at the mention of manual flying. 'Could you show me a bit of how that works, when we get nearer?'

'Yes, sure, but only for a bit. Flying in any debris field is dangerous and out here there's nowhere to put in for repairs.'

'OK, I'm up for that.' He was surprised that Gar-ran had agreed, although he knew he liked it when he showed an interest in the Scarab. *I'm going to fly an actual spaceship!*

'If you like, I can give you a quick lesson now?'

Tim stared up at Gar-ran.

'Seriously?

'If you want to.'

'Let's do it.' Tim couldn't believe his luck. Gar-ran must really trust him. There was a faint click and the previously redundant steering and flight control console in front of Tim unfolded itself and extended until he could reach it easily. The console was an ellipse shape, split in two and connected by a silver tube. It was full of buttons and switches.

'Later I'll activate your controls but for now just watch me. The first thing to learn is …'

The next hour flew by and Tim was slightly aggrieved when Gar-ran said that was enough for one day. He went to his room and made some notes while it was all fresh in his mind. Later Gar-ran asked him to meet him in the lab room and showed him another console unit with a viewing screen. Through this he was able to access a giant database filled with information and images of different stars, planets and their inhabitants and overall position in the universe. It was mind-blowing.

'How come you never showed me this before?' he asked.

'You already had enough to think about. You can use it now to find out a bit more about where we're going.'

Tim needed no further encouragement. This was even better than the internet, and he was soon so absorbed he lost all track of time. Eventually though, hunger got of the better of him and he headed off to the galley. Gar-ran came down a little later and they hung out for a while. These were some of the best times, he decided, chilling out before the next big day. He felt part of the team for sure now. He knew he was making a difference, and instead of apprehension about tomorrow, Tim realised he was looking forward to it.

Back in his quarters, he stretched out on his bunk and fell into a dreamless sleep.

***

The descent to Dimantia was bumpier than he expected. Tim knew from his reading that the planet had an unusually dense atmosphere, but he was unprepared for the turbulence they encountered. Finally, the shaking eased off and Gar-ran flipped on the viewing screen. There was still a lot of cloud cover, making it difficult to see, but the terrain looked mountainous. There were no spaceports so they were going to have to land on whatever level ground they could find.

The viewing screen showed they were in a shallow valley. Gleaning what they could from Tim's dream, Gar-ran had suggested they start the search in the south-eastern sector of the planet. There was no known name for the region, so Gar-ran had dubbed it the long valley and they were at the southernmost end.

'Ready?'

'Ready.' All the gear they needed was already stowed in the airlock. Nerissa had reported an atmosphere close to Earth's so they could breathe unaided. Plasma pistols, securely fastened, were their choice of weapon, although Tim knew Gar-ran would also carry the restored laser lantern in case of emergency. Slowly the door to the new world opened, flooding the little chamber with bright light.

Tim stepped out and gazed all around. There were no settlements, no traffic, no sign of any life. There was hardly any sound except the whisper of the faint breeze, and it felt like they were the only living beings that had ever stood there. It was an unexpected, eerie feeling, and to distract himself he studied the nearest cliff face, which was steep, but looked climbable. Thin, sea-green patchy grass grew in between some of the cracks and fringed the summit some 200 feet above.

'Well, this is as good a place to look as any,' Gar-ran said. Tim nodded. He felt sure he could manage the climbing and hiking they were going to have to do, but would Gar-ran? It was something he hadn't considered till now.

'Maybe we should go further along, see if we can pick up a trail?' he suggested. Gar-ran agreed and they started off. After ten minutes they reached a section that was easier to ascend. Gar-ran went first. He climbed slowly to start with, which wore Tim's patience, although he resisted the temptation to say anything, but then Gar-ran got into a rhythm and began to move with more confidence. It was pleasantly cool and the weather clear, but the trek got tougher and soon Tim was shoulder to shoulder with Gar-ran.

'I think we'll take a little breather,' Gar-ran said, slinging off his pack.

'Yeah, OK,' Tim said, although he could have happily carried on. As he shrugged his backpack off, a small rock clattered down from above and, as Tim looked up, he froze. There was a large boulder right above them, balanced just on the cliff edge, and he was certain it hadn't been there before. He was just about to alert Gar-ran when the huge rock toppled over the edge. Tim threw himself forward and hauled up Gar-ran, who yelped in surprise and then, seeing the danger, pushed himself and Tim hard against the rock face as the massive stone crashed past them and down the path they'd just climbed. It landed with an ear-splitting crash somewhere below. Smaller rocks now clattered down the cliff face and Tim covered his head with his rucksack. Then Gar-ran gave a sharp gasp of pain and Tim realised with dread he'd been hit.

Gar-ran's right arm hung limp and his suit was torn at the shoulder.

'One of them got me. Collarbone's broken,' he murmured.

Tim was stunned. He'd wondered at odd times on their journey from Earth what he would do if Gar-ran got sick, or injured, and now it had happened for real. Gar-ran was hurt and they'd barely started. He suddenly felt small and alone, but then mentally shook himself. His friend needed him; he was going to have to step up and get through this.

Staying as close to the cliff face as possible, Tim rooted in his bag for first aid supplies. Using a thick bandage, he was able to fashion a crude sling which at least would partially support Gar-ran's arm and minimise aggravating his injury further. He found that having something practical to do focused his mind, although his hands shook a little as he knotted the sling.

'You realise that was no accident?' Gar-ran said, grimacing.

Tim nodded. 'Someone doesn't want us here.' He drew his plasma pistol.

Weapons ready, they slowly ascended the slope. Tim's eyes darted all around, but there was no sign of the unknown assailant. He felt that he should be leading now, but Gar-ran had insisted on taking point. They hiked upwards in silence and Tim's pistol felt puny and inadequate in his hand.

They slowed as they reached the summit crest and Gar-ran gingerly peered over onto the rim. He looked around for what seemed like ages, and Tim had to bite his tongue to stop his questions, hating not being able to see. Finally though, Gar-ran signalled for him to approach and he scrambled onto the plateau.

Ahead he could clearly see the furrow where the boulder had been rolled and, within that, the deep impression of a pair of giant, oval footprints. The prints headed away and became fainter as the ground got firmer until, finally, they were scarcely visible. Tim shuddered as he imagined the size of the giant that somehow must be close by, but yet unseen. It worried him that there they were continually breaking new ground; there was no chance to plan an exit route or strategy as it was all virgin territory to them.

There was no choice but to press on. He wiped some of the rock dust from his face and took a few deep breaths to calm himself as he trailed Gar-ran. The ground was becoming much harder and uneven. Pockets of stubby grass covered some of the larger rocky mounds around them, but there was little other vegetation and he felt exposed. Ahead of them and to the right was a large natural arch spanning a gorge eighty feet across.

Tim looked all around but there was no other way across the chasm. He didn't like the idea of the rock bridge at all but could see no alternative. He turned to Gar-ran, who stared ahead grimly.

'We're going to be very exposed as we cross, so best to get over as quickly as possible,' he said.

'Let me take the lead.'

'No Tim, I can manage. Here though, you take this, although I pray it won't be needed. Gar-ran dug in his bag and slowly withdrew the laser lantern. Tim reached out and took it from him. He felt a pang of unease with the sudden shift in responsibility. He now had possession of a banned, deadly weapon he didn't even know how to operate.

'How do I work it?'

'I've modified the controls to make them simpler. You see that lever on the side? Pull it hard back to focus, then flip the switch on the top, and hold tight.

Remember though, it's only to be used in an absolute last resort.' Gar-ran looked stern and Tim knew it wasn't the time for wisecracks.

'I understand.'

Together they moved up to the base of the arch and looked around carefully. The stillness and silence still revealed nothing. They raced up, Gar-ran leading. Within ten seconds they were nearly halfway across and Tim wondered how Gar-ran could run with his bad arm. Forty feet to go. Then something from above caught his eye and he looked up in horror to see several rocks the size of grapefruits hurtling towards them. Where had they come from? He hesitated, unsure whether to wait out the barrage, or turn back.

'Keep going!' Gar-ran yelled, his voice ragged with pain. Tim threw himself into a flat-out sprint, teeth gritted as the first rocks smacked into the arch with frightening force. He pushed harder, certain that any second he would be sent flying like a skittle, over into the abyss without even time to scream. Twenty feet to go. The barrage seemed to be slowing. Ahead, Gar-ran had reached the other side and was covering Tim with his pistol. Moments later Tim was across, nearly colliding with his friend as he skidded to a halt. They'd made it. Gar-ran though was sweating heavily and looked pale.

'I have an idea what's going on,' he gasped.

'Me too. Some maniac's trying to kill us!'

'Yes, but it's more than that. I'll explain in a minute. Let's keep moving.'

That sounded like a great idea to Tim and they jogged onward. Tim scanned all round but there was still no sign of their attackers. He had a strange feeling that the whole planet was hostile, that it resented their presence and would not stop tormenting them until they left. He shook his head to dispel the debilitating thoughts. He had to stay sharp; Gar-ran was counting on him.

They followed a broad slope which took them up into another wide plateau. Tim froze as he saw the figure standing ahead of them. He brought his pistol up but Gar-ran's hand on his shoulder stayed him.

'Look.' Gar-ran pointed to other nearby figures.

Tim stared, puzzled, then looked more closely. The stone giant dead ahead would never move again. Its legs were partially melted into the ground. The pale grey face was flat and would have been expressionless except for the wide black mouth which was open and contorted as if silently screaming. Tim noticed too that the giant was weather-beaten, as if it had been stuck there for a long time.

The other figures were also in similar states. He counted five of them. The smallest was still at least eight feet high. Some had lost arms. One figure was half-lying, its back heavily indented and scorched to a charcoal colour. Tim touched the fallen giant's shoulder and recoiled as a piece of it crumbled away. Looking further ahead, he noticed the cave for the first time. It was big – at least eighty feet high.

Realisation came in an instant: 'They were trying to protect something.'

'Yes. And I think that's what's happening now.'

Tim nodded. What were they protecting though? The relic, or something else? Perhaps in the past others had searched for the relic, invaders who were ruthless and powerful.

'We've got company,' Gar-ran said, jolting Tim from his thoughts.

Tim spun round and gasped. There were three of them. But these stone giants were very much alive. Somehow, they'd snuck up silently.

The middle one was gigantic, at least eighteen feet tall, and the two others must have been over fifteen feet. They were a dark grey slate colour. The giant's forehead and brow jutted forward and their eyes were slanted and black as coal. Their slit mouths were firmly closed.

Tim scanned the area with his peripheral vision. There was nowhere to run. Gar-ran stepped forward with his arms open and wide. In a loud voice he said something incomprehensible to Tim's ear. Then his translator kicked in.

'... did not mean to trespass. We mean no harm.'

The two smaller giants turned to their bigger companion. After what seemed like an age, one of the smaller ones shook his head and began stalking towards them with surprising speed. The other guardians shouted for him to stop but he ignored them.

'Damn. I think we've stumbled into one of their sacred areas, and he's not happy about it. I think we'll have to try and outrun them, get back to the ship, and try to open communications from there,' Gar-ran whispered.

I probably could outrun them, but can Gar-ran? Tim was doubtful. They were going to have to try anyway. He stepped back to get a better view of the path and bumped into one of the fallen giants. There was a cracking sound and Tim looked up in disbelief as the giant's blackened head wobbled, then snapped off, falling to the ground with a heavy thud.

'Defilers!' The big stone guardian roared and bounded towards them.

'Run!' Gar-ran shouted and Tim darted off, needing no further encouragement. *Of all the bad luck.* The giants were spread out in a line and, putting on a burst of speed, Tim was able to race between them, ducking as a pair of huge hands swiped at him. He turned to see Gar-ran duck through the biggest guardian's legs, nutmegging him, which would have been funny if he'd had enough breath to laugh.

He tore down the path back towards the arch, with Gar-ran labouring his way behind. *What if there's others ahead, waiting for us?* He pushed the worrying thought from his mind and ran harder. He could hear Gar-ran churning on behind him. He was at the arch now and paused to let Gar-ran catch up.

'Keep going,' Gar-ran spluttered, sounding tired and in pain. Tim's lungs were burning. He was nearly across when a shadow from above engulfed him and he looked up in trepidation. The Scarab hung in the air at the other side of the bridge and was slowly descending. Gar-ran must have signalled Nerissa, he realised. Already he could see the airlock opening. Gar-ran caught up and they bundled themselves inside and flung themselves down the corridor to the command hub.

Something hard hit the ship's hull and, as he took the co-pilot's chair, Tim turned to Gar-ran.

'They're bombarding us. We have to get airborne,' Gar-ran spat as he hammered the ignition sequence into the console. Tim's stomach flipped as they lifted off. Gritting his teeth, he switched on the viewing screen, just in time to see the largest giant striding across the bridge, which was shaking with every step.

'Oh no you don't,' Gar-ran muttered as he engaged the weapons panel. Isolated in the command hub, Tim didn't hear the boom of the plasma cannon, but watched in amazement as the bridge exploded in front of the giant, sending him tumbling into the chasm below.

'He's tough enough to survive.' Gar-ran's voice was little more than a dusty croak and Tim turned to him in concern.

'Remind me to teach you the ignition sequence,' Gar-ran muttered.

'Your arm ...'

'Later. Let's get away first.' Gar-ran was about to engage the thrusters when something massive filled the screen – something so big it was like a solid wall of rock.

'Oh no!'

Sixteen
Grom

Where did that come from? Tim stared at the vast stone wall that blocked the viewing screen. They'd nearly flown directly into a cliff, but he was sure it hadn't been there before. He opened his mouth to speak when a ripple ran right through the ship.

'What was that?' Things were getting weirder by the minute.

'One minute.' Gar-ran rapidly typed in a command on the control console. The sound that came through the speakers was deafening, making them both recoil. Gar-ran hastily dialled down the volume. The sound was a deep, sonorous rumbling which reminded Tim of whale song.

'What the hell is that, Gar-ran?'

'That, is Grom, if I'm not very much mistaken.' Gar-ran typed more commands into the console and then spoke in a loud voice.

'We come in peace; we didn't start the fight! There are only two of us: an elder and a young one!'

There was silence for a few moments and Tim wondered who on earth, or in this case, who on Dimantia, Gar-ran was talking to. Then the voice came through again and the same rippling sensation gently shook the ship.

'I'll translate to English,' Nerissa said, her face appearing briefly on the viewing screen before the translation manifested. Tim stared at the text and felt dread seep into his bones.

LEAVE NOW OR BE CRUSHED.

'Please may we speak with you? We have come far on a mission of life and death; we only ask if you can assist us?' Gar-ran spoke urgently.

There was silence for several minutes. Tim leant across and whispered.

'Who's Grom?'

'He's the leader of the southern stone guardians, and he's truly ancient.'

'Will he understand you?'

'Yes, as I speak Nerissa will translate and broadcast in their language.'

Tim gazed at the viewing screen, which was still entirely filled with slabs of grey rock.

'He must be massive?'

'Yes. The oldest ones are as big as mountains. Over a long time, they begin to petrify, and may only move every thirty years or so.'

Tim shook his head. Living, hostile mountains with personalities. *What next?*

Grom's voice came through again and the translation appeared across the top of the viewing screen.

WHAT DO YOU SEEK HERE?

'We're looking for a segment of the dimension bomb, which you know as the Calcis. A great calamity is upon the young one's world and we need every piece of the Calcis to fight the evil that is coming. I am a star marshal and the young one is a champion of his people.'

WHAT MAKES YOU THINK WE HAVE WHAT YOU SEEK?

'The guardians have long been the protectors of precious and sacred things; I can think of no better place to search.'

Tim was about to speak but Gar-ran motioned him to stay quiet. Champion of his people? What was Gar-ran playing at?

There was silence again for several minutes and a trickle of sweat ran down Gar-ran's face before Grom spoke.

OTHERS CAME BEFORE, THEY ALSO SOUGHT, BUT THEY TRIED TO TAKE WHAT WAS NOT GIVEN. THEY WERE DEALT WITH, BUT

SEVERAL YOUNG GUARDIANS PERISHED. YOU MET WITH THEIR REMAINS ON THE HILLTOP.

'I am sorry for that; we had no idea.' Gar-ran looked uncomfortable and Tim shifted uneasily in his chair. *Trapped between a rock and a hard place, literally.*

I WILL SPEAK WITH THE OTHER ELDERS. WE WILL THINK ON WHAT YOU HAVE SAID. DO NOT ATTEMPT TO LEAVE IN THE MEANTIME OR YOU WILL BE CRUSHED.

Tim read the last sentence and turned to Gar-ran. If he was worried, he was hiding it well.

'We understand. Thank you,' Gar-ran said. He switched off the communicator and sat back in his chair, breathing a sigh of relief.

'Well that went as well as it could. Now we wait.'

'How long do you think it will be?'

'That's just the thing; time has an entirely different concept for the guardians. We're going to have to wait it out.'

Tim nodded. He could understand that. If you lived for thousands of years and were virtually indestructible, you wouldn't need to rush anything much. 'Could they really crush us?'

'Yes. Easily. But they won't attack unless the elders give the go ahead. So, we wait.'

'OK. What was that stuff you said about me being a champion of the people?'

Gar-ran looked sheepish and Tim realised that maybe this time Gar-ran had miscalculated.

'I got a little carried away; they value strength.'

Tim didn't reply. He had the feeling Gar-ran's words may come back to haunt them. 'We need to get your arm sorted.'

'I have just the thing.'

***

A few minutes later, they were sat in the lab. Tim was supporting Gar-ran's arm. Gar-ran, stripped to the waist, was holding a round, torch-like device in his left hand which emitted a weak light. He passed the light over his shoulder area several times, occasionally flinching. After a few more minutes he turned it off.

'So that will help it heal?' Tim was sceptical.

'Yes, it helps to repair tissue and knit bone. I'm going to lie down for a little while.'

'OK, I'm going to hang out in my room. Do you want anything?'

'Not at the moment thank you.'

Tim left Gar-ran to it and slowly headed back to his quarters. He felt like a hostage, which of course they were of sorts. Part of him wanted to go outside while Gar-ran rested, just to see how big this Grom really was. He knew that would be a bad idea though, maybe fatal. Safer just to go to his room and wait things out.

The rest of the afternoon slowly slipped away and became the evening, but there was still no response from the guardians. Eventually Gar-ran turned to Tim and said: 'Get some sleep; this could go on for a lot longer.'

Tim tried unsuccessfully to stifle his yawn.

'I think I should stay. I'm the people's "Champion", after all.'

Gar-ran laughed softly. 'Go on. Even champions need their rest.'

'OK, but I'm coming back here the moment anything comes through.'

But the night remained silent and, after tossing and turning for a couple of hours, Tim drifted off into a restless sleep.

He awoke suddenly, early the next day, and jumped straight out of bed and quickly got dressed. Gar-ran was already in his chair in the command hub and Tim wondered if he'd been there all night.

'Nothing yet,' he said, as Tim sat down.

Tim felt a mixture of relief and disappointment. How much longer would they have to wait? He noticed Gar-ran wasn't wearing his sling.

'How's your arm?'

'Much better thanks. But it's going to be stiff for a few days. I can't lift much with it.'

Tim stared at him. 'But it's broken. Your collarbone is broken.'

'*Was* broken, but now it's almost healed. You saw me with the re-knitter yesterday? You saw me using it.'

Tim blinked in surprise; he had of course seen the torch thing Gar-ran had scanned his arm with, but he'd never imagined it could possibly work so fast. If only they had such things back home! People would hardly need hospitals.

'That's amazing,' he murmured.

Gar-ran was about to speak when Nerissa burst in.

'Incoming transmission.' She sounded perfectly calm but a jolt of adrenaline shot through Tim, rooting him to the spot as the now familiar ripple shook the Scarab.

I AND THE COUNCIL OF ELDERS ARE AGREED. WE WILL TEST YOUR CLAIMS. IF YOU PASS THE TRIALS, WE CAN ENTER DISCUSSIONS. THOSE ARE OUR TERMS. ACCEPT OR BE CRUSHED.

'He doesn't mince his words, does he?' Tim said, clutching humour from their dark situation.

'No, no he doesn't. Seems like we'll have to accept,' Gar-ran murmured, almost to himself.

'Let's do it.' At least this way they had a chance, Tim thought, although all he really wanted to do was stay on board where it seemed safe.

'I agree. Lord Grom, we accept your terms,' Gar-ran raised his voice.

Several minutes staggered by before Grom spoke again. Tim was feeling tenser by the minute. What else did these things want from them?

LEAVE THE SHIP NOW AND COME TO US. WE ARE READY.

'We will do so, but Lord Grom, your voice is so powerful, so strong, we feel it will shatter our ears and deafen us without the safety of the ship.'

Tim hadn't considered that. Fear began to creep into the dark corners of his thoughts.

WE KNOW THIS. OTHERS WILL SPEAK. COME.

Gar-ran puffed out his cheeks as he sat back. 'Damn. We've got to go.'

Tim nodded. He was afraid, but anything was better than the endless waiting on board. At least outside they had some kind of chance. *Maybe*. It seemed a long walk to the airlock though. Bright daylight streamed in as they stepped out to meet the guardians. Tim wondered if the big one they'd blasted off the bridge would be there, and would he want revenge? A faint breeze was blowing and the air was pleasantly warm. He stopped dead as he looked up at the gigantic figure of Grom, leader of the southern stone guardians.

The giant soared above him, easily over 300 feet tall. His hands alone were bigger than the ship. He was a paler grey than his companions who, while still massive, only reached up to his shoulders. Tim realised they must be the other elders.

Ahead of them another sixteen-feet guardian approached. Tim listened intently as the strange, sonorous voice was converted to English and relayed through his earpiece.

'I am Von. You are young to be the champion of your people. You must be a great warrior. Unless the older one is lying.'

Tim looked at Gar-ran as his heart hammered in his chest. He hadn't expected to be addressed.

'I ... I will do whatever I have to.' *That sounded lame.* He clamped his mouth shut and didn't meet Gar-ran's eye.

The guardian did not reply but instead turned to Gar-ran.

'You. You claim to be a star marshal.'

'Yes, for many years now.'

'Repeat the oaths you swore when you first wore that badge.'

Gar-ran frowned for a moment then stood to attention. 'I swear to serve and protect the powerless. To bring the fugitive to justice. To avenge the fallen. To help the helpless. To expand our order. To seek truth and knowledge, and to stand by my brothers and sisters.'

Von nodded slightly. It was a full minute before he spoke again.

'Show me your badge.'

Gar-ran held up the engraved disc. Von nodded again. Tim wondered if that was it, but in fact it was just the beginning. Von began to question Gar-ran in more and more detail. To Tim, some questions seemed bizarre. A whole half an hour passed, and then again. Tim's legs ached and his attention wandered. He studied Grom, noting that there were small cracks and fissures in his mighty legs where different-coloured mosses had taken root. His huge knuckles too were covered in lichen, reminding Tim of the liver spots on his grandad's hands. Finally, he became aware that Von had stopped. Von looked up at Grom, who slowly nodded.

'You have passed the trial of knowledge.'

Von turned to Tim. 'Now you will face your trial. Come.'

What trial? He didn't like the sound of that one bit. He glanced at Gar-ran, who was looking both guilty and worried.

Von led them back towards the wide-open plateau. It was cooler now and Tim was cold and stiff from standing for so long.

'Are you OK?' he whispered to Gar-ran.

'Yes, I'm glad that's over.' He seemed subdued.

'What d'you think is coming next?'

'They're going to test you. I'll do whatever I can to help.' Tim nodded. He looked around but there was no way out.

Just then Von stopped and Tim saw that ahead stood six guardians, each around fifteen feet, three either side.

It was unnerving to walk through the colossal sentinels who at any moment could crush them both like bugs. Tim thought he recognised one of them as one of the three they'd encountered yesterday, and kept his gaze firmly on the ground. Ahead, an area had been marked out with round stones the size of bowling balls. They were arranged to form a circle forty feet wide. He realised it was like his dream, but what came next? If only Gar-ran had hypnotised him, like he'd asked him to, he'd know now what was in store. He felt a surge of resentment against the stupid, stubborn old man, and then guilty at having such a thought; they both needed each other if they were ever going to get out of this.

Von stopped and turned to face them. The silence hung in the air for what seemed like long minutes before the guardian spoke.

'Here we will test your quality. Larn, a young guardian, has been given the honour of facing you.'

Tim's stomach clenched and his hand drifted towards his pistol. The ground began to tremble beneath as Grom slowly approached. Each step he took covered fifty feet. Gar-ran immediately appealed to him.

'Surely this isn't necessary. Let us talk some more, Lord Grom, please!'

But Grom just stared down impassively on them.

'No more talk,' Von said and beckoned Tim forward.

'Surrender your gun.' Tim turned to Gar-ran, who nodded. Reluctantly, he handed over the pistol. His hand shook and he hated to seem weak, but he couldn't help it. He prayed silently that, whatever happened, he wouldn't wet himself.

Another guardian stepped forward. In each hand he carried a large, heavy axe. He handed one to Tim, who nearly dropped it. The handle was made of a shiny metal and was over three feet long. The blade was crescent-shaped and made from a duller metal, its edge wickedly sharp and tipped with some kind of clear, hard stone. It was a good weapon, if you had the strength to wield it.

At that moment Larn, Tim's opponent, stepped forward to take the other axe. He was at least nine feet tall. He held the axe easily in one massive hand and made a few practice cuts through the air.

It's David and Goliath for real, Tim thought, as his legs shook. He didn't rate his chances much.

Von turned to Tim.

'During combat you will not step outside the marked area or there will be consequences. You may have a few moments to prepare.'

Tim tottered back to Gar-ran on his wobbly legs. He dared not show how scared he really felt. How on earth was he going to deal with this? He hefted the axe up so Gar-ran could inspect it.

'It's diamond-tipped. See here?' He leant forward and whispered, 'Tim, I'm sorry I've got you into this. They'll be watching me too but I have a plan if things look desperate. Remember, although he's big, he's a lot slower than you. Use your speed and stay out of range.'

He raised his voice for the benefit of the guardians standing close by.

'In the meantime, let's shake hands and I wish you the best of luck.'

Tim felt Gar-ran press something into his palm as they shook hands.

'Find a way to use it,' he muttered.

Tim pretended to adjust his translator and sneakily dropped the mini-bomb into his breast pocket. Just knowing it was there made him feel better; now all he had to do was survive long enough to find a way to use it. His opponent was already waiting in the enclosure. Tim walked to the opposite side and Von stood in the middle, between them.

'This contest will continue until there is a clear winner. BEGIN!'

Larn came straight towards him and Tim warily circled around, staying away from the edge of the enclosure. Without warning, the giant leapt into the air with his axe held high. Tim darted forward and did an awkward forward roll just as the massive axe smashed into the ground. He spun and swung as hard as he could but only succeeded in clipping the back of the giant's leg. That was enough to stagger him though, and he was about to dash in and try to seize the advantage when a vicious swipe from his enemy's axe forced him to duck and back off.

He heard Gar-ran urging him to keep moving but didn't dare to look round. His whole world now was the arena and the danger in front of him. He had an idea about how to deploy the mini-bomb, but it would mean getting dangerously close. His opponent suddenly stopped moving and, just as Tim began to question why, the guardian flung his axe at him. Somehow he manged to block it, but the impact sent him reeling backward and, unable to keep his balance, he toppled over. The giant advanced towards him with a surprising turn of speed and desperately Tim threw his own axe as hard as he could, but Larn swatted it away and continued coming. Tim hefted the other axe up and scuttled to the side. He had a horrible sensation that, even if he swung with all his force, he still wouldn't be strong enough to stop the giant. He knew he should strike, but it felt wrong to attack someone unarmed, even if that someone was trying to kill him. Gar-ran was screaming at him to attack and, taking a deep breath, he lunged forwards. Feinting right, then darting left, he swung the axe as hard as he could, but the stone warrior blocked it with his massive hands and grabbed the axe shaft. Tim wouldn't let go and the next thing he knew he was flung in the air like a bull tossing a matador, and crashed down hard, chest first.

The impact stunned him for a moment, but his mind screamed at him to use the mini-bomb before it was too late. Doing his best to mask the movement, he reached into his breast pocket. There was nothing there. He felt again frantically, but it was gone, and he saw it lying on the on the ground behind the advancing giant and close to his axe.

An idea hit him and, without stopping to think, Tim forced himself up and ran full speed at the giant who stopped, as if confused. At the last moment Tim dropped down and slid feet first through the guardian's legs, scooped up the mini-bomb and reached for the axe. He nearly had it when a cold, hard hand grabbed his collar and lifted him high off the ground. Tim wriggled and kicked but couldn't shake the warrior's grip. Larn bellowed in triumph and, as the cave-like mouth opened, Tim rammed his fist into the giant's face and dropped the mini-bomb down his throat.

At once Larn dropped him and Tim scrambled back out of range. A tiny, muffled explosion signalled the detonation, and the baying crowd quietened as the young guardian slowly dropped to his knees. He swayed for a few moments then fell face forwards and lay still. Tim stood, mesmerised, hearing nothing at first other than the sound of his own ragged breathing. The silence was broken by Gar-ran's cheers and Tim turned to face the watching guardians. It was over.

Von walked towards Tim and two other giants clumped into the arena and carried out their fallen comrade. It dawned on Tim his position now might be more dangerous than ever. The guardians wouldn't have imagined him winning. How would they react?

'Congratulations. An amazing and … unexpected victory. You must have incredible power in your hands to stop Larn with one punch.'

Tim stared at Von. The guardian's expression revealed nothing. Did he suspect?

'I … I had to win.'

'Yes. Yes you did. THE TRIAL OF STRENGTH IS OVER!' he boomed, making Tim flinch.

'Go, and rejoin your friend.'

Tim ran over to Gar-ran, who was looking mightily relieved.

'Well done, you did brilliantly! I'll treat that graze on your chin when we get back on board. Are you hurt from the fall? When you went up in the air like that …'

'I'm OK, just glad it's over.' He glanced round and saw that Von was headed towards Grom and the other elders.

'Now what?'

'I have a feeling there will be one more test.'

Tim shook his head; he'd been afraid of that. He looked up at Grom, who made a series of hand gestures that were watched closely by Von, who then nodded and made his way over.

'You will await notice of the final trial.'

Tim looked at Gar-ran, who from his expression was probably thinking the same thing. *How long will that take?* Before either of them could speak, Von continued.

'We are aware your concept of time is different from our own and this will be taken into consideration. You will now be separated. Do not resist and do not attempt to board your ship.'

Instantly, a sixty-feet-tall guardian stepped forward and hoisted Tim up and tucked him beneath his arm. Tim yelped with surprise and, despite the warning, kicked and struggled.

'Put me down! Gar-ran!'

Gar-ran sprung forward and then stopped as a shadow fell over him. Tim craned his neck around to see the immense hand of Grom scoop Gar-ran up with surprising delicacy. He lost sight of his friend as Grom's huge back blocked his view. Tim yelled and beat his fists against his giant until his hands ached, but the guardian strolled onwards remorselessly. They journeyed down the mountainside into a wide canyon and, with a swiftness that took his breath away, Tim was hoisted high up and dropped onto a stone pillar. He did his best to break his fall but still banged his knee hard. Anger made him jump up immediately, but he stopped dead when he realised the platform was no more than six feet in diameter, and below was a mighty drop.

The stone column began to tremble and, for a horrible moment, Tim wondered if an earthquake was about to strike but, turning, saw it was just the approach of Grom, still clutching poor Gar-ran.

Over eighty feet away was a taller stone pillar, although it barely came up to Grom's waist. Gar-ran was dropped down onto that pedestal.

Far below, Von had appeared. 'YOU BOTH WILL REMAIN HERE. DO NOT ATTEMPT TO LEAVE OR APPROACH YOUR SHIP. YOU WILL AWAIT THE FINAL TRIAL,' he shouted and Tim's heart sank. They were totally trapped up there, isolated and exposed to the elements for who knew how long. *At least we can see each other.* The thought consoled him a little as Grom strode away, shaking the ground with every step. Von and the other guardians followed and eventually disappeared from sight.

'They'll never be able to sneak up on me,' Tim muttered, then laughed to himself. But his laughter quickly died as he realised the light was going and he had no idea how long the nights on Dimantia were.

Seventeen
The Verdict

The gap between was too far for conversation so, after a shouting match to establish that they were both unharmed, they lapsed into silence. Within half an hour it was completely dark and he couldn't see Gar-ran at all. The floor of the column was uneven and it was impossible to remain comfortable for long, and all the time there was the awareness that a fall to death awaited on every side. Sleep was out of the question. What if he were to roll off the edge while dreaming? Would he wake up before he hit the ground? Would it hurt?

He tried to focus on more positive things, distract himself with other thoughts and memories. Whatever the next trial was, at this rate they would both be exhausted before it even began. Maybe that was the idea. To pass the time he went through everything he'd learnt about the ship, where everything was, basic navigational procedures, and the layout of the command hub. Gar-ran would let him fly soon, he was sure of it. Now that was something to look forward to. With no sign of dawn, he lay back and turned onto his side. There was no way he was going to sleep up there, but he would just try to relax for a few minutes.

***

It was the breeze that woke him the next morning. It felt cool and fresh as he blinked his eyes open. He had a moment of utter confusion until he felt the hard rock digging into his face and remembered where he was. Carefully, he sat up. Every muscle and joint seemed to protest against movement. It would be even worse for Gar-ran. Gar-ran! Had his friend survived the night? Tim pushed himself up and called out as loudly as he could. It was getting light, but the other column was too far away to see properly.

He called again and this time Gar-ran answered that he was OK, his voice echoing along the canyon. The sun rose twenty minutes later, bathing the valley in its amber glow. Tim's column trembled faintly and he tensed; either an earthquake was building or Grom was on his way. Turning, he saw him, approaching from behind a bend in the canyon which his head and shoulders reached above. The trembling in the column increased and Tim was sure he would be shaken over the edge. Then Grom stopped and extended his enormous arm. His hand opened, forming a platform, the fingertips now a foot from where Tim stood.

What if Grom accidentally crushed him? Or worse, dropped him? Was this part of the test? One thing was sure: he had little choice but to obey. He took a breath and ran into Grom's palm. Instantly he was thrown off balance and fell into a sitting position as he was carried along. Within a few moments Gar-ran stumbled down one of the giant stone fingers towards him.

'Tim! Are you all right?'

'Yes, yes, I'm OK. Thirsty though. What about you?'

'I'm OK. I've had better nights though.'

They shared a smile and then all conversation stopped as they felt themselves lowered down. Von stood before them, flanked by several guardians.

'Out-worlders! Are you ready for the final trial?'

Despite his exhaustion, Gar-ran stood up straight and Tim did likewise.

'We're ready,' Tim said, surprising Gar-ran, who'd just opened his mouth to reply.

Von was silent for a few moments, then slowly nodded.

'THE TRIAL BY PATIENCE IS OVER!' he proclaimed. Then, slowly and deliberately, he began to strike his chest with his fist. Each strike resounded like a bass drum and one by one the other guardians began to repeat the gesture until the booming sound filled the valley. Tim shivered. The tremendous noise was one of the most intimidating sounds he'd ever heard. Was it good or bad? Gar-ran looked anxious too. The noise reached a deafening crescendo, then Grom struck his own chest once. The blow was as loud as a thundercrack and silenced everyone.

'I think we've passed,' Gar-ran whispered.

Tim frowned. 'But ... but what about the final trial?

'Last night *was* the final trial. The trial of patience.'

Tim was about to reply but Von cut in again.

'You have proven yourself worthy. It was foretold this day would come. You may have what you seek.'

Elation pulsed through Tim. Gar-ran was right: they'd done it. Now what?

Slowly Von unfolded his hand and Tim immediately saw the golden gleam of another segment. It looked perfectly preserved.

'Take it,' Gar-ran urged.

Tim stepped forwards. His fingers tingled the moment he grasped the shining segment. 'Thanks. Thank you.' He looked up at the guardians who surrounded them like a silent stone forest.

'You may return to your ship. Lord Grom will speak to you,' Von said.

Another guardian returned their weapons and they were escorted back to the Scarab. Once on board, they immediately raced to the command hub. Within seconds the rippling vibration flowed through the ship and Grom's words appeared on the viewing screen.

GO IN PEACE OUT-WORLDERS. BLESSINGS OF KNOWLEDGE, STRENGTH AND PATIENCE TO YOU. MAY YOUR QUEST SUCCEED.

'Thank you. Thank you Lord Grom.' Tim and Gar-ran spoke practically in unison.

'Let's get out of here before anything else happens,' Tim said as Gar-ran switched off the broadcaster. He couldn't wait to get airborne. They had another piece and he was another step closer to home.

Eighteen
Nexus-3

Slothra allowed himself a small smile of satisfaction as his ship tore through the upper atmosphere of Moloco and into space. He was getting closer. Many of his past targets had thought they'd escaped, but in the end, he'd caught every one of them. The job would soon be complete, payment would be made and honour satisfied. The designer had agreed to turn them both over to him when he'd finished with them, and that meant more trophies for his collection. It was just a case of deciding between removing their heads, or their hearts. Perhaps both. He grinned as he adjusted his course.

***

A part of Tim's consciousness knew he must be dreaming, but it seemed so real. He was lost within a vast forest. Far above, in the jungle canopy, something was moving at speed, raging through the thick overgrowth towards him. He turned and ran, but blundered into a swamp. The cold, fetid water began to seep through his flight suit as he sunk deeper into the mud, then with a huge splash something heavy landed behind him and he yelped in alarm, but as he turned around the jungle faded away and he found he was in the galley on board the ship.

It was just a silly dream after all! He finished sipping his hot chocolate but, as he stood up, he saw his left leg had been replaced with an artificial, metallic one. It looked robotic and alien and he wanted to scream but no sound came out.

He clasped hold of his leg. It felt hard and cold. The cold increased and spread throughout his body and, from nowhere, a powerful gust of wind rocked him. He blinked in confusion as the galley dissolved, to be replaced by towering, snow-clad, jagged mountain peaks. In the valley below he saw the remains of a large spacecraft buried in the snow. The sky flickered with blue and green light, and two great moons shone brilliantly. He realised he was holding another segment of the dimension bomb and felt a moment of pure joy, but then he fumbled it and it fell into the snow, and it disappeared from view.

Everything around him began to tremble, and fear clutched his heart, but then he was awake and it was Gar-ran shaking him.

'Wake up Tim, wake up. You're dreaming.' Tim sat up fast and the room span around him. His head felt like it weighed a ton, so he swivelled his eyes until the anxious face of the marshal came into focus.

'Gar-ran? Where am I?' he whispered.

'You're in your quarters on the ship. You cried out. What did you see?'

'Lots of things.' Tim rubbed his face hard. Was he awake, or still dreaming? His hands tingled like mad.

'Come to the galley. You must tell me everything you can remember.'

Gar-ran insisted Tim drank some of the hot, sweet tea he'd made and Tim gulped a few mouthfuls before relating his dream. He'd felt embarrassed when he realised his cries had alerted Nerissa who woke Gar-ran, but now, talking about what he'd seen, he felt better. He didn't tell him about the part where he'd seen his leg had been replaced though. That was too scary to think about.

Gar-ran listened gravely, nodding a few times. 'Would you be willing to try another hypnosis session, if needs be?'

'Yeah sure, definitely,' although he didn't relish going back into that forest again with whatever had been lurking in the canopy.

'I'm going to run all this through Nerissa and see what she comes up with. Go back to bed; try to get some sleep.'

Tim nodded. He was feeling sleepy now. 'What about you?'

'I'll be fine.'

***

Tim woke up mid-morning and, after a shower, found Gar-ran in the lab. He was scrutinising a printout and Tim knew immediately he'd found something.

'Morning Tim. Did you get some rest?'

'I'm fine. Did you find something?'

'Yes, I think so. I've been going through things with Nerissa. You remember that you saw yourself on a frozen planet with two moons, and there was a crashed ship in the mountains?'

'Yes.' Tim replied cautiously as he recalled the biting cold of the wind and the eerie shriek it made as it blew down through the icy peaks.

'I think that's Corax, one of the winter worlds, and that's good news because it's relatively close. The crashed ship you described sounds like a deep space freighter, which would make sense. There could well be another segment in its hold. So, we're headed there now. First though we're going to stop for a few hours in the Nexus system. It's the last point of civilisation before the winter worlds and I need to get the ship checked out. There doesn't appear to be any serious damage to her hull from the guardians' attack, but some of those rocks hit us hard, so I want to make sure. We'll be there tomorrow afternoon.'

'OK. What's Nexus?' The last point of civilisation, as Gar-ran termed it, made it sound like some frontier town in the American Wild West. Maybe there would be other marshals there.

Gar-ran smiled broadly. 'You'll like Nexus. Nexus-3, to be precise.'

Tim decided he'd read up on it in the lab after breakfast. Right now, he had something more mundane on his mind.

'I've been meaning to ask you. Do you know anything about watches? Mine's stopped working.' He held it up for Gar-ran to see.

'Ah. We've been through some areas which are subject to strong magnetic fields. I think your watch has succumbed to them.'

That didn't sound good. 'But you can fix it?'

'No. You'll need a new one, I'm afraid.'

Tim's heart sank a bit. His mum had given him the watch for Christmas. However, he wasn't that surprised that something made for earth might fail in the outer reaches of the galaxy. *Outer reaches of the galaxy.* He still could hardly believe he was there.

'I may be able to get you a replacement when we stop. Something more robust. And advanced.'

A space watch? Now that would be something. 'OK. That'd be great, thanks. I'll keep this anyway though. Just in case.'

***

Nexus-3 was not actually the third planet in the Nexus system. It was, rather, the third largest and the one Gar-ran was most familiar with, Tim discovered as he scanned the database in the lab. It was described as an exotic world, populated with yellow-skinned humanoid inhabitants. *Yellow-skinned.* There wasn't a lot of info though, and Tim suspected that another reason for stopping was for Gar-ran to broaden his knowledge.

'So, what are the people like there?' he asked as Gar-ran came in.

'They're quite different, but it's an advanced, democratic society, and Nectar, where we'll be stopping, is beautiful.'

'Nectar?' Tim smiled.

'That's as close to English as I can translate. It's a capital city and the one I know best.'

'OK. Sounds cool. I'm looking forward to it. There's something else though I wanted to ask.'

'Yes?'

'The other day, when Von asked you to repeat the oaths you swore, what was that about? How did he know about them?' Tim had wanted to ask this before but there hadn't been time.

Gar-ran pulled up a chair. 'Every marshal swears the oaths when they finish their cadetship and take up their first commission. The integrity of the marshals is one of our biggest assets. The stone guardians are ancient, and in their youth often travel widely, so it's not that surprising Von would know about us. The guardians have been entrusted with many secrets over the years.'

Tim nodded. He didn't really feel like a true cadet as his association with Gar-ran and the marshals would most likely end when and if they dealt with the threats back on Earth, but it was awesome to be part of this huge, secret, intergalactic order. He was probably one of the youngest members too. And all because of that day down on the beach which already seemed like an age ago. He felt a twinge of homesickness, but pushed it away, something he was learning to do more and more lately. Part of growing up, he supposed. He stretched his leg out, smiling as he felt the muscles contract. Still flesh and blood for now.

It was early evening when they touched down in the spaceport but the sun was still bright. They were both dressed in light grey jumpsuits. Tim's was brand new and the collar felt a little stiff against his neck.

'The atmosphere is virtually identical to Earth, so we won't need breathing equipment. At the moment though it's light for twenty-two hours a day. The native inhabitants are known as Nexians. They'll be the tall yellow ones,' Gar-ran said as they made their way to the airlock.

'Just how yellow?' Tim wondered aloud.

'You'll soon see. Is your translator turned on?'

Tim checked and nodded.

The spaceport was practically empty. Gar-ran must be deliberately choosing the quietest times, Tim reckoned. He tried not to stare at the entry official. This was difficult though, as he was extremely tall and saffron-coloured. He wore a black and red-edged robe and his bare arms were well developed. His facial features were surprisingly earth-like, though. Other than his colour, the most striking thing was his head. It was smooth and bald, etched with crescent-shaped tattoos. This was going to be a very educational trip, Tim thought, and realised that for the first time since he'd stepped aboard the Scarab, he wasn't feeling anxious. He'd heard the expression travel broadens the mind, and reckoned it must be true.

***

He left all the talking again to Gar-ran, who explained he wanted to have the integrity of the ship's hull evaluated and that they'd return in a few hours' time for the report. They were directed to the right-side exit.

'We can pick up some transport here.' They stepped outside, where another Nexian, this one shorter and slimmer and garbed in a silver-coloured robe edged with emerald green, awaited them. His bald head was completely covered on one side with dark blue ink. He smiled as Gar-ran handed him a printed form and showed them to a vehicle unlike any Tim had seen before. It was hovering two feet above the ground, pure white, and wedge-shaped, the front of the craft tapering to resemble a bird's beak.

'Bit of a tight fit for us in there,' Tim observed.

'It's built for speed, but there's more room than you'd think,' Gar-ran replied as he signed the form.

The Nexian touched the side of the craft and, to Tim's amazement, a small instrument panel and screen appeared. A few buttons were pressed and the Nexian stepped back and gestured to Tim and Gar-ran to move forwards. Gar-ran bent down and placed the palm of his hand on the small, raised screen. It lit up with a red light at his touch.

'Do as I did,' he said.

Tim crouched down and placed his hand on the screen, which again glowed red. Confused, he looked quizzically at Gar-ran.

'Just a security measure. Now only the three of us have access to the transport.'

Tim stared at the vehicle. What a clever idea; much better than worrying about keys. He noticed the still-smiling alien.

'Don't worry, he won't be coming with us,' Gar-ran whispered, making Tim laugh.

Minutes later they were zipping along to the city centre. Tim was shocked at how fast they were moving, but Gar-ran handled the craft with such skill and precision that Tim's anxieties soon melted away and he sank back into his felt-lined seat to enjoy the ride. In no time at all they slowed down and stopped.

'We'll have a little tour, visit a couple of places where we may pick up some information, then we'll head back to the port and get an update on the ship,' Gar-ran said as they got out.

'All right. We don't have any weapons, is that going to be OK?'

'It should be. The habitants here are quite relaxed. I'm not expecting trouble.'

Trouble may be expecting us, Tim thought, but said nothing.

Tim soon realised that the females of Nexus were beautiful. They were paler-skinned than the males and with tall, slender figures. Many wore their hair long and in a range of startling colours: powder blue, purple, indigo. Their bare arms were decorated with bracelets of fantastically varied designs. Many smiled at Tim as he passed by and the scent of their perfumes was intoxicating.

They wandered through a small market which specialised in different silks, satins and other expensive materials. Others displayed an array of different accessories and adornments, badges, broaches, bracelets and finely worked beads and pendants. Tim was impressed by how happy and relaxed everyone appeared.

Then he caught sight of the figure standing at a stall at the edge of the market. Instinctively he reached down for his pistol, which of course wasn't there. The hyena stood threading some beads together and hadn't noticed them. Tim touched Gar-ran's arm and whispered.

'There, on that stall at the end.' Gar-ran, who'd been chatting to a glamorous older Nexian, turned to look.

'He's harmless,' he said after scrutinising the hyena for a few moments 'They're not all bad. Well spotted though.'

Tim wasn't entirely convinced, but as they passed the hyena's stall, he turned out to be as friendly and engaging as any of the other traders.

'There's somewhere I want you to see,' Gar-ran said, pointing at the needle-shaped tower in the distance.

As they got closer, Tim realised there were two enclosed escalators travelling up and around the tower like silver snakes entwining a tree. Each escalator was encased in a clear glass tube so the passengers could admire the view.

'Is there another way up?' he asked Gar-ran.

'No, just this one. It won't be so bad.'

Gar-ran was right again: the escalator was an incredibly smooth ride. You could hardly feel it move and it was fun to look down on the market, which now appeared the size of a postage stamp. Tim was tall for his age, but was dwarfed by the Nexians all around. He grinned at Gar-ran who, as always, was watching everything.

'Where are we going?' Tim whispered.

'To the very top. There's a famous bar up there with spectacular views of the city. It's a popular place for people to meet and socialise. I think you'll like it after the trials of Dimantia.'

The escalator deposited them in a wide foyer flanked by striking blue-green foliage and tall, fern-like plants. There was a single entrance at the end of the foyer leading to what Tim presumed to be the famous bar.

Gar-ran nodded to the Nexian who stood on guard outside the entrance and slipped him something that Tim couldn't quite see but guessed was money.

They strolled into a big circular room with a sophisticated-looking bar in the middle. The rich pink carpet felt springy underfoot, and soft, comfortable seating was arranged around the windows.

'The view from the east side is the best.' Tim followed Gar-ran to the enormous tinted windows. The view was stunning and Tim saw that the city was smaller than he'd imagined. In the distance, just below the horizon, was a vast series of inter-linked lakes. Other, similar-sized cities were also just visible, and to the south a great forest rolled way into the distance.

A waitress came over and asked if they would take refreshments.

'You'll like what's coming, Tim,' Gar-ran said as he placed an order.

While they waited, Tim scanned the area. There were around forty or more patrons, the vast majority being native Nexians, but Tim saw a man who reminded him of Zarox, Gar-ran's friend from the space station, and a young woman who could have passed for an earth girl except for her huge, round eyes and amazing shoulder-length hair which looked exactly like seaweed.

The drinks arrived. Tim's was a creamy orange colour, smelt delicious and tasted incredible, like all the best fruits in the world added together with a double dose of fresh cream. 'Better than coke?' Gar-ran winked. They moved to a large, peach-coloured, semi-circular sofa.

There were three Nexians engaged in conversation to their left and, after a few minutes, a young couple came and sat close to them. Tim let their voices become a blur as he sipped his drink and relaxed.

As he gazed around the room, his eyes fell on a large black panel fixed to the far wall. Different-coloured lights flickered on and off along its entire length. He turned to Gar-ran but saw he was chatting to someone, so he got up and wandered over to investigate.

On the side of the panel was a series of instructions but, as usual, they were in a totally incomprehensible language. Tim caught the scent of perfume and looked up into the eyes of a very pretty young Nexian girl who was only eight or so inches taller than him. He was so stupefied by her beauty, he didn't hear what she said.

'I'm sorry, what?'

'Do you have change?' She held up an elaborately decorated note and nodded to the black panel.

'Ah no, sorry.'

'It's OK, I can, wait, I've found some!' The girl smiled and held up a smooth blue disc which she fed into the money slot. Immediately the music in the bar changed.

It's a jukebox, Tim realised, laughing to himself. This new tune was an instrumental piece composed of electronic beeps at different frequencies.

'This is one of my favourites,' the girl said, smiling down on him.

Tim wasn't keen on the music at all, but smiled back at the girl. If only he could think of something to say.

'This is your first time here, isn't it?

'Yes,' he admitted.

'I come here every week. It's wonderful, isn't it?'

'Yes, it is.'

'Which sector are you from? I hope you don't mind me asking, but it's just that I haven't seen many like you here.' She leant down and touched him on the arm.

'I'm from far away. I'm here on a trip with my ... uncle.' Tim pointed at Gar-ran. *That was lame.* Why didn't he say he was a marshal cadet? That would have sounded more impressive.

'Oh how wonderful! Can you believe I've hardly been off planet, except for when I was very young, and that doesn't really count, does it? You must tell me about your adventures. Are you staying long?'

'No, no not really, just a flying visit.'

'Oh, what a pity. It must be wonderful to fly along visiting different planets. I suppose you'll be off to Nexus-1 next?'

'Oh no, I don't think so. Just here. My name's Tim by the way.'

'I'm Tanara.' She leant in again and Tim caught another waft of perfume.

'Well, wherever you go, just stay away from Nayra.'

'Who's Nayra?'

Tanara threw back her head in amusement. Her laughter had an eerie, discordant sound that was at odds with her looks.

'It's a place, silly. On the other side of the city. Let's just say they're not as friendly as we are here.' Tim was about to ask for more details but Tanara stalled him by placing her hand on his shoulder.

'It was nice to meet you. Perhaps I'll see you again before you leave.' She smiled and slipped away. The bar was noticeably busier and Tim soon lost sight of her. A moment later, Gar-ran joined him.

'Nice to see you making friends. Pretty girl.'

Tim smiled. He felt quite hot. 'She told me to stay away from Nayra. Wherever that is.'

'Interesting. Why did she say that?'

'Well I told her I was a tourist. She thinks you're my uncle.'

Gar-ran chuckled at that. 'Nayra isn't all bad, but we won't be going there anyway. Our next stop is much nicer.'

'Are we going then?' Tim wasn't in any hurry; he wouldn't have minded chatting to Tanara again.

'Finish your drink first.'

He ambled to the window and took in the view again. The sun was brilliant and, from so high up, everything looked bright and fresh.

This is the best place so far, he decided.

***

They squeezed their way back to the escalator. Tim looked around for another glimpse of Tanara, but the golden girl was gone.

The descent down seemed much quicker. The streets were still crowded and they weaved their way through groups of cheerful, brightly dressed Nexians. After ten minutes or so they rounded a corner and came upon a huge, open plaza far bigger than anything Tim had seen or ever imagined. It was the size of five football pitches and comprised of gargantuan, pastel-coloured flagstones. Everything was spotless and gleaming. In the centre was a massive fountain, as high as a five-storey building. The water glittered and dazzled in the sunlight. Innumerable shops fringed the giant square and Tim spotted what looked like row upon row of sun loungers.

'Impressive eh?' Gar-ran said. Tim just nodded, too bowled over to speak. They walked close to the shops on the west side of the square and the shop awnings provided some welcome shade. A lot of the merchants sold clothes, bags and decorative home items like handsomely designed vases and ornaments.

After about fifteen minutes they were level with the fountain and, almost in a trance, Tim moved towards it. It was built in three separate tiers of white, silver and pale blue stone, like a colossal wedding case. A sweet scent reached his nose and he realised the water was perfumed. It was all a bit too much, he decided.

'They'll have finished checking the ship now, or would you like to stay for a while?' Gar-ran asked.

'No it's OK.' Tim had had enough for now; everything was just too perfect.

As they left the square, they passed a large video screen. Tim glanced at it and caught a glimpse of something that stopped him in his tracks. He called Gar-ran but then the picture changed to display a holiday advert full of smiling Nexians relaxing on the world's longest beach.

'Ah, we haven't got time to go there,' Gar-ran said.

'No, not that. I've just seen a picture that looked like us.'

They stared at the screen until the picture came up again. It was a composite image but their likeness was unmistakable. Gar-ran scanned the text and Tim read the concern in his eyes.

'What does it say?'

'Someone has murdered a storekeeper in Terran and they're looking for two aliens in connection. One old, one young.'

'What! But we didn't do anything ...'

'No, but someone clearly thinks we did. We have to leave immediately. It won't just be Slothra after us now.'

They walked quickly back to the car. Tim resisted the urge to look back to see if they were being followed. What if Tanara saw the posting? Would she believe it? Certainly, she'd tell her friends. Gar-ran gunned the engine and they whizzed off, in seconds going so fast that the outside was a blur of light. After a few minutes they slowed abruptly.

'We've got trouble.' Gar-ran sounded vexed and Tim peered over his shoulder to see. The spaceport had been cordoned off. Barriers topped with red flashing lights had been erected and several big, well-armed Nexians in bright blue uniforms stood guard.

'Uh-oh.'

'They're local police. They'll be holding the scene until the more senior investigators appear.'

They sat in silence for a few moments. A sick feeling seeped into Tim's gut as he racked his brain trying to think how they could get in.

'Could you call the ship to us again?'

Gar-ran shook his head. 'The more sophisticated spaceports have a blocker in the roof dome to prevent the signal getting though. It's a security measure.'

Tim thought for a few moments more. 'They're looking for two people, so maybe we can disguise ourselves in some way, and go in separately?'

'I was just thinking along those lines.' Gar-ran smiled enigmatically.

Nineteen
Shadebellum

‘ut isn't this place dangerous?'

'Only sometimes.' They were in Nayra, the bad side of town, and it was decidedly less glamorous than the centre. Although once well made, the grey buildings surrounding them were a lot smaller and more utilitarian in design, with none going higher than three storeys and well weathered in places. There was no one around except for two tough-looking Nexians watching them from an open doorway across the road. The taller of the two whispered something to his companion and moved further back, out of sight.

'We need to look as if we know exactly where we're going,' Gar-ran said quietly.

'Do we know?'

'More or less.'

Tim fell into step, resisting the temptation to glance back at the watcher in the doorway. He wished they'd stayed in the car.

'There's a growing element in this part of the city who reject the way the city centre residents live their lives. More and more people here believe that the more affluent members of Nectar have become hopelessly decadent, more interested in fashion and nice material things than the advancement of the society. They fear they're falling behind the other local planets.'

'So ... they want a change, a revolution?'

'Things aren't that bad yet, but the view here is that the wealth and natural assets are hoarded by a privileged few who contribute little. If things remain as they are it will lead to some kind of confrontation.'

Hopefully not while we're here, Tim thought.

They turned a corner into a narrower street which contained a few small shops.

'Anyhow, that's none of our concern; we're here for something very specific.'

Midway down the street they stopped outside a shop which looked like it had been closed for years. Above the door was a badly faded sign with shabby crimson lettering.

'This is the place.' Gar-ran glanced around and, when satisfied there was no one else watching, banged five times on the door. After a short time, the door opened a few inches and an elderly Nexian peered out. He was pale-skinned and his black eyes were suspicious and hostile. He regarded Gar-ran for a few seconds.

'Go away.' The door was about to shut in Gar-ran's face, but he held up a small red disc. Tim couldn't make out the engraved image but noticed the disc was the same shade of red as the shop sign.

The old Nexian's eyes widened as he peered at the token. 'Inside,' he murmured as the door opened just enough to admit them.

Three steps up led to an open doorway on the right. As they walked through the door, a wide beam of blue light engulfed them for a second.

'You're both clean. Can't be too careful nowadays,' the old Nexian said as he shuffled along.

The room was brightly lit. The far wall contained a massive shelving unit which was crammed with an abundance of different plants and flowers. Some of them reminded Tim of lilies, but with richer and more vibrant colours. He wondered how they could live in a room without natural light. There were also some cactus-type plants with purple spines six inches long growing in a cluster in the corner. The aged Nexian was now standing behind a grey metal counter that was as tall as Tim.

'To have the token you must have been here before, though I can't say I remember you.'

'It was a while ago,' Gar-ran answered. 'My young friend and I are in a situation where only one of your products can help.'

Tim had the uncomfortable feeling Gar-ran was about to start a lengthy haggling session. He didn't want to stay in this place much longer; it was too hot, too odd.

'Which product?'

'Shadebellum.'

The merchant stared hard at Gar-ran, piquing Tim's interest. 'Shadebellum is now prohibited on Nexus-3,' the merchant said cautiously.

'That's why I'll be paying you so handsomely,' Gar-ran said, tapping his pocket.

'And what makes you think I have any prohibited substances?' The merchant looked suspicious as his eyes kept flicking towards the doorway.

'Like I said, this is the only establishment that can help us.'

'Show me.'

Gar-ran pulled out a thick wedge of Nexian currency and placed it on the counter. The Nexian looked at the pile but made no attempt to pick it up.

'How long would you need it for?'

'At least half an hour and enough for the two of us. And of course, we need adequate amounts of antishade.'

Tim was following the conversation with interest now, wondering what plant could be so expensive.

'Let me see that token again.' Gar-ran handed over the red disc, which was carefully perused. Flipping the token back to Gar-ran, the merchant opened a drawer in the counter and carefully lifted out a small tray on which lay two rows of blue flower buds the size of a Malteser chocolate. Tim frowned; they'd come all this way for that?

'Two buds for yourself and half of one for the boy,' the merchant said, dropping the buds into Gar-ran's hand.

'Afterwards drink this before the hour is up, half each,' he added as he placed a small, green, glass bottle on the counter.

'We have a deal then?'

'Take them and go.'

'Thank you.'

The Nexian didn't reply. Thirty seconds later they were back on the street.

'What was that all about?'

'You'll see. I'm glad he's still in business. Now, back to the spaceport. I have a plan.'

A plan sounded good. Tim felt a blast of relief; he shouldn't have doubted Gar-ran.

***

'You must be joking.' Gar-ran had just explained his plan and it was the craziest thing Tim had heard so far. They were parked in a discreet street close to the spaceport.

'No, it should work.'

Tim snorted. 'You're telling me that those little buds can turn us invisible and we'll just be able to sneak in there and back to the Scarab?'

'More or less.' Gar-ran gave him a tight smile. 'We'll have to move quickly though. There's no telling for sure how long the effect will last. Are you ready?'

'Not really, but I'll give it a go.'

'Good man.' He passed Tim a half bud of Shadebellum. It tasted bitter but he chewed it down. Gar-ran took his.

Nothing happened at first and Tim was about to speak when he saw with astonishment that Gar-ran had become translucent and was fading before his eyes. Within moments you could barely see him at all. He gazed at his own hands; it was happening to him too.

They slipped out into the main road and hurriedly made their way along, taking care not to bump into anyone. The area around the spaceport had been largely cleared of people but there was still a gaggle of onlookers straining for a better view of what was happening behind the blockade.

Tim soon realised they weren't entirely invisible, just superbly camouflaged. When Gar-ran moved the air around him seemed to ripple slightly, but you'd only notice if you were watching carefully.

Approaching the main entrance from the side, they saw that other police officers dressed in dark green tunics had arrived. *These must be the senior investigators Gar-ran had mentioned.* They were almost at the hangar entrance when Tim sneezed. The guard nearest them turned around but Tim had already ducked down, and stayed crouched until the guard turned back. Gar-ran tugged at his sleeve and they edged their way into the main hangar.

The tension was getting to Tim, but there couldn't be far to go now, he just had to keep cool. But then he saw a gang of police surrounding the ship. One stood directly in front of the airlock.

What they needed was some kind of diversion, and an idea pinged into his head. As they'd passed through the entrance, he'd seen a Nexian engineer on the far side repairing an engine, his tools spread out around him. He tapped Gar-ran on the shoulder to get his attention.

'I have an idea; I'll be back in a sec,' he whispered, and moved off, ignoring Gar-ran's hissed command to come back.

Stealthily, Tim stalked toward the engineer, whose attention was fixed on his work. Ever so gently, he selected a tool that looked similar to the socket wrenches he knew from his dad's garage and deftly picked it up. He moved sideways until he was in line with the small, wall-mounted control panel ten feet away, then he hurled the tool towards it. It missed but clattered onto the floor noisily. Straightaway, three of the guards raced forwards. Crucially, one of them was the one blocking the airlock. Steadily, Tim made his way back to Gar-ran and they crept forwards.

***

Gar-ran was just about to disengage the lock when there were shouts from the far end of the hangar. Two guards were forcibly detaining the engineer and the third was brandishing the tool Tim had thrown. The other guards around the ship raised their weapons and moved forward. The airlock popped open with faint woosh and Tim piled in, bumping into Gar-ran. One guard turned and shouted a challenge which was cut off as the door closed behind them. Gar-ran tore ahead to the control hub and had fired the ignition sequence before Tim gained his seat. They shot forward, forcing the investigators to dive aside.

'I'm engaging cloaking so they can't track us,' Gar-ran said as they roared out and soared up. Within minutes they were in orbit and Gar-ran set a course to quickly take them beyond the Nexus system. Tim lolled back in his chair, finally allowing himself to relax a little. He felt a pang of regret as he realised he may never see the beautiful Tanara again, but being captured and imprisoned was a thought too horrible to contemplate.

Suddenly he felt violently sick. Gar-ran, too, looked rough.

'The antishade, we must take it,' he murmured, pulling out the small green bottle. 'Drink half.' He thrust the bottle at Tim.

Tim took a big gulp. It tasted vile, but he forced it down and handed the bottle back to Gar-ran, who drained the rest. The terrible nausea began to subside, but it was a long ten minutes before he felt right again.

'That was a close one,' Gar-ran said, mopping his brow with the sleeve of his suit.

'You take me to all the best places,' Tim replied, sending them both into a fit of relieved laughter.

'I'm setting a course to take us to Corax, the winter world.' Gar-ran leant forward and began to plot their way.

Twenty
The Winter World

———◆———◉———◆———

'No, it's too far away, and there's no known intelligent life.' Gar-ran tapped the on-screen map of the Milky Way in the command hub in reply to Tim's question as to whether the inhabitants of the Winter Worlds would be aware of their fugitive status.

Their destination, Corax, was located in the upper Cygnus arm of the Milky Way, apparently a region Gar-ran knew little about.

'Corax is like Earth during the last ice age really. Of the four planets in the system, it's the only one which can support sustainable life.'

'How would one of the pieces of the relic end up there?' Tim wished a segment of the dimension bomb was stored in a museum or gallery, any place they could just slip into and grab it without too much risk.

'Well, it's only a theory, but supposedly decommissioned dimension bombs were spilt up and auctioned off piecemeal to wealthy collectors. It could be that one of the transporters had the misfortune to crash on Corax. It's possible even a hijack attempt was made and they tried to outrun their attackers and pitched down. We'll know more when we get there.'

Tim blew on his tea to cool it while he mulled this new info over. 'When will that be?'

'In seventy-two hours.'

Three more days in deep space, Tim thought. He'd have to keep himself busy.

'You mentioned teaching me the ignition sequence?'

The time slipped away. As well as the flight training, Tim spent hours in the lab reading up on more planets and civilisations, and practised on the weapons range. It was late in the afternoon on the third day when Gar-ran summoned him to the hub.

Corax stood before him on the viewing screen: a white and blue disc streaked with cloud cover. From his studies he knew it was half the size of Earth, but there were no reliable maps. Gar-ran punched in a new command and they began their descent. Tim took his seat quickly and watched as Corax bloomed in size until it filled the whole screen.

***

The hub trembled as they raced through the atmosphere, and Tim clutched the armrests of his chair until his hands ached. After what seemed like too long, Gar-ran slowed the ship to coasting speed while Nerissa built up a detailed picture of the surroundings, encompassing terrain, weather, air quality, levels of oxygen, and any presence of harmful elements. This was collated into a detailed report she displayed on the viewing screen.

There was a lot of information about Corax's composition, which Tim found incomprehensible but which interested Gar-ran, who summarised.

'We can breathe the air here, although it's very cold. Temperature minus 20 Celsius with the wind chill. No visible settlements. Native inhabitants unknown. Some flora consisting of perennial grasses, lichens and mosses. Fauna unknown.'

'It's not much to go on,' Tim said, surprising himself with his bluntness.

'We'll be breaking new ground,' Gar-ran said mildly.

Classic understatement, Tim thought.

From the dream, Nerissa had deduced the crashed transporter was most likely to be in the uncharted Tarpang mountains. Gar-ran was confident they could find it and directed the Scarab in a series of low passes over the northern peaks while Nerissa scanned the terrain. Several hours went by and Tim was thinking about dinner when the alarm sounded.

'I have something, building picture … coming onscreen now,' Nerissa announced.

'It's hard to tell what it is,' Tim said, staring at the grainy image.

'Yes, but I think it's definitely some kind of ship. It's buried by a lot of snow and ice. We'll have to try to find a way inside when we get up there. Judging from the terrain, it's not going to be easy. You see here?' Gar-ran pointed to a dark streak. 'That's a narrow ravine. Too awkward to fly into. We'll have to set down where we can and hike from there. We'll travel as light as possible but with a good supply of rations, just in case. Best to take some weaponry and motion detectors and move slowly to start with, I think.'

Tim nodded. He had the uneasy feeling Corax was going to be their most dangerous stop yet.

***

Gar-ran chose a variant on the jumpsuits that Tim hadn't seen before. These suits were far thicker and more padded and contained an automatic, built-in heating system. There was the usual utility belt, but also a hood with a black fur trim which you could pull up and tighten. Gar-ran also handed him a pair of thick blue gloves with silicon grips on the palms. They both wore advanced hiking boots whose sole automatically adapted to the terrain and would provide a crampon-like grip against the dangerous ice.

'These are great,' Tim murmured. Maybe Gar-ran would let him keep them.

Tim's pistol hung in its holster at his right hip and a foot-long ice axe was securely fastened to his belt. Gar-ran had the same gear but, in addition, would carry their GPS wayfinder, which doubled up as a motion detector. Both of them had a rucksack with rations and sleeping bag. Finally, they fitted a stocky fur snood around their necks and the all-important ice goggles to prevent snow blindness.

***

Light snow fell intermittently around them and the air was so cold that Tim was half afraid to breathe in case his lungs froze. The jagged peaks of the Tarpang mountains loomed before them.

'It's a three-hour hike or so to the ship and we have about eight and a half hours of daylight left, so we'll have to get a move on,' Gar-ran said.

Tim nodded. They had discussed the possibility of having to spend the night on the transporter if they ran out of time. It was risky though; they had no idea what could be on board, or if they could even get inside.

At first they made decent progress and were able to maintain a good pace. Tim scanned the desolate landscape as they marched but it remained entirely devoid of any form of life and the chill he felt was not just from the wind. The route became icier and more treacherous and it wasn't long before he slipped over. The adjusting grip on the boots helped, but sometimes the terrain was so rough they had to take a long diversion to find more walkable sections. It started to snow again and the cloud cover blotted out the weak sun entirely. Turning around, he could no longer see their trail.

Gar-ran was marching on ahead and Tim laboured to keep up but, without warning, the ground gave way and he was falling. Desperately, he dug his ice axe into the bank and tugged hard. The hook bit in and he stopped with a bone-jarring suddenness. Opening his eyes, he was surprised to see he'd only slipped a few feet.

Cursing, he hauled himself up and brushed off the wet snow.

'DON'T MOVE!'

Tim jumped, then froze. Gar-ran looked down from the ridge.

'Don't move a muscle. You're right on the edge of a crevasse.'

Startled, Tim looked down, but the ground appeared firm, no different to the last mile or so anyway. But Gar-ran had the wayfinder, so he could see more.

'Take half a step to the left and then one step forward.'

Moving gingerly, Tim stepped as instructed. 'Now, turn to me and take a step forward. Good, now retrace your steps up here.'

Following the directions, Tim clambered up alongside Gar-ran.

'Let's take a short break.'

'OK.' Tim slipped off his rucksack and took out his water bottle. The bottle was insulated so wouldn't freeze.

'Sorry about that.'

'It's OK. This place is treacherous. I shouldn't have carried on. From now onwards, we move together...'. He broke off in mid-flow.

'What is it?' Tim asked as the adrenaline suddenly kicked in.

'I'm not sure; I thought I saw something out of the corner of my eye.' He consulted the motion detector. 'No, nothing. You OK to carry on?'

'Sure.' Tim wondered what Gar-ran could possibly have noticed in all the whirling snow.

They continued their trek upwards. Finally, ahead of them was a cleft between two ragged snow-swept peaks which led to the ravine where the buried ship lay. The gap was narrow, less than eight feet across. Gar-ran went first, pistol out and ready. Tim followed close by, checking that nothing had come up behind them. He shivered as he peered down into the ravine; his dream had come real again. The back section of the wrecked transporter was just visible some way below. The tips of its tail fins poked up through the thick snow and Tim estimated the width of the ship to be around 100 feet across.

'Somewhere there must be an entrance,' Gar-ran said as they gingerly made their way down to level ground. 'The scanner should be able to detect it even through the ice,' Gar-ran murmured, adjusting the controls.

Tim nodded, hoping they could find the way in soon. The cold was getting to him, despite his suit. Long minutes went by as Gar-ran continually swept the detector up and down, but the signal never changed. They decided to climb up onto the transporter and at last the detector beeped a different tone. Tim's heart thumped in anticipation, but there was no visible trace of any entrance.

'It's down there somewhere. I have an idea. Switch your pistol to wide beam on the lowest setting. I'll cover you. Now, crouch down and fire into and across the ice. Fire one shot every ten seconds.'

Tim did as directed. He felt nervous but excited that Gar-ran was trusting him with something crucial. His first shot melted the ice a few inches deep in a two-feet radius. He waited the ten seconds and fired again. More ice melted away. Ten more seconds passed and he fired again. Now he could see what looked like the top corner of a metal panel.

'Hey, I can see something!' He turned to Gar-ran, who was looking down at something.

'Keep going,' he said. Three more blasts and a rectangular hatch entrance was fully revealed. There didn't seem any way to open it though.

The sound of Gar-ran firing shocked Tim and he nearly lost his footing as he whirled around. He brought his own weapon up into the ready position but couldn't see the danger at first. Something moved in the corner of his vison and he gasped as the two dog-like creatures trotted closer. They were Labrador-sized with white shaggy coats, large ears and strange, milky, opaque eyes. They stood some way off, as if sizing up him and Gar-ran.

'What are they?'

'I don't know. Some kind of hunting dog, I think. Cover me while I take a look at what you've found.'

'OK.' Tim's heart drummed against his chest. The dogs had moved nearer. *Can they jump? What if they jump up here?*

'We're going to have to blast our way in.' Gar-ran opened one of the pockets on his belt and bought out lump of clay-like putty which he fastened to the hatch.

'Keep watching them,' Gar-ran cautioned.

Tim snapped his head round. There were three of the dogs now, and they'd edged closer.

'Brace yourself,' Gar-ran called out, and Tim tensed for the bang, but the blast was less than he expected. It terrified the dogs, though, who sprinted off, yelping.

'Good to know,' Gar-ran smiled. The hatch had blown back on its hinges and there was easily enough space for them both to go through. Turning on his torch, Gar-ran stepped through first.

It was eerie to stand in the wide, silent corridor. Their torches were powerful but could only light so far ahead. To compensate, Gar-ran fished out two headtorches from his rucksack. Tim had tried one out the day before and, once strapped on, they were pretty comfortable. It was much better being out of the wind and chill, and Tim adjusted his headlamp to cast a wider beam as Gar-ran wedged the hatch door shut.

The floor sloped sharply down and, without the special grips on their boots, it would have been easy to plunge headlong. Tim winced at the stench of burnt oil. The metal cladding on the wall to their right was cracked and buckled from the crash impact.

'There could be anything in here, so stay alert,' Gar-ran whispered, his face pale in the torchlight.

Bracing themselves against the wall, they continued to pick their way down until their path was blocked by a huge mound of compacted snow and ice.

'The roof must have breached in the crash,' Gar-ran murmured.

Tim shone his torch and saw that a section of the floor ahead to the left had collapsed, leaving a jagged hole.

'What do you reckon?' He didn't like the look of it at all, but could see no other way.

'We may not have a choice.' Carefully, Gar-ran crouched down and peered down to the level below. He picked up a small chunk of blackened, twisted metal and dropped it through the hole. It hit the floor below with a dull clang.

'About sixteen feet. We could rope down. I'll check it out first.'

Tim moved closer. He couldn't help thinking about the scene from *Alien* where the crew of the Nostromo explore a seemingly derelict ship and step into a nightmare. He shuddered, and busied himself with selecting a good section of rope. He spotted two thick pipes running above and, after checking they were stable, he fixed the rope through them and passed it to Gar-ran, who carefully climbed down. He moved slowly, to avoid collision with the sharp edges of the broken floor. Tim stood over him shining his torch down. Gar-ran reached the floor below without incident and shone his torch all around.

'It seems pretty intact down here. Come on down, but carefully. Watch the edges.'

'All right.' Tim took hold of the rope and sat down on the edge of the hole. He half-slid, half-climbed his way down and saw that the corridor in which they stood was half as wide as the one above. The floor was composed of light grey metal tiles, some of which were loose.

'Let's try up here first. There should be some way of getting down to the lower deck.'

Twenty feet ahead, the way was blocked by a large metal door. On the upper right was a small electronic panel which was long deactivated, judging from the look of it.

'Shall we just blast it?' Tim asked.

'No. It wouldn't do any good. There must be a failsafe system in place, to allow entry to the other side in the event of electronic failure or deactivation.'

Tim crouched down and scanned the floor. There weren't any signs or markings, but he noticed one of the tiles was a darker grey. Pulling out his penknife, he cut around all sides and peeled the tile back. In the space below was a round chrome button. It had to be the failsafe, but he hesitated. What if he was wrong?'

'Go on, trust your judgement,' Gar-ran said softly.

Tim pressed the button and moved back. There was a gentle clunk sound and slowly the door slid back, grinding its wall through the accumulated detritus. Tim felt a surge of achievement which vanished when the door stopped abruptly, leaving just enough space for them to get through if they went single file. He pressed the button several more times but the door refused to budge any further. He exchanged a glance with Gar-ran and they both drew their pistols.

'I'll go first,' Gar-ran whispered.

The corridor led around to the right and it seemed to get colder with each step. The passageway narrowed and, dead ahead, the way was blocked by another metal door. Tim moved ahead of Gar-ran and something crunched under his feet. He shone his torch down and saw the floor was covered with loose, mud-coloured gravel. A faint mist began to rise from the floor.

'Run! Run for the door!' Gar-ran pushed Tim forwards.

'What is it?' Gar-ran's sudden urgency unnerved him and he felt the first flicker of fear.

'Gas, released by the crushed gravel.' He shone his torch at the celling and they saw the roof was perforated with dozens of holes like a colander.

'Unless we can get through, we'll either be poisoned or sedated.'

Wishing he hadn't asked, Tim ran to the metal barrier. Gar-ran frantically scanned the floor but this time it all looked the same.

'What about higher up?' Tim realised with a shock he was slurring his words and already felt woozy.

'Yes! It could be.'

Gar-ran scanned the upper section wall next to the barrier and immediately the scanner beeped.

'Tim, I'll lift you up. Use your knife and try that section there,' Gar-ran indicated the area and squatted down, cupping his hands together.

Clumsily, Tim placed his foot into Gar-ran's hand and was hoisted up. Protruding from the wall was a metal box the size of a pack of cards. He worked the knife blade around all sides as he tried to wrench the cover off, but it was stuck fast. He could feel Gar-ran begin to sag beneath him. He twisted the blade harder and the box snapped off, revealing another chrome-coloured button. He slammed his hand onto it and immediately the barrier slid back and they tumbled through. Gar-ran spotted the lever on the other side and had just enough strength to throw it to seal the door and trap the sedative gas inside. He sunk to his knees. Tim was already flat out on his back, his head spinning. He could feel a slight breeze and gulped down the fresh air.

'There must be another breach in the hull,' Gar-ran said, his breath ragged.

They lay there for some time, letting their heads clear.

'That was nasty,' Tim said.

'We were lucky.'

'Lucky? We walked into a trap.'

'Every ship has some kind of defence system. There's usually defences on a transporter like this. It could have been they were triggered automatically by the crash. There's something in here they wanted to protect and that's good news for us.'

'What's the bad news?' Tim smiled despite the anxiety of their close shave.

'Let's press on,' Gar-ran said, dragging himself up.

They moved further down the corridor, which widened into a larger, open area.

'There,' Gar-ran said pointing.

To the far right was a curving walkway. It corkscrewed down to the right, disappearing from sight. It reminded Tim of the helter-skelter ride at the county fair back home when he was younger. He was hit by an intense wave of homesickness. Tears sprung into his eyes but he blinked them away, relieved that Gar-ran wouldn't notice in the semi-darkness. He forced himself to concentrate on now.

'Let's take it slowly. Be ready for anything, Tim.'

As they descended, the torchlight picked out whole sections of the walkway that were warped and ruckled up, forcing them to watch every step they took. They remained silent with weapons drawn as they headed further down into the unknown. After a couple of minutes, it began to grow lighter.

'Where's that light coming from?' Tim whispered.

'Walkways like these would normally always have lighting from a type of energy crystal. Once charged, they can stay alight for decades, even if there was a total power failure. It's a safety design to help find your way around. These are starting to fail though; this ship's been here a long time.'

Tim wasn't sure if that was a good or bad sign. At the bottom of the walkway they stepped out into another wide corridor and he noticed that the floor to the right was different. It was elevated and painted pure white and marked with black diagonal stripes.

'This could be it. I think we can access the ship's hold through there,' Gar-ran said, moving ahead.

A closer inspection revealed two metal wheels fixed to opposite ends of a raised floor section.

'Take the wheel at the far side, Tim. We'll turn clockwise to start with.'

Tim hurried to the other end and, crouching down, clasped hold of the metal wheel. On the count of three he turned the wheel hard. Surprisingly, it spun around easily like a nut fitting onto a bolt and, after a few seconds, stopped dead. There was a faint clunking sound and slowly half the floor folded downwards with a gentle whir. Gar-ran shone his torch down.

'This is it,' he said.

Twenty-One
Hounded

Slothra checked the reading again. The signal was weak but consistent. He typed the coordinates in the control console. The computer would be able to analyse the distance to where the signal originated and predict the likely course of the fugitive's ship. Then it would just be a case of closing in fast, and striking with speed and surprise. Time to sharpen his claws.

***

Eight steps led down to a big, open area. Dozens of different-sized rectangular metal cases lay piled up haphazardly on top of one another. Some had burst open. One long crate contained what looked like a set of solid silver cannons. Other shattered containers revealed an assortment of rich silks and oddly patterned fabrics. There was also a strong spicy smell and some sections of the floor were coated with a mustard-coloured powder.

'Don't worry; it's only a type of spice,' Gar-ran said, reading Tim's expression.

'It's going to take *ages* to go through all this.' That meant they would probably have to find somewhere onboard to spend the night, not that they were likely to get much sleep.

'Not necessarily.' Balancing precariously on two upturned cases, Gar-ran pulled out a metal disc the size of a side plate from his bag and fitted a telescopic pole to it. The top of the pole was shaped into a handle with an integrated control panel.

'What's that?' Tim asked.

'It's a kind of metal detector, but I've set it to only detect the rarest metals and alloys.'

Tim smiled, he was used to people metal detecting on the beaches back home after the crowds had gone, but he never expected to encounter one out there.

'The good thing is we know what we're after. However, we may have to do some heavy lifting ...'

Half an hour went by as they slowly clambered and scanned the chaotic tumble of packing cases. Tim was just about to ask if he could have a go when suddenly it beeped and Gar-ran peered closer at the screen.

'I think I'm onto something. Two layers down,' he murmured.

The first case that needed shifting was flat and thin like a table top and, by each taking one end, they could lift it easily. The metal cube container underneath though was a different story. Try as they might, it was much too heavy to be lifted. In the end, they resorted to clearing out a gap to one side and then pushing as hard as possible. Inch by inch the cube slid towards the gap, and then finally fell in with a resounding clang.

The case below was smaller, the size of a briefcase. Two thick straps fixed the lid down firmly and, in the centre, strange letters and markings were painted in green ink. 'Can you read that?' Tim asked.

'No. Let's hope it doesn't say, do not open.' Gar-ran cut through the first strap with the multi-tool blade. Tim did the same on his side. The lid came off easily.

The beeping from the detector intensified as Gar-ran reached in and scooped out handfuls of shredded black rubber and threw it to one side. 'It's just packaging material.'

Tim joined in, and gradually as he dug through the rubber chips, he saw the first golden gleam. He scooped the last few handfuls of packing aside and saw not one but two segments of the dimension bomb nestled snugly together. That meant they had all the pieces they needed! He turned to Gar-ran for confirmation.

'Yes, we can start the journey home now.' Gar-ran smiled as he lifted the relic out and passed it to Tim.

'We should be able to get back to the Scarab before nightfall,' Gar-ran said as they picked their way back to the cargo entrance.

Tim was delighted; finding the remaining pieces together was a massive bonus. Now all they had to do was get back to the Scarab. For the first time he had the feeling everything was going to work out.

They retraced their way back to the upper decks. It was hard work climbing up the rope but Tim managed it without help. He shuddered though as Gar-ran opened the hatch and the icy wind ripped in. The weather had deteriorated quickly. Gar-ran went first, carefully checking on all sides for the dogs.

'We've got three and half hours of daylight left, so we'll go straight down and to the west and that will take us back to the ice field. We should just do it if we get a move on.'

Tim nodded. He was feeling bullish now and even though it was freezing, he was relieved to be outside. Fresh snow had fallen and they sank a foot deep in some areas. They were just over halfway down the trail when the ground collapsed beneath them and they tumbled head over heels down towards the rocky base of the mountain.

Frantically, Tim dug his heels in and lashed out with his ice axe. The point drove deep into the ground and slowed him slightly. He bumped over some sharp stones and yelped as he felt them cut him. Finally he slowed and came to a halt. He gasped for breath, and felt a moment of real terror when he found he couldn't move. Was he paralysed? He thrashed wildly and realised that it was thick, wet snow that held him fast, sparing only his head and shoulders. He kicked and thrashed some more and was able to free one leg and, after several minutes of wrenching and scrambling, he pushed himself out of the snow's bitter embrace.

Gar-ran? Where is he? Tim spun around but the marshal was nowhere to be seen.

Stunned, he stood there, wanting to call out for his friend but fearful of making any noise that could trigger another deadly snow slide. He had to do something though. He began to call his friend's name, first quietly but then more loudly. He stopped after every call for a moment to listen, and when no answer came, he carefully made his way further down. The minutes ticked by and panic began to rise in Tim's chest. He fought it down. He had to think.

He carefully scanned the slope below. There was a large bank of churned-up snow and something else. He gently slid further down. A scrap of green fabric stuck out. Gar-ran's rucksack. Tim headed down as fast as he dared. It was impossible to tell if the rucksack had been wrenched free or if Gar-ran was still wearing it and buried below. He began to scrape and dig frantically, scooping the impacted snow away. More of the rucksack became visible and then he saw the blue of Gar-ran's flight suit. He dug harder. Suddenly an idea hit him. He lay down on his side and brought out his laser pistol, which was still set for wide beam. He dialled it down to its lowest setting. What he had planned was risky, but Gar-ran could be injured or, worse, suffocating.

The first beam melted the snow several feet across and, encouraged, he fired again and again. The heaped-up snow was melting quickly, revealing Gar-ran lying on his side. He swept the snow from his friend's face and supported his head. Gar-ran's eyes flicked open. Tim sighed in relief. Gently, he helped him sit up.

'Are you hurt?'

A coughing fit racked Gar-ran and he shuddered. It was some moments before he could speak.

'No, just bruised and shaken. But if it hadn't been for you …'

'I had to find you; how would I get home otherwise?' Gar-ran returned Tim's smile but a moment later a look of concern filtered across his face.

'What is it?' Tim asked. Maybe he was hurt after all.

'The wayfinder. I must have lost it in the fall.'

Tim's stomach dropped as he realised they'd lost their only accurate means of navigation. Maybe not lost; perhaps he could find it. He patrolled around the immediate area while Gar-ran got his breath back. When Gar-ran was able to stand, they checked further down but there was no sign of the scanner. Soon it would be dark. Tim felt the bite of anxiety but said nothing as they carried on searching. After a fruitless half an hour though, Gar-ran called a halt.

'We'll have to press on. We won't make the ship before dark, and it's too dangerous to climb back to the transporter, so the priority now is finding some shelter. I noticed something on the hike up. If we can find it, it could be exactly what we need.'

'OK, let's go.' Tim hoped he sounded more certain than felt. At least Gar-ran was thinking clearly, so he must be OK after all. They were on even ground now but, looking up, Tim was shocked at how far they'd slipped.

'I'd better check my pistol,' Gar-ran said. He didn't add, 'In case the dogs come again,' but the thought was already in Tim's mind. He had some mini-grenades too, but dare they use them in these conditions? He hoped that was one choice they wouldn't have to make.

'No damage. Good. We'll head west. We're looking for a large, overhanging section of rock. Beneath that I'm sure I saw a cave earlier, although I couldn't tell its size. We'll have to assume the dogs are still out here somewhere and they could be hostile. We must keep checking all around us, especially as the light goes.'

Tim agreed. There was no way he wanted to be surprised. The snow was firmer and they could move more easily, although the temperature was falling rapidly.

Two hours dragged by and the light was going fast. Tim was finding it harder to concentrate. The chill and the constant strain of checking for the dogs was debilitating and he had moments of walking along in a daydream of being warm at home in front of the TV. Then an icy gust would blow his hood back and jolt him into the present.

They stopped for a few moments to rest and, almost immediately, there was a sharp, whining howl from somewhere in front of them. Another cry tore through the air and one by one more of the strange and unseen dogs joined in. It was impossible to tell how many there were as the sound came from all around.

'Let's keep going, but slowly, no running at all, and keep checking around you,' Gar-ran urged.

Tim nodded. He wanted to speed up but knew it was crucial he remained as calm as possible. The howling persisted but the dogs remained out of sight, occasionally they would glimpse pairs of gleaming eyes in the distance but the dogs would run off before they could get a bead on them.

The darkening sky also forced them to move with care; the last thing they wanted now was to fall over or down something. Abruptly the howling ceased and Tim and Gar-ran exchanged glances. The sudden silence was even more unnerving as they had no idea where the dogs were. Gar-ran stopped suddenly and Tim bumped into him.

'What?' Tim whispered.

'The overhang is directly ahead but they're blocking us,' Gar-ran said.

Tim moved up behind Gar-ran. A snarling wall of white-furred dogs, their eyes aglow, blocked the way. He swept his torch around and saw the hounds were spread out in a semi-circle, surrounding them. There had to be at least a dozen of them.

'What are we waiting for? Let's shoot!' Tim whispered.

'No! We don't know how many are out there and how they'll react. Shoot only if necessary.' Tim stared at Gar-ran as if he was mad, and began to wonder if actually his friend was really OK. Maybe he'd banged his head on a rock during the avalanche and had concussion. Out of the corner of his eyes he saw two dogs edge closer. He turned sharply to face them and they stopped, then slowly moved back. Tim turned to Gar-ran, who was holding something in his left hand.

'Last one,' Gar-ran said and tossed something small and shiny toward the dogs. It sank into the snow before Tim had time to see what it was. Then Gar-ran pulled out the handheld digital detonator and he understood. He turned his head away a split second before the explosion half deafened him and splattered him in snow. There was a collective yelp from the dogs and they sprinted away, soon becoming lost in the dim light.

'Move now!' Gar-ran shouted. They ran for the shelter of the overhanging rock and saw some way back the entrance to a shallow cave. Tentatively they moved further in, still watching to make sure no dogs had slinked back. The cave was about twenty feet deep and slightly less in width. It widened in the back and they saw that fifteen feet or so up was a natural stone platform. It would be an awkward climb but worth it.

'We should be safe up there,' Gar-ran said. He took a step forward and wobbled slightly.

'Are you OK? I'll take your bag …'

'I'm fine. We'll have something to eat and get some rest. It's been quite a day.'

Twenty-Two
Exodus

S
now blew into the front section of the cave for another half an hour and coated the floor below them. Under the beam of the torches it looked like a rich, luxuriant carpet. It was eerie though as, in the growing darkness, the cave entrance resembled a giant mouth.

'Our suits' heating batteries should be good for another nineteen hours, so we won't freeze, but it's definitely time for some food,' Gar-ran said.

Tim realised then how hungry he was. Thirsty too. Breakfast seemed liked a lifetime ago.

'Great, I'm starving.' He sat down and, with an effort, tugged off his heavy boots. His feet felt stiff and sore, so he gently massaged them while Gar-ran sorted through the food rations.

'It's important to rehydrate. You have three bottles left?'

Tim nodded and dug down into his bag to produce one of his insulated water bottles. He pulled out the stopper and took a long drink.

'We'll get away at first light tomorrow. If the weather is clear enough.'

Tim had been wondering about the weather conditions too. About what would happen if the foul weather accelerated into a real blizzard and they were trapped there.

'Tim!' He realised Gar-ran had been saying something but he hadn't heard a word. He smiled sheepishly.

'Which one do you want?'

'Sorry?'

Gar-ran waved the foil ration pouches he was holding. 'This one is like chicken and pasta and the other one is a kind of vegetable soup. Both my own creations.'

Tim was tempted to ask what 'like chicken' actually meant, but decided he was too hungry to care. 'Like chicken sounds good to me.'

'See this little button here on the side? If I break the seal and press it, the packet will heat up from inside. Here's a spoon. It will be ready in thirty seconds. Just rip along the top of the pouch when it's ready.' Gar-ran passed the pouch over.

Tim pressed the button and marvelled at the warmth that spread through his fingers. 'This is great. This must be like the food real astronauts have.'

'Well we are real astronauts, aren't we?' Gar-ran smiled. He seemed better now they were inside and Tim was glad; he'd been worried, but the marshal seemed fine.

The food was tasty and filling. He had to give Gar-ran credit; he went to every effort to make things as easy as he could. They chatted for a while and, before long, Tim's eyes began to droop and it was time to call it a day. He got into his sleeping sack and lay down using his rucksack as a pillow. Sleep came quickly. He awoke with a start once in the night but Gar-ran was sound asleep, his breathing deep and even, so he relaxed and nodded off again.

When he next opened his eyes there was another foil food pouch on the floor next to him. *It must be morning and that's breakfast*, he thought. The hardness of the floor had taken its toll on his muscles and his neck and shoulders ached. He stretched out full length and rolled onto his back and sat up. He was alone. There wasn't a lot of light in the cave but he could hear movement somewhere below. Still half in his sleeping bag, he grabbed his pistol and pointed at the door. What settings had he left the gun on? There was no time to check. Rolling over, he took aim.

'Morning Tim. Bit early for target practice, isn't it?' Gar-ran smiled up at him.

'It's never too early,' Tim muttered, feeling foolish. He noticed the melting snow on Gar-ran's suit. 'How bad is it?'

'Worse than yesterday. We'll have to hope it stops later and we can make a break for it.'

'Any sign of the dogs?'

'No.'

'That's something I suppose.'

***

Tim's food pouch turned out to be a mixture of cereal and a type of stewed fruit that tasted like prunes. Definitely an acquired taste. After breakfast he decided to have another check on the weather. Beyond the shelter of the cave, the wind blew so violently it was difficult to stand, let alone move. The driving snow meant that visibility was almost nil, so he quickly headed back inside. *How long will our suit batteries last now? Should we be worried?*

The morning dragged by. There was nothing to do and the waiting only increased the tension they both felt. Finally, in the early afternoon, the weather began to clear. After a quick lunch of vegetable stew, they gathered their equipment and moved to the entrance. The blizzard had blown itself out and the day was now clear and bright and very cold. Tim calculated they had about five hours left before the batteries that powered the internal heating system inside their suits ran down.

'I reckon we're about a half a mile off the trail. If we head up this way and then to the right, we should be able to see it. Once we're back on track it should take us two hours to get back to the Scarab.' Gar-ran pointed out the route. It seemed fairly straightforward, Tim thought, unless of course the unexpected struck again. They'd have to carry on anyway, as another night outside was unthinkable.

They continued to slog upwards, weaving in and out of a series of snow-covered boulders. They'd regained a lot of the height they'd lost and Tim recognised one of the peaks off to the right. Mustn't rush though. A lot of snow had fallen and the last thing they wanted was another avalanche.

After what seemed like a very long hour, Gar-ran stopped.

'This is it, as best as I can tell. I'll take the lead and we'll take it slow and steady. Step where I step.'

The ice paths stretched before them: a great white broken expanse of churned-up snow, rock and ice, and sickening hidden drops. But on the other side would be the ship, and safety. As quickly and as carefully as they could, they picked their way across the treacherous frozen landscape.

Somewhere behind, a piercing howl broke out and they turned to see the dog pack gathered in the small valley far below. Despite the risk, they quickened their pace. The dogs never moved closer but their howls continued to reach up towards them until they looked down and saw the pack drifting away like ghosts in the night until finally they were lost from sight. Tim let out a big sigh, puffing his cheeks.

'Let's hope that's the last of them,' Gar-ran muttered.

Several times they both slipped and stumbled and Tim knew his body would be bruised black and blue in the next few days, but they hiked on and finally, over two hours later, Gar-ran said: 'There she is!'

Tim peered into the distance. At first, he couldn't see anything much, but then was able to make out the outline of the Scarab. Heavy snow had almost covered her, masking her elegant form. Immediately his mood brightened. *Not far now.* Gar-ran brandished the ship communicator in his gloved hand.

'I've been trying to call her to us, but the sensor's not transmitting. Must be the snow or the cold.'

'Maybe it's the batteries?' Tim said smiling. His feet hurt and his shoulders ached and it was bloody freezing, but he was happy.

They jogged the last twenty feet. Gar-ran activated the airlock and ramp without breaking stride and soon they were inside. Tim flung his rucksack down and raced to the command hub. Home! He was heading home.

Twenty-Three
The Fugitives

Tim was still elated the following day as they ate breakfast in the galley, but Gar-ran was taking a more cautious view.

'It's a long way back and don't forget we're still wanted fugitives. Of course, we can prove that we were gone from Ter-ran before the storekeeper's murder, but we can't afford any delays. I won't feel truly happy until we're back in Earth's atmosphere. There's something else as well.' Gar-ran put his cup down and looked solemn.

Uh-oh. What now? Tim thought. He spooned down the last mouthful of rice pudding and gave Gar-ran his full attention.

'A few hours ago, I picked up a distress signal. As far as I can tell it originated from the Karanagan system. That's not too far from here. As a marshal, I'm honour-bound to lend aid to any ship that needs assistance within a reasonable distance of my field of operation.' He paused, watching Tim's reaction.

'In other words, we're going to help someone, or something.'

'Yes. However, there is a chance it might not be genuine. Slothra is out there somewhere; it could be a ruse to lure us in. Nonetheless I think we should investigate, but I wanted to talk to you first before I set a course. What do you think?'

Tim's initial thought was to say no. They had enough on their plate with the journey and what they would find when they got back to Earth, but he started to think what if it was them who were in the position of needing help? Wouldn't he want someone to come to his aid? Right now, they needed all the allies they could get.

'I guess we can take a look.'

'Good lad. If I suspect anything untoward, I promise you we'll be out of there.'

'All right. What is this Karanagan place?'

'It's a system of five planets, named after the largest one. It's a primitive world, mostly covered in jungle and rainforest. If we push it, we can be in orbit by tomorrow.'

Tim remembered his dream, where he was high up in the canopy of a forest, and began to feel uneasy. Still, he'd made his decision to support Garran and he didn't feel it would be right to back out now. He just hoped they weren't making a mistake.

***

Slothra listened intently. The signal was definite now. He'd been incensed earlier when, for several hours, he'd lost the connection to his target's ship, but he had it back now, stronger than ever. That could only mean they were closer. He drooled at the thought; the thick black spittle ran down his chin into the matted fur. He typed in a few instructions to adjust his course and settled back to wait.

***

'Coming up on the screen now,' Nerissa announced.

Tim sat with Gar-ran in the command hub. 'Can you zoom in please, Nerissa.'

'Yes Gar-ran, enhancing now.'

The strange craft had clearly seen better days. It drifted stealthily at a funny angle and they could see clear damage to the nearside. It was unlike any ship Tim had seen so far, being almost entirely flat, and resembling a giant, floating clamshell.

'I've been calling on all frequencies but no response so far,' Nerissa said.

'Hmm. It's a type of cruiser but normally I wouldn't expect to see one this far out. OK, engage the shields and let's take a closer look,' Gar-ran said.

Tim was nervous. Why would a space cruiser be here in such a remote location? Had it been abandoned? A space equivalent of the *Mary Celeste*? Half of him wanted to ask Gar-ran to turn around, but the other half was curious.

'It could be something to do with the sanctuary,' Gar-ran murmured.

'What's that?'

'It was a research project on Karanagan some years ago. Based in the Karang forest in the southern hemisphere. They sent regular reports back at first but then they just stopped. So, they sent another team out to investigate and they never came back either. At some point the whole project was abandoned and ...'

Gar-ran never got a chance to finish because, at that moment, something hit the ship hard. They were thrown violently forwards and only their seats' restraining straps stopped them from smashing into the control panel.

'Shields disengaging!' Nerissa shouted.

'Hang on!' Gar-ran rolled the ship to the right; Tim saw a white flash on the viewing screen and realised they'd just missed being hit a second time. What the hell was happening? He felt totally helpless. Even if he could resist the terrific pressure of the G-force, the flying instruction he'd taken hadn't included defensive actions.

'Nerissa, white storm!' Gar-ran yelled.

'Affirmative.'

Tim watched amazed as Gar-ran wrestled the Scarab level. A white ball of crackling energy burst ahead of them and enveloped their attacker's ship. It bloomed so quickly there was no time to evade. The enemy craft shook violently then veered down and out of view. Tim felt a savage joy and couldn't help whooping in delight.

'You got him, Gar-ran!'

'Maybe.' Gar-ran looked angry and was about to say something else when Nerissa cut in.

'Forty per cent power loss. No comms.'

'How far to Karanagan?'

'Three hours.'

'That's cutting it fine, but we should just do it.'

'What just happened?' Tim asked, and was alarmed to hear how shaky his voice sounded.

'A classic ambush. I should have expected it.' He banged his fist on his chair arm.

'Was it Slothra?' Tim wasn't used to seeing Gar-ran rattled and it made him nervous.

'I think so. We're going to have to land on Karanagan while I get the power restored. Shouldn't take too long. I'm sorry Tim.'

'It's OK, we survived. It'll be all right.' He didn't know what else to say. He hated having to make this diversion, but wanted to appear encouraging. One thought nagged him: *how bad is the damage?*

***

It was a fraught three hours until they made planetfall on Karanagan. The ship brushed the tops of the trees as they whipped along and then shakily rose up before levelling out. The problem was going to be finding a place to land before lack of power forced them down. Tim stared at the seemingly endless green sea of trees that made up the massive ancient forests of Karanagan. Nerissa's face popped up in the top right corner of the viewing screen.

'Nerissa, what do you have?'

'Loading now,' she replied.

Tim couldn't read the data on the screen but Gar-ran scanned it avidly, before taking the ship up for a better view. Tim saw that the canopy below wasn't so uniform as the surrounding forest; instead the trees were different heights and some were growing at odd angles.

The outlines of a large rectangular structure appeared on the screen and gradually more detail became apparent. There was an incomplete outer wall surrounding a central building which appeared to have several rounded towers. Two other small buildings were located near the far surrounding wall.

'Is that the sanctuary?' Tim wondered aloud. It reminded him of the AutoCAD drawings he'd seen his dad work on.

'It must be. We can take shelter in there and there's a chance I might be able to signal Nectar one, they could then relay a message through to the marshal command, but we must get the ship down first,' Gar-ran murmured.

The frustrating thing was there was nowhere to land the ship close by; the canopy layer for miles around was too dense to get through. They had to fly some distance before they discovered an area clear enough to take the Scarab into. A huge tree had fallen, taking out its two neighbours, giving them just enough room. Tangled branches grazed the ship's hull as they descended to the forest floor.

'We're miles away,' Tim blurted out. He didn't mean to sound like a sulky kid, but it was clear they were in for another long hike. If only they hadn't gone to the other ship's aid! He kept that opinion to himself though.

'I know. Best I can do. Right, we'll have to sit tight while Nerissa runs a full diagnostic.'

Gar-ran was putting a brave face on things but Tim could tell he was concerned. He felt guilty for moaning. The only way they'd get out of this was by sticking and working together. He made a mental note to try to not lose his cool.

'So, this sanctuary place, you said it was a research centre once?' he asked as they headed to the lab.

'Yes, Karanagan was only discovered around fifty years ago by scientists from Nectar one, the sister world of where we visited. As it's mostly forest, there's a good chance any plants here could be harvested for medicinal purposes, just like back on Earth. That was the plan anyway, so they built a research centre called it the sanctuary, but for some reason it didn't work out and the place was abandoned. However, if I can get the sanctuary's comms hub online, I should be able to connect to Nectar one and ask them to signal marshal command. That would make for a smoother trip home.'

It sounded like a good plan to Tim. The marshal command might send in backup.

'Somehow we're being tracked. I'll check the hull, then we'll press on. We're a sitting target here. Nerissa will engage cloaking and a full lockdown while we're away.'

'What's it like outside? Can we breathe?' He didn't fancy marching through a steaming jungle with an oxygen tank fixed to his back.

'Yes, we can, but it's going to be hot and humid. There's a good amount of daylight left so we can cover quite a lot of ground, but we'll have to camp before last light. This time we'll both wear wristband local location finders and map generators. That way we can always find our way back. It's best we wear the full cover flight suits as we want to be as protected from the rainforest and its inhabitants as much as possible. Also, we don't know what plants or ferns are poisonous, so it's best to be safe.'

Tim was getting fired up now. He could do this. Gar-ran was in full-on mode and it was good to see him recovered.

'What weapons?' he asked.

'Pistol and rifle, but modified ones which are waterproof and should be able to cope with the forest's humidity. They fire exactly as the ones we used on Corax. Here, before we step outside, rub this over your face and neck, and ears too.' He handed Tim a small white tube with a metal cap.

'What is it?'

'Insect repellent. Put plenty on and keep it with you.'

Tim did as advised. The gel was clear and had a faint disinfectant smell. It left his skin feeling sticky.

Nerissa reported the shield generator had been badly affected but the damage to the lower hull was largely cosmetic.

'We were lucky. If we hadn't had shields up it would have been much worse.'

'Do you think whoever attacked us is dead?' Tim hoped so, which wasn't a nice thought, but he was beginning to realise he would do anything to get back home.

'I don't know. It's safer to assume not. They would have gone down on the other side of the planet if they made it, so we have a head start for now. Let's get ready.'

Forty-five minutes later they stood in the airlock making final checks.

'Ready to go?' Gar-ran asked.

'Yeah, let's do it.' He was apprehensive now but the quicker they could get to the sanctuary the better. The airlock popped open and they carefully stepped onto the forest floor. The heat and humidity hit him instantly, like stepping into a gigantic greenhouse on a summer's day.

High ahead in the forest canopy, creatures which had been frightened away by the ship's descent were beginning to return to the upper branches and call to one another. Tim caught a flash of a bright red and yellow bird that darted into cover high up. The ground was thick with leaf litter and the damp soil clung to his boots. Gar-ran carried a machete to cut through any dense vegetation. At the level they were at though it was more open than Tim had expected. There were many trees, some with huge trunks and twisted roots, but it was relatively easy to see and move around.

'Right, there's only a few places on the hull a tracker could be fixed. I'll check, you keep watch.'

Gar-ran ducked beneath the hull, and Tim brought his pistol into the aim position, checking first it was ready to fire.

Slowly he turned on the spot, maintaining all-round awareness. That was the plan anyway, but his eye was continually drawn to the richness of the landscape which surrounded them. Strange, brightly coloured fungi grew thickly at the bases of many trees, while others were so smothered with climbing vines it was hard to tell where the vine ended and the tree began. Some trees he knew could live more than 400 years and grow to over 200 feet tall, but the vine-clad trees wouldn't last so long. There was something about the sheer majesty of the forest which was engulfing them that compelled them to a reverent silence.

The forest itself is never quiet though, and there was a perpetual chorus of unseen insects clicking and buzzing. Something ran across a branch above and Tim saw a long, furry tail before the creature disappeared behind the leaf cover. Already the sweat was trickling down his face and the collar of his suit felt damp against his neck.

'Got it,' Gar-ran announced after fifteen minutes. He held up a silver cube the size of a sugar lump.

'Is that it? I was expecting something bigger.'

'Small but effective. It had to be planted at either Nectar 3, or back at TX-1450.' He flipped the tracker in the air like a coin and caught it on the spin.

'The service station? By who?' Tim wondered if it was something to do with Zarox; perhaps he didn't believe their cover story. He wondered if the idea had occurred to Gar-ran.

Gar-ran shrugged. 'Could be anyone. A bounty hunter like Slothra relies on informers; he's probably got many paid retainers in areas where there's a lot of traffic. Anyhow I've disabled it now.' He tucked the cube in his belt and took a bearing from his wrist map. 'Right, this way.'

He pointed ahead to where the treeline began again. It would be darker beneath the canopy and Tim felt a tingle of excitement, or was it fear? He shrugged that thought off and fell into step with Gar-ran.

Two hours passed and the heat and humidity became more oppressive. The straps of the rucksack cut into his shoulders and he felt almost unbearably hot in his flight suit. The forest was beginning to all look the same and Tim started to feel a peculiar sense of indifference.

Gar-ran stopped. Tim halted too but, peering ahead, couldn't see anything amiss. Then he looked down. A vast trail of ants cut across the forest floor in front of them. There were thousands upon thousands of them, and they were huge: each one at least two inches long and more angular-looking than any ant he had seen before. The trail stretched back for at least fifty feet. Tim was astonished to see something he recognised on an alien planet.

'Where are they all going?' he asked.

'Foraging for food. They'll try to take anything they come across, and they will not stop.'

There was no walking around them, so they leapt over instead. The ants paid no attention. Another hour slipped past and they stopped to rest and drink. He eased his rucksack off and massaged his aching shoulders. They sat on an old dead tree. Something brushed his leg, making him jump. A foot-long grey millipede scuttled by.

Tim backed away. He knew back on Earth millipedes were harmless, but he'd never liked them. Too creepy looking.

'It won't bite,' Gar-ran said, smiling at his distaste. He checked the digital map.

'We're a third of the way there; if we go for another two hours then call it a day, we can set up camp before last light.'

'OK.' Tim wasn't sure how he felt about camping in the jungle. They had the equipment, of course, and weapons, but it would be totally dark and they were miles from the safety of the ship. He pushed the troubling thoughts aside. *Just try and enjoy the experience,* he told himself. As they continued, the first rain began to fall. At first, he hardly noticed it as most of the downpour was absorbed by the canopy, but as the deluge grew in intensity, more and more rain filtered down and they were soon drenched. Thankfully, the wrist maps were waterproof, but it was hard to keep the pace up. He hoped the rain would ease before they stopped to camp.

***

Occasionally they'd come across a truly massive tree with huge, fat roots so large they had to clamber over them to continue. The roots were often coated with a dark green moss that was very slippery, and once Tim fell backwards, landing heavily in the leaf litter. His rucksack cushioned the impact but he was still winded. He lay there for a second as Gar-ran climbed back to help. Out of the corner of his eye he saw something twitch and turned his head to see a large beetle with a shimmering blue body close to his head. The beetle's antennae probed the air and its pincers clacked together. Tim was up like a shot but, when he turned round, the beetle was gone.

'I'm OK, just lost my balance.' He seemed to be making a habit of falling down or over something on their expeditions, but Gar-ran just smiled and carried on. Tim tried to brush himself down but his suit was so wet it was pointless. He was beginning to seriously dislike this rainforest.

They carried on without further incident until Gar-ran called a halt.

'We can make camp here. We'll get set up and then have something to eat.'

Finally. Tim shrugged off his rucksack and massaged his aching shoulders.

Shelter was the first priority and he was keen to get cracking. The rain had slackened but showed no sign of stopping. They'd practised setting up mock camps while on the Scarab, but never in these actual wet conditions.

Working together, they unrolled the waterproof shelter sheet which would serve as a tent cover for the hammock that would be slung underneath. The sheet was a big square with thin, strong ropes attached to each corner. Underneath the sheet, pulled tight across the centre, was another strong rope. Each end of this was lashed securely five feet high between two young trees. They reached up and each took a corner and pulled down, pegging the corner ropes to the ground with a hammer Gar-ran had brought.

Ducking under, they pulled the other side down until the sheet was taut and pegged that side to the ground too. Now they had a tent under which to sling a woven hammock. That didn't take long and, when Tim tested it, it held him fine and was surprisingly comfortable. They repeated the whole process for Gar-ran.

The rain stopped. 'Typical,' Tim muttered as he laid groundsheets beneath the hammocks.

Dinner was a meat stew which they ate from the self-heating packets they'd first used on the ice planet Corax. Gar-ran crumbled salt tablets into their drinking water and reminded Tim to drink plenty. The light was beginning to fade and it was time to build a fire. Tim watched fascinated as Gar-ran hacked down some thin green branches and chopped them into logs. He then cleared a three-feet-square section on the forest floor from leaves and other detritus and built a little platform from the logs. He covered this with a layer of soil.

Throughout their trek Gar-ran had collected seed pods from the large trees which had fallen to the floor. The pods were encased in a cream-coloured fibre which looked like cotton wool. Tim had wondered at the time why Gar-ran was collecting them, only to be told. 'You'll see.' It was this fibre that Gar-ran pulled from the pods and unravelled into a pile.

'This is very useful stuff. It's water-resistant but highly flammable.' Sure enough, once lit, the fire burnt well. It was nearly dark and, as well as light and heat, the fire had the effect of making the forest seem less scary and threatening. Tim smiled to himself. Maybe camping wasn't so bad after all.

'The smoke will also keep insects away. On the subject of which, it would be a good idea to put some more repellent on.'

Tim squeezed a generous glob of repellent from the tube and massaged it onto his face and throat. He reached around to the back of his neck and was shocked to touch something soft and squidgy. Something had attached itself and, when he jerked his hand away, there was blood on his fingers.

'There's something on my neck!' Gar-ran jumped up to look and led Tim towards the fire so he could see better.

'You've acquired a leech.' Gar-ran relayed this information as if it was a perfectly normal occurrence to have a bloodsucking parasite attached to a delicate area.

'Whaaat? Get it off!'

'Wait a second. Don't try to pull it. Hold still.' He pulled out a small packet from his rucksack, tore it open and poured the yellow powder over the leech. After a few moments it dropped off. Gar-ran picked it up and tossed into onto the fire, where it sizzled and writhed in the flames.

'That was disgusting. Are there any others?' Tim asked.

'No, I checked, just that one. They're mostly harmless, but leech bites can bleed for a while, so I'm putting on an antiseptic pressure dressing.' After applying the dressing, he wrapped a length of bandage lightly around Tim's neck. 'Keep this on.'

'I don't know how it happened; I didn't feel anything.' Thank god Gar-ran had got it off; the thought of spending an entire night unaware he was harbouring a parasite made him squirm.

'Probably dropped down when we put the tent up.'

'Filthy thing.'

'We'll likely encounter more before this trip is over. You know you could collect a couple as souvenirs to take back home and show your friend.'

'What are you, crazy?' *What friends does he think I have?*

'Only joking,' Gar-ran chuckled. Tim scowled, unable at present to see the funny side. Later, as he lay in his hammock under a mosquito net, he reflected it could have been worse: without the all-over cover of his flight suit, a leech could have got in *anywhere*. Before turning in they had changed into dry suits and put the wet ones on a rope line near the fire. It felt odd to go to bed fully clothed, but he was taking no chances against biting insects. Gar-ran had insisted on being sentry while Tim slept. Sleep, however, proved elusive.

There was too much noise. Without the rain to drown them out, the sound of the insects and other forest creatures was unbelievable. After a while a new voice joined the night chorus. Tim lay awake for ages wondering what it could be. A high-pitched, rasping, croaky, rattle-like call that seemed to come from everywhere. Sometimes the calling would die down and he thought it was finally over, but then after a few moments of relative quiet it began all over again. Eventually, through sheer exhaustion, he dozed off.

'Tim! Wake up!' He opened his eyes and saw it was getting light. Gar-ran stood there.

'We need to get going.'

Reluctantly, Tim rolled out of his hammock and nearly tumbled over as he slipped his boots on. His neck felt sore.

'Are you OK?'

'Yeah, tired. I couldn't sleep last night. It was so noisy.'

'Yes. I'd forgotten how the nights can be in these places. It was male tree frogs calling. They often call at night after rain, and there's always more of them during the mating season.'

'So ... it will be like that again tonight?'

''Fraid so. I'll get breakfast ready.'

Tim yawned. He felt like a zombie, and the prospect of a long day's trek through a steaming, hostile jungle was doing nothing for his mood. Still, there was nothing that could be done, so he busied himself with packing his gear up and getting ready to face the day.

Twenty-Four
Jungle Journey

A fter two hours' trekking, Gar-ran asked Tim if he'd like to lead for a while.

'Can I really?' This was a bonus, Gar-ran trusting him to navigate.

'Yes. Just remember as well as checking the map, keep checking the ground and what's ahead and around. We don't want to walk into anything unexpected.'

He handed Tim a straight, sturdy branch which came up to his shoulder. The offshoots had been hacked off. 'Take this as a staff. It's strong enough to beat back vegetation and you can test the ground ahead to see how waterlogged it is.'

Tim regarded it dubiously. 'Can't I have the machete?'

'No. It's lethal, and any cuts out here would get infected.'

Tim was about to protest but thought better of it. He moved to the front and was soon absorbed by his new responsibility. From time to time they had to skirt around dense vegetation which hung from the forest understory above. Walking past one hefty tree, he saw the trunk was smothered in small, climbing insects.

'Termites I think,' Gar-ran said. One great feature of the wrist map was that it calculated the remaining distance to your target, and Tim now saw they were two thirds of the way there and still had hours of daylight left. High above, something shrieked and he caught another glimpse of a furry tail. He hadn't seen the creature fully but it moved like a monkey. At first the shrieks had unnerved him, but whatever it was always stayed high up in the branches so he was almost used to the piercing cries by now. He was beginning to tire though; the jungle heat sapped your strength.

As he was leading, he supposed he could call a break whenever he wanted, but he was determined to show Gar-ran what a good job he could do when given the responsibility. So, let Gar-ran be the one to suggest a break.

Two more hours slipped by and Tim was flagging now. Still, it was Gar-ran that suggested they take a break. They'd made good time and Tim was proud. It felt great to take off the heavy rucksack for a while and he stretched to take some of the tension out of his muscles.

'Another couple of hours and then we'll break for lunch. We should reach the sanctuary by mid-afternoon if we can keep the pace,' Gar-ran said.

'I think you'll be able to keep up,' Tim replied, and broke into laughter at the shocked look on Gar-ran's face.

'There is some way to go yet, young man ...'

***

Slothra's ship shook violently as it cut down through the atmosphere. He'd finally got it back online but he needed to slow down before it was too late. The weather made the entry much tougher, but there was no time to wait. Another warning light blinked on. It was going to need all his skill to pull this off. Another fifteen seconds should see them clear. There ... he was through. He grunted with relief, and flicked the viewing screen on. A heavy blanket of thick grey cloud hung below. Good. It would hide him nicely. It was highly improbable he'd entered anywhere near where his prey was based, but he was sure he could track them.

Whatever he'd been hit with had done a lot of damage. He'd lost the signal from the out-worlder's ship, although that could be due to the weather. Data indicated the storm would end by the next day and he would soon have a much clearer picture. It would be good to get outside. Being cooped up for so long had sharpened his appetite though, and his hunger for the hunt. They were down there somewhere, and he was coming.

***

Forty-five minutes of daylight left. Gar-ran had taken the lead again and they'd been forced to take a major detour to avoid a large, boggy area filled with swarms of insects. Tim had wanted to press on but hadn't argued when Gar-ran said they should make camp. This they were able to set up far quicker than the previous night and had a good fire blazing in no time. Gar-ran changed the dressing on Tim's neck and applied more healing cream.

'You said whoever was at the sanctuary originally had disappeared, and so did the team that went after them. What do you think happened?' The question had been nagging at Tim as the day had worn on.

Gar-ran added more kindling to the fire before answering.

'No one knows. It's years ago now.'

Tim had the impression he knew more than he was letting on, but he didn't press it. 'I guess tomorrow we'll find out.'

'Perhaps.' Gar-ran then slept for a couple of hours. He'd insisted on taking the overnight watch and Tim was too tired to argue.

***

Tim woke early the following morning and felt much better after a decent sleep.

'If we can avoid detours, we should reach the sanctuary before midday,' Gar-ran said as they ate breakfast. 'We've got enough food and water for now but if it looks like we'll be out here longer, we'll need to start collecting water. Somewhere back there must be a stream feeding into that swampy ground we avoided.'

'Will it be safe to drink?

'We can test that, and I have some purifying powders that I can add to anything we collect.'

Tim nodded. He wanted to get on with things now; it had started to rain again and, as far as he was concerned, the quicker they got to the sanctuary the better.

Breakfast over, they packed up the camp and set off. They fell into a rhythm, alternating who took the lead every hour. It seemed hotter than ever and Tim was distracted by the many flowering plants with brilliantly coloured blooms of red and deep orange that hung from some trees. Many flowers where shaped like a bird's head and had long, slender stems like the neck of a stork. Others flowered higher up in the canopy and looked similar to orchids. They were a welcome distraction from the tension that was building in his gut as they got closer to the sanctuary.

'We're a hundred feet out. We'll close in to fifty feet and see if we can make a circuit before heading in. Silent approach and only speak if it's essential,' Gar-ran said. Tim drew his pistol and checked the settings.

They avoided some low-hanging vines and, side by side, moved forwards. They got to the fifty-feet mark and, even though it was directly in front of them, it was still hard to make out the stone walls of the sanctuary or gauge its size accurately. The relentless growth of the jungle had all but hidden it from view and soon it would be entirely covered. It was definitely quieter in this part of the forest. Tim tripped on a branch and nearly pitched over, but Gar-ran grabbed him in time. Something squealed and darted past, making them both jump. It was gone in a flash but looked like a hairy pig, about the size of a house cat. Tim couldn't believe how quickly it raced through the tangled undergrowth.

They edged around the ruins of the sanctuary and, after several minutes, Gar-ran signalled to move in. They closed in another ten feet and listened. Other than the usual buzz of insects, nothing seemed untoward. They continued their circuit around and soon it was just possible to make out a wide expanse of steps leading up to a small courtyard. Gar-ran leant over and whispered.

'That must be the main entrance.'

They trekked for another five minutes but then their path was blocked by a huge fallen tree. Luminous green and yellow fungi were growing around the toppled giant, and fat red beetles crawled over the damp bark. 'Let's go back,' Gar-ran whispered.

Thick clusters of ferns obscured the beginning of the steps that led up the entrance to the forgotten sanctuary. Gar-ran scythed them down with the machete while Tim followed behind, laser pistol drawn and ready. The steps were crumbling and covered in a thick carpet of bright green moss. It reminded Tim of the very slippery seaweed you would see coating the rocks on the beach at low tide back home. He felt a pang of longing for something safe and familiar instead of this unknown alien world, but pushed those thoughts aside. It was here and now that mattered.

Silently he caught up with Gar-ran. Ahead of them was a small, heavily overgrown courtyard. Roots from trees either side had grown right across the cobbled floor like an outstretched, withered hand. Many of the stones had been forced out and displaced as if the jungle resented their intrusion and was determined to claw back its territory. At the other end was an open entrance carved into a wide, two-storey building with a sloping, stone-tiled roof. The entrance too was festooned with jungle growth that would need hacking down.

The smaller roots and leaf litter snapped and rustled despite their efforts to move with care. As they approached the door, Tim noticed the sweet, sickly smell of rotting fruit.

Gar-ran sheathed the machete and brought up his plasma rifle and switched on the attached torch. Keeping his eyes ahead, he whispered to Tim.

'I'm firing in a low-level shot, which should flush out anything immediately inside. Be ready.'

'All right.' Tim nodded. His mouth felt completely dry and his heart was pounding heavily in his chest. There was a bright flash from the rifle muzzle and the chamber beyond the doorway illuminated for a second with a soft orange glow. Tim strained his ears but could hear nothing at first, but then he detected a faint shrieking note, that quickly grew louder and nearer. He realised it wasn't just one cry: it was many, a shrilling cacophony of sound. In a thick, dark blur, the first wave of bat-like creatures burst through the doorway straight towards them.

'Down!' Gar-ran yelled and Tim threw himself to the ground. Muscular, leathery wings brushed over his back and he shuddered. The noise from the escaping creatures was ear-splitting.

He didn't dare look up but covered his head with his hands. Finally, the bat things were gone, up through a small gap in the trees overhead.

'That was horrible,' he said.

'Yes, I wouldn't want to get trapped inside with them. They'll come back later or after we're gone.' Gar-ran stood and brushed himself down and they continued into the threshold of the sanctuary. It was very dark in the corridor beyond. Fortunately, just inside was a wall-mounted torch which, although long burnt out, still smelt faintly of pine and oil. They'd brought plenty of seedpod fibre with them and when this was added to the torch it lit easily. Opposite was another wall torch which they lit as well. The floor was littered with droppings from the bats, which accounted for the terrible smell. Tim's eyes watered and he stepped carefully. To their left was a door divided into three panels. Tim tapped it gently. The door was made of a green, tinted metal and carved with patterns that resembled climbing vines.

'Some kind of alloy,' Gar-ran said. 'Wood would be no good here. It's too damp. A wooden door would warp and eventually rot. So, this is a better alternative. Now let's see if we can get inside.' Gar-ran inspected the door closely and then pressed firmly on the third panelled section. After a moment the section collapsed in on itself and Tim realised it was in fact a folding door.

'Let me help.' Tim pulled while Gar-ran pushed and slowly the door folded back until they could fit through. A small brown lizard skittered out and over their feet and down the corridor. Nothing else stirred. A long metal table on a rectangular pedestal stood in the centre of the room. On one wall was a series of metal hooks and, below, the desiccated remains of various dried plants and flowers. The fragments of a smashed stone bowl lay on the table, and several tall, yellow, glass jars that were covered in dust. Three long shelves contained stone jars of various sizes.

'It's like a lab,' Tim said.

'Yes, this must be where they dried the plants and then broke them down to study their compounds. Interesting.'

They spent some time fully checking out the room but it proved to hold no clues to what they sought. There was another chamber to explore further along the corridor and they lit more torches as they continued. Two heavy doors marked the entrance into a new room.

This chamber was very similar but had two long metal cabinets each containing two drawers which were both full of various preserved plants and seeds.

Behind the two large brass doors, which were surprisingly easy to open, lay a series of rooms. These comprised of a communications room, what seemed to be a medical room, a small accommodation block with rotted torn items of clothing strewn across the floor, a kitchen which contained a rack of rusting utensils, a bath facility and a large empty room. Here, a section of the ceiling had collapsed and huge roots and plant tendrils had snaked down and were starting to spread across the floor.

Tim didn't like it at all. It was stiflingly hot, for one thing, but also, with the years of neglect and the unexplained disappearances of the previous residents, the sanctuary was a sinister place to explore. At least Gar-ran had been pleased to find the comms room. If they could restore power, he could call for backup. He noticed at the end of the building were two more large bronze doors. One of them was buckled, as if something heavy had banged into it.

'That will lead back outside. I'm thinking that there must be some kind of generator out there. It's a long shot, but if we can get it powered up, I might be able to broadcast a signal to some of my colleagues. Get us some backup. Although, this far out, we're pretty isolated. Also, I'd like to access the data and see if it sheds any light on what happened here.'

'What are they like? Your colleagues, the other marshals?'

'Most of them are good. I haven't always seen eye to eye with them but they'll come if they can.'

Most of them are good? Tim had to know more. 'What, are some of them rogue agents or something?'

Gar-ran paused and looked uncomfortable. 'Well, occasionally we've had a few bad apples, like any big organisation. I meant really that the nature of our work can lead people to form strong opinions and views, and that can cause conflicts with those of us who prefer a more moderate, or reasoned approach.'

'I see.' *A politician's answer,* Tim thought.

'Now, let's see what's outside.'

Tim moved to help him but something made him glance back at the big communal room. He frowned; it was crazy, but he could have sworn that the thick tendrils which were growing down from the hole in the celling had spread out a little further. Impossible in so short a time. Must be the heat getting to him. There was a loud metallic scraping and Gar-ran wrenched the unbuckled door open. Dead vines and ivy-like plants had grown down over the doorway and it took a couple of vigorous machete swipes for Gar-ran to hack though them. The forest had almost entirely reclaimed what had once been a courtyard area cleared by the researchers.

Tentatively, they walked a little further from the facility. The trees were younger there but still tall and strong. Dead ahead was a huge tree, one of the biggest Tim had seen so far and thick with moss and vines. Its bark was richly textured and it seemed out of place with other trees whose trunks were smooth and pale. Tim wondered why; did it have some special, lost significance?

'Something over there.' Gar-ran pointed with the machete. About twenty feet to their right was something cube-shaped. It was two feet square and covered in leaf litter and moss but clearly made of metal.

'The generator?'

'Must be.' The device was fitted in dark grey metal housing with a lockable door. The lock wouldn't budge, but the hinges had nearly rusted out, so together they were able prise off the door from the other side and reveal the generator inside. It looked pretty dilapidated.

'Hmm. It's not one I'm familiar with. This may take me some time,' Gar-ran said.

Tim watched Gar-ran work for a few minutes but then got bored and wandered away.

'Don't go too far,' Gar-ran said.

Tim ambled back to the sanctuary. Why was one door buckled and bent? He moved closer. Both doors were engraved with elaborate designs of ferns and flowering plants. He tapped the bent door. It seemed so solid. Something moved out of the corner of his eye. Before he even had time to shout, he was yanked back with great force. His head hit the ground and he passed out.

Twenty-Five
The Natural World

Slothra leapt across and into the next tree, his claws easily cutting into the soft bark and giving him a sure grip. He couldn't have asked for a better place to hunt in. The forest there was very much like the jungle he'd been born in, and already he felt at home. The pain from his injuries nagged him at times but he ignored it. He'd found the fugitives' ship the day before and picked up their scent immediately. He'd waited for them, but when they failed to return at nightfall, he realised they must be hiding out somewhere. Maybe injured too. He began to follow but then the rain came and it was hard to make out their route in all the beguiling scents that the rainforest unleashed after a storm. It didn't matter though: sooner or later he would find them.

***

Tim came round with his head pounding. His face felt as if it was being squeezed between two massive hands. He blinked his eyes open and realised that he was hanging upside down. *What's happening*? He couldn't move his right arm and, looking down, he saw a thick green plant tendril wrapped around him, pinning his arm tight to his body so he couldn't draw the laser pistol. Lifting his head, he saw he was being dragged up through the ruined roof of the sanctuary towards a giant red flower. The central bud of the flower slowly began to unfold its petals to reveal a gaping black mouth lined with two rows of wickedly sharp thorns, or were they teeth? He twisted violently and managed to grab a section of metal piping that ran across the ceiling and, for the time being, was able to resist the plant's incessant pull. He knew, though, he wouldn't be able to hang on for long and shouted for Gar-ran at the top of his voice.

Long seconds ticked past until Gar-ran burst into the room. Tim was still clutching onto the pipe, but the plant was shaking him, determined to break his handhold.

'Shoot it!' he screamed.

Gar-ran took aim but, just as he pressed the trigger, Tim was yanked to the side and the shot went wide. Gar-ran moved in and took aim again but, before he could fire, something grabbed his leg and he was pulled off his feet. Tim watched, horrified, as what he thought were dead tendrils were now very much alive. Gar-ran was lifted up and then slammed down hard on the broken floor. His plasma rifle went flying and he lay still.

'No!' Tim's grip slackened for a second but the plant sensed it and tore him free and upwards again. He lost sight of Gar-ran completely. He twisted around and saw he was only ten feet away from the first row of enormous, spine-like teeth. Then he suddenly remembered the multi-tool Gar-ran had given him after they found the relic on Moloco. It was in his utility belt. He quickly found it and frantically tried to open out the sharp blade, but it was awkward to do with his left hand and he nearly fumbled it, but finally the blade opened and locked into place. Seven feet away now. He twisted and stabbed into the tendril that was pinning him as hard as he could. Pale green sap oozed out but still the plant drew him up.

He stabbed again and again. He was just a few feet away, too afraid to look up, but he could see the terrible spine teeth out of the corner of his eye. The tendril loosened slightly and he has able to grip the pistol but didn't have enough leverage to withdraw his arm. He bellowed in frustration and pounded the knife again until at last he was able to withdraw his hand. The tendril immediately tightened around his waist.

He was almost right inside the mouth; the thick petals were beginning to close around him. Panic threatened to engulf him; it couldn't end like this. He clicked the laser pistol to full power and fired down the gaping maw of the plant. Immediately he was flung backwards and fell several feet, hitting a thick tree branch. He was winded but managed to grab hold. The pistol clattered down and landed on the roof of the sanctuary below. Above, the plant writhed and jerked. It was dying. He hoped so, anyway.

He clambered along the branch until he was above the sanctuary roof. It was a drop of about six feet. He landed on his feet but immediately tumbled over. Scrambling up, he grabbed his pistol and climbed carefully down through the hole in the roof. Gar-ran was extracting himself from a mass of roots and tendrils and Tim ran over to help him.

'Tim! Thank goodness! I thought it had got you.'

'It nearly did.'

He picked up the plasma rifle and tossed it to Gar-ran. Suddenly, two huge green tendrils smashed their way down into the room.

'It's still alive! Run!' They sprinted out and back towards the main entrance.

'It's dying but it's determined to take us with it. We'll have to make sure it's dead,' Gar-ran said. They stopped and turned to face their enemy. The monstrously thick tendrils were snaking across the floor towards them.

'Fire!' Gar-ran shouted, and they both blasted in unison. The combined power of the weapons incinerated the tendrils, which frantically tried to withdraw themselves, but within seconds were turned into blackened stalks.

'We'll have to make sure,' Gar-ran said, his expression hard.

'You mean go back in there? To the room?' Gar-ran nodded. Slowly, they moved ahead. A foul-smelling sap had pooled into a puddle on the floor and they were forced to jump over it. They crouched in the doorway and peered into the room.

'I'll aim high, you cover the floor,' Gar-ran said. He fired repeatedly through the jagged hole in the roof and Tim concentrated his fire on the roots and tendrils which covered the floor. After several seconds there was a muffled explosion above them and burning chunks of plant stalks, blackened petals and several broken spine teeth fell down into the room. It was half a minute before the detritus stopped falling and then it became very quiet and still.

'I think we know now why this place was abandoned,' Tim said.

'Yes … the likelihood is that there will be other plants around. We can't stay here, it's too dangerous. I couldn't get the generator to work either.'

Nervously, Tim glanced around. It was scary to think that there could be more giant carnivorous plants about, maybe even surrounding them. He shook the thought away.

'So, back to the ship?'

'I don't think we have a choice now. Nerissa will have as much of the system as possible back online now, and there's a couple of components I can replace. Once we get airborne again, I'll try to signal the marshal council.'

Tim wasn't looking forward to the long trek back, but anything was better than staying there. He heaved his rucksack on again. 'Better get started then.'

Twenty-Six
Long Way From Home

The first rays of light filtered down to the forest floor, waking Tim. It was never very light at the level they were at but he was beginning to get used to it. Despite the excitement and stress of the previous day, he'd slept well. After a quick breakfast they struck camp and plunged ahead again.

It got muggier as the morning wore on and Tim was sure it would rain again before long. They'd seen two young wild boars a little while before but, after a curious glance, the hogs had lost interest and returned to rooting around in the forest litter for something to eat.

The feeling though that there was something out there watching them had grown stronger by the hour, so much so he was about to mention it to Gar-ran, when he remembered the danger amulet. Better check it, he decided. He whipped it out from his belt pocket and his breath caught as he saw the stone was glowing a fiery red.

'Gar-ran!' The marshal spun round and tensed as he saw the stone.

Something enormous jumped down from the tree next to them and leapt onto Gar-ran, pinning him down before he could even lift his rifle.

Slothra! Tim's mind screamed to him as he gazed in disbelief. The creature seemed even bigger and more powerful than he remembered. But he wasn't quite the same. There were several ugly bald patches throughout his fur and the skin looked puckered and scorched. One of his great yellow eyes was damaged too. Rather than diminishing him, though, these changes made him more frightening than ever. Tim absorbed all this in a moment as he brought his pistol up.

'Let him go!'

Slothra was using Gar-ran as a living shield. He'd crouched down to reduce his massive bulk, preventing Tim from a clear shot. One thick arm was wrapped around Gar-ran's neck and his other claws were held menacingly close to Gar-ran's face.

The creature spoke, its voice a deep, harsh croak. Tim, who wasn't wearing his translator, couldn't understand. Slothra's claws moved closer to Gar-ran's face.

'Ssshoot him,' Gar-ran managed to say and then choked as Slothra tightened his grip, cutting off his air.

338

'Don't!' Tim shouted. His hands were trembling but he fixed his aim on the beast. It was clear that if he didn't drop his weapon, Slothra was going to choke Gar-ran to death or simply rip him apart. With the way his hands were shaking, Tim didn't think he could get a shot in without the risk of hitting Gar-ran too.

Slothra barked out more words that Tim didn't understand. He was getting angrier. Gar-ran's face was turning red as he fought for air. Tim lowered his weapon and let it fall to the ground. He felt terrible, but what choice did he have? Slothra disarmed Gar-ran and, without warning, hurled him at Tim, who fell back heavily with the force of the impact. He tasted blood in his mouth and lay there stunned for a moment. Terror arced through him as he realised they were now both defenceless. He scampered up as quickly as possible, but Slothra had already picked up his pistol.

Casually, Slothra drew his own plasma rifle. Gar-ran stepped in front of Tim. Then Slothra emitted a low croaking sound, like he was laughing. He bellowed something unintelligible and gestured to their rucksacks.

'What's he saying? Tim asked.

'I don't know. He wants us to drop our rucksacks, I think.'

Tim felt a burning anger building in him. They had come so far and now this?

'It's not over yet,' Gar-ran whispered, almost as if he could read Tim's thoughts. With reluctance they shrugged off the rucksacks and tossed them at Slothra's feet. He stepped over them and, with sudden violence, broke his own rifle over his huge knee, letting the two pieces fall to the ground. He did the same with Gar-ran's rifle and Tim's laser pistol.

Tim exchanged a puzzled glance with Gar-ran, who looked pale.

Slothra barked out some other command and pointed away from them.

'He's letting us go?' Tim asked. It seemed incredible.

'No. I'm afraid not. He's just giving us a head start. He's going to hunt us in the old way. No modern weapons.'

Tim's heart began to bang harder in his chest.

'So ... he's not just here to capture us and take us back?'

Gar-ran shook his head. 'He wants some fun first.'

Slothra bellowed again, making them both flinch. He was pointing vigorously in the direction he wanted them to run. The thought flashed into Tim's mind that at least this way they had a chance, however small. If he wanted, Slothra could have just killed them then and there. Maybe, just maybe, he and Gar-ran could figure out a way to survive.

'Come on, let's go.' They walked away quickly, keeping their eyes fixed on Slothra, and then they both sprinted as hard as they could, soon lost from sight among the endless trees. They ran hard for several minutes. From somewhere behind them rose a deep, growling howl which echoed through the air. It sounded like a cry of triumph.

***

There was a little under two hours of daylight left. It was hard to tell how far they had come, how much distance they had put between themselves and the bounty hunter. They'd stopped briefly to get their breath but were on the move again.

Sweat poured off Tim, but still they had to ration their water carefully, having only one bottle each clipped to their belt. Gar-ran had hoped, if they could get closer to the ship, they would be in range to call it, but their GPS showed they were still too far away. At some point soon they would have to make a stand.

'Maybe we should split up, or pretend to,' Gar-ran said suddenly. 'Our GPSes are linked so we can always keep track of each other, but you could head for the ship and I'll head west, that way it could confuse him and buy us some more time.'

'No way, Gar-ran. I'm not leaving you to that thing.' Tim was appalled Gar-ran would even think it. 'We stick together.'

'If we stay like this, we're making it easy for him. I don't want to split up either, but it might give us more of a chance, or buy some time.'

'Gar-ran, it will be dark in less than two hours.'

'Then that's time we can use to our advantage. At least this way it's not what he would expect and if I don't make it, maybe you can get out of here. Nerissa can get you back. She could contact the other marshals and explain what's happened.'

Tim hesitated. It was true. They had to do something different. He made up his mind.

'One hour, no more than that. Then send me send coordinates to for us to meet.'

'OK, that's a good idea. Here, take these.' Gar-ran pulled out two mini-bombs. 'You remember how they work?' Tim nodded. 'We have two each, and you still have your knife.'

'Yes.' Tim patted the pocket where it was stashed.

'All right, in one hour then. Get going.' Gar-ran clapped him on the back. Tim checked his map and, taking a deep breath, ran on again.

***

The rain came again and Tim's feet squelched and slipped as he jogged. He'd blundered into the swampy ground in the middle or the forest and had been forced to backtrack and find a way around. Since then he had been plagued by flies and biting gnats and supposed that the combination of sweat and rain had washed off the insect repellent, making him an irresistible target for the myriad swarms which had emerged as the sun sank lower. He stopped and leant against a huge root buttress. He needed a few moments to catch his breath and think.

He'd gotten away from Slothra the first time around and he could do it again, he told himself. He closed his eyes for a few seconds. No, that was no good, he daren't risk falling asleep, although he could feel exhaustion begin to wrap around him, urging him to sit, rest for a little while longer. He shook himself and stood up straight again. He had to find a way to turn the odds in his favour. If he could get to somewhere where he was in control, or hidden, and lure Slothra in … but then what? The only way he could stop him was to kill him. It seemed unthinkable, but that's what it boiled down to. Either he or Gar-ran had to stop him once and for all. He wiped his face again and moved on.

Twenty-Seven
The Wild Hunt

G ar-ran didn't think he could run any further. And where else would he run to anyway? It was time to prepare himself. He wasn't afraid to die; he just wanted the chance for it to be on his own terms. If he had to go, though, he'd make sure he took the beast with him; anything to keep him away from the boy. He hoped it wouldn't come to that. On his wrist map he studied the surrounding terrain. He saw a place where they should be able to meet and plan the next moves. He sent the coordinates to Tim. It would take about half an hour to get there, maybe longer moving in the dark.

There was a tiny sound behind him. He whirled around but didn't see the thick net of woven vine leaves that dropped from above and fell heavily around him. The edges of the net were weighted with thicker vines. Something heavy smacked into the back of his head. His vision blurred and, unconscious, he fell face forward onto the wet ground.

***

Slothra dropped down. Another perfect capture. Gar-ran's wrist map beeped and, intrigued, the hunter grabbed hold of Gar-ran's limp arm and scanned the information on the display. He couldn't read the text but he could read the map layout. Coordinates for a rendezvous. He grinned, exposing his yellow fangs. Tugging the device off Gar-ran's arm, he clipped it to his own belt. He could be there in no time. He just needed to finish up here.

*****

Tim's wrist map beeped loudly, making him jump. He adjusted the volume settings to the lowest level. It would still vibrate if any more messages came through. He felt a wave of relief sweep through him that Gar-ran was still alive and able to communicate. He quickly plotted a course for the location he'd been directed to and set off. It would be last light by the time he got there. He pushed that frightening thought away and instead focused on navigating though the darkening forest. He was tuned in and more aware of what was happening around him. *This must be how the tribes that live in the Amazon and other forests survive*, he thought. Although, of course, they were born to that life and he would never achieve their deep understanding of the ways of the forest. Still, he was gaining confidence with every moment he avoided capture.

***

Twenty minutes later he slowed as he saw two forest hogs snuffling in the soil twenty metres ahead. They grunted loudly as they saw him and he froze. These were bigger than any of the hogs he had seen so far and powerful muscles rippled under their sleek coats. Their faces were encrusted with mud but, even from this distance, their two-inch tusks stood out. They looked at Tim without any trace of fear. Tim dropped his eyes and slowly moved back. After ten paces he sidestepped, planning to go around. He could see the hogs in his peripheral vision but they appeared to have lost interest. He would have to watch out, as clearly this was their territory. He cursed at the thought of having to slow down when all he wanted to do was cover as much ground as fast as possible. He had enough to think about already without running the risk of antagonising more wild beasts.

After another ten minutes, Tim decided to risk picking up the pace. He wished he still had the stick Gar-ran had given him or, better still, the machete. Sometimes the fat leaves and vines which trailed down from the understory were too thick to push through and he had to go around, losing valuable time. The area Gar-ran had selected appeared to be a small clearing. He hoped by the time he got there his friend had come up with a plan.

***

Slothra peered down from his viewpoint overlooking the clearing. He was well hidden by the thick foliage and knew that if he remained still, he wouldn't be seen. Not that it mattered anyway; the boy was defenceless. A massive tree had fallen some time before, taking out two of its smaller neighbours, and the area below was relatively clear and easier to move through. That suited him as well. The boy would arrive in about fifteen minutes. He settled back to wait.

***

The half-moon was rising as Tim edged his way into the clearing. He'd run across another pack of hogs and had been forced to divert again. Clusters of bright stars were beginning to show in the great, dark sky overhead, and he could see fairly well. The forest insects still clicked and buzzed but the birds had fallen silent and Tim felt very exposed as he walked further into the open space. A large tree lay diagonally across his path, its trunk reaching up as high as his waist. He rested against it and consulted the map. He was definitely in the right place, but where was Gar-ran? He daren't risk calling out. His heart was pounding so much he felt sure anything within ten feet would hear it. Reaching into his pocket, he withdrew the multi-tool and unsheathed the blade. It wasn't much of a

347

weapon, but holding it made him feel better. Something moved behind him.

***

Slothra relished the look of dawning horror on the boy's face as he realised it wasn't his friend who was there to meet him but his worst nightmare instead. He tossed the out-worlder's wrist map to him and the boy stared at it dumbly for a moment before realisation flooded over his face and the fear intensified. He wondered if he would start to cry. But no, despite his despair, he held the puny blade steady and Slothra felt a trace of admiration for the boy's courage. Many of his previous targets had begged to be spared when he caught up with them. Some offered money in a vain attempt to save their miserable lives. Sometimes he let them prattle; it was amusing, knowing that whatever they said wouldn't stop him from taking them. Something hit him in his chest and dropped to the forest floor, something the boy had thrown. He realised his mistake a split second too late.

***

Tim ran as hard and as fast as he could. He hadn't waited to see the results of the explosion, having dived over the giant fallen tree just before the mini-bomb exploded. He knew Slothra wasn't dead though; his screeches still rang in his ears, but he must be badly hurt or incapacitated at least. He stopped and turned on his wrist map just long enough to get his bearings before shutting it down again. He had to keep going. His only priority was to reach the ship. He couldn't stop or think about Gar-ran even for a second or he knew he'd break down. His side ached but he forced himself onwards as the tears streaked his face.

***

It was the rain that woke Gar-ran. He was surprised to find himself still alive. The sharp ache whenever he moved his head was further proof of that. What really puzzled him was the fact that he was staring up at the forest floor instead of the trees, but then he felt the grip of the net and he understood. He was hanging upside down in Slothra's net, which hung from a thick branch, and the pain in his wrists was from the mesh restraints that the bounty hunter must have used to tie his hands. He felt a surge of hope for Tim. Maybe Slothra wanted them both alive, perhaps as ransom. He had to escape somehow and find Tim before Slothra did, if it wasn't already too late.

***

Tim shivered as he sat in the darkness beneath the giant tree. The rain had eased off slightly but he was soaked and filthy. He was surprised that he didn't feel hungrier. Maybe all the adrenaline coursing through him had wiped out his appetite. It had been some time since he'd escaped from Slothra.

He couldn't believe Gar-ran was gone. Tears came into his eyes but he cuffed them away. He couldn't think about that yet, because if he did it would be to acknowledge that he was utterly alone and as good as dead, lost and stranded millions and millions of miles from home. He was still alive right now though, and if he could only get to the ship, he had a chance. The ship that was still a long way away. There was no question of sleep tonight. He wiped the mud and rain from his face with his sleeve and set off again.

***

Sweat ran down Gar-ran's face and into his eyes. He shook his head to clear his vision.

It had been a great moment when he realised that Slothra hadn't searched him before stringing him up or he would have surely found the multi-tool in his side belt pocket. Although his wrists were bound together, he'd been able to extend the blade and was trying to hack and saw through the thick vine which was threaded through the net and wrapped around the tree branch. The movement caused him to sway back and forth, so he was forced to work more slowly than he wanted to.

Metal mesh cord was impossible to cut through with just a small blade, so he had turned his attention to the vine. Of course, if he was able to sever it, he would crash head first down onto the forest floor and possibly break his neck, but it was best not to dwell on that too much.

The blade snagged and, as he yanked it back, he nearly lost his grip and dropped it. Anxiety flared through him and he stopped for a few moments while he regained his composure. He found that a slow and firm sawing motion was best, and the blade at last began to work through the tough skin of the vine. Then it snapped so suddenly he didn't have time to cry out before he smashed into the forest floor and lost consciousness.

Twenty-Eight
The Lord of The Forest

Tim stared at the danger amulet as it turned orange. He whirled around but could see nothing. The remaining mini-bomb was tightly held in his fist. He heard the snuffling and snorting of the forest hogs before they came into view. His eyes had adjusted to the forest gloom, but it was still hard to make out how many of them there were. It had to be at least six or seven. Was this the danger the necklace was warning him of? Or was Slothra watching him right now? A deep grunt louder than any of the others startled him and, squinting, he saw the hogs make way for a gigantic beast three times their size.

Tim gaped at the size of the brute; it had to be the dominant male, or whatever the top hog was called. He edged back carefully, trying not to panic. If the boar charged, he would have to throw the bomb. He'd cranked it up so that it would explode on impact, but it was his last one, so his aim had to be perfect. He was hoping the huge hog wouldn't take any further interest in him. He moved further and further back until the beast was out of sight and then cut east to try to clear their territory.

He'd been jogging for five minutes when he realised he'd totally lost his bearings. Could he risk turning the map on again? Did he have any choice really? With shaky hands, he switched on and studied the glowing screen.

***

Gar-ran's eyes flickered open and the world slowly came into focus again. He didn't know how long he'd been out, but there was no time to waste. Ignoring the pain in his shoulder, he forced himself into a sitting position. The net was still around him but he was able kick his legs out and drag it up and over him. That was a start, he told himself, as he sat shivering on the wet earth.

With an effort he managed to slide the heel of his boot back to reveal the hidden compartment. A small package wrapped in white plastic dropped out. Quickly unwrapping it, he took out the silver compass. There was also a strip of painkilling tablets, antibiotics and water purification capsules. He rewrapped these and replaced them in the heel compartment and resealed it. It was awkward holding the compass between two hands but, with its luminous markings, it was easy to read. He remembered the direction he needed to stay on to make it to the rendezvous point

in the clearing, and set off, feeling desperate to get
there, although part of him dreaded what he would
find.

Twenty-Nine
Strange Meeting

Gar-ran ran into the clearing. He'd stashed the compass and now clutched a mini-bomb in his fist. Immediately he saw the small crater and corona of scorched and blasted grass. A trail of sticky blood which looked like tar led up into nearby tree and he let out a sigh of relief as he realised the blood was Slothra's. He walked back to the blast area and saw the wrist map nestling against the fallen tree and recognised it as his own. The screen was badly cracked but it came on when he powered it up. He waited a few minutes to see if it picked up the signal from Tim's device, but nothing was detected.

What had happened there? Awkwardly climbing over the fallen trunk, he saw the indentation in the grass and realised Tim must have lain there, perhaps shielding himself from the bomb blast. Scuff marks and a fresh footprint indicated he'd run off fast, that should make him easier to track. Had he been injured? Where was he now? He clipped the wrist map onto his belt and followed the trail.

***

Exhausted, Tim slumped down against the tree close to the edge of the swamp. He would have to find a way around, but for the moment he was too knackered to think about it. He batted away the insects that flittered across his face and tried to coax his tired brain into deciding what to do next. Despite the distance he'd come, he was probably still a day's journey from the ship. His rucksack, the hammocks and the other supplies were most likely where Slothra had first ambushed them.

He could in theory find his way back to them, as the coordinates were logged on his map. He could rest up there before heading back to the ship. But backtracking meant he may come across the hogs again, and that would be pushing his luck too far.

Is Slothra really dead? He must be. After a few more minutes, Tim forced himself up. He'd nearly dozed off. Despite the risk, it made more sense to go back and get his gear. He was also starving and there was food and water in his rucksack, and his hammock was there. He twisted and snapped off a thin, low-hanging branch which had grown out straight and stripped the leaves off. Using the knife blade, he whittled one end into a sharp point. It wasn't much of a weapon, but he felt better for having something with him.

The glow from the screen of the map was bright and lit up the immediate area and went a little way to making the forest seem less frightening, although it would have been nice to have someone to talk to. He yawned hugely. The energy which had previously driven him on had dissipated in this last hour as tiredness seeped through him. He was beginning to stumble and totter as if drunk.

Not that he'd ever really been drunk, of course. He and Josh had smuggled a big bottle of cider down to the beach to share with friends during the last holidays, but he hadn't enjoyed the taste much. It was rough stuff, but there had been plenty for everyone. He laughed at the memory and bumped into a tree; thick wet leaves smacked into his face, bringing him forcibly back to the present. He'd wandered off course. *Must concentrate.* He admonished himself as he staggered on.

***

The screen on Gar-ran's wrist map continued to flicker and sometimes the image of the terrain scrambled before reassembling. It was definitely failing, but he needed it to last a little while longer. He changed the view so that a greater area was revealed and then, on the top of the screen, he saw the tiny red dot. He zoomed in; the dot was definitely moving. Tim was still alive, Gar-ran shouted in relief. He had to get to him. What had happened to Slothra? Was he still trailing them? These questions buzzed through his mind as he broke into a jog and then ran as quickly as he could, forcing his way through the snarled vines and muddy ground.

***

Tim stared at the red dot that had appeared at the side of his screen. It was moving towards him. Fear and disbelief exploded in him, banishing the tiredness that had numbed him. Somehow the bounty hunter had survived. He must have hung onto Garran's wrist map and he was coming towards him and would soon be there.

He turned off the scanner, although he knew it was already too late. He turned to run but then changed his mind. There was no point. Slothra would catch up with him anyhow. He'd have to make a stand there. He still had his spear; if he could get one strike in, it might be enough. Silently, he crouched down and pressed his back into the trunk of the tree. He was trying to control his breathing but it wasn't working. His one consolation was that the bounty hunter must be badly injured, and surely that gave him some chance. He could hear something; it was faint but it sounded like someone calling. He strained to listen.

It sounded like his name, but it was too faint to be sure. How could that be? Then he heard the call again; it was nearer and clearer. It couldn't be Gar-ran because he was dead. Unless it was Gar-ran's ghost. He shivered and gripped the spear even tighter.

'Tim, it's me, Gar-ran. Where are you?' the voice said again. It was very close. Tim slowly drew in a deep breath. He was ready; just let the thing get a bit closer and he would strike.

'Tim, check the amulet.'

Confused, Tim did nothing for a moment. He dared not look down. Grasping the spear in his one hand, he brought the danger amulet up until it was level with his face. The stone glowed blue! He jumped up and around the tree, spear ready just in case. Gar-ran stood a few feet away, looking round. His friend turned and jumped slightly when he saw him.

'Tim!' Gar-ran rushed over and Tim saw his hands were bound. Tim opened his mouth to speak but was so astonished that no words came.

'Are you all right?' Gar-ran's face was a picture of concern.

'I … I thought you were dead,' Tim said falteringly as he regained his voice. Then he hugged Gar-ran hard.

'I thought so too for a while. Slothra ambushed me and knocked me out. When I came round, I was tied up.' He then explained about the compass and how he managed to navigate to the clearing.

'We've got to free your hands,' Tim said, drawing the multi-tool.

'That won't do it, I tried already. But never mind that now. I saw the blast marks back at the clearing. You got him?'

Tim frowned; he couldn't say for sure. 'Yes, I think so ... I don't know. He's hurt, but I don't know about dead.'

'You've been very brave. Now we must try and get back to our gear. Do you think you can make it back there?'

'Of course I can.' Tim bridled at the suggestion he wasn't up to it, although he knew that Gar-ran was just concerned. He patted Gar-ran's arm and they set off.

**

It took over two hours to reach their discarded rucksacks, and Tim felt his legs begin to sag as he unravelled the hammocks. Gar-ran tried to help as best he could but of course was hampered by his restraints. After what seemed like an age of fumbling, Tim was about to clamber up when Gar-ran reminded him to change into dry clothes to sleep in. He quickly did so and it was a relief to get out of the damp jumpsuit which was now filthy and reeked of sweat. He hung it up to dry and crawled gratefully into his hammock. *What a night.* He curled up and quickly slid

into a sleep as dark and deep as the forest around
him.

Thirty
If You Go Down to The Woods Today

◆————————————◎————————————◆

Tim awoke feeling ravenous. Their rations were beginning to run low but Gar-ran too was hungry so they feasted on a thick, ready-to-eat porridge straight from the heated packets. Tim had to feed Gar-ran, which was pretty funny, especially as Gar-ran was doing his best to maintain an air of dignity, which only made Tim snort with laughter. It would be a full day's hike at least to the ship so, after they finished eating, they packed up quickly. Gar-ran asked Tim to bring him his rucksack and, with difficulty, Gar-ran extracted a green bottle resembling a small fire extinguisher.

'I hope we don't have to use this. It's untested, but it could make all the difference. I want you to have it.'

'What is it?'

Gar-ran explained, and Tim's eyes widened in surprise as he listened. The bottle was cool to the touch as he stashed it in his bag. While in good spirits, he was feeling the physical toll of the previous day's ordeal. There were more cuts and scratches on his hands than he'd realised, and a painful red welt on his face from where a vine had lashed him. His knee ached and he was still dog-tired. On the plus side, his leech bite was healing nicely.

Gar-ran's back seemed to be troubling him, Tim noticed, and by midday they hadn't covered as much ground as he would have liked. The weather stayed dry but it was muggier than ever and soon they stopped talking, finding it better to save their energy. The course Gar-ran plotted was meant to take them clear of the swamp ground but it proved to be a bigger area than they realised and that cost them time. Eventually, though, they were back on track and, a little while later, Gar-ran called a halt for the day.

'It's just over an hour and a half till last light. Let's set camp now and have something to eat before it gets too dark,' he said.

'At last,' Tim murmured, grateful to slip off the rucksack and massage his aching shoulders.

'Keep your spear handy, just in case,' Gar-ran cautioned. He'd been able to retrieve the machete the night before and it now hung from his belt. Instinctively, Tim checked his amulet, but the stone remained a steady blue.

The night was long and the raucous calls of the tree frogs and other eerie cackles from high up in the canopy often awoke Tim with a start, so his sleep was fitful and uneasy. It was a relief when dawn came and they could get up and on with things.

'I've had enough of the jungle now,' he remarked to Gar-ran after unleashing a huge yawn. They were traipsing through thick, wet leaf litter which clung obstinately to their boots. Tim trod on a concealed giant millipede which shot out of cover, making him jump as it scampered to safety in the undergrowth.

'Well,' said Gar-ran, 'the good news is we should be close to the ship in about three to four hours.'

'Is there bad news?' Tim asked. He tried to make his voice seem light and easy, but didn't quite succeed.

'No, not exactly. You've picked up a hitchhiker though.'

Tim looked blankly at Gar-ran, wondering what he was on about. Gar-ran pointed at Tim's shoulder and Tim looked down to see an enormous yellow jungle cricket perched there. He yelled and the cricket somersaulted off, landing perfectly in a soft bank of moss, its colour providing excellent camouflage. Gar-ran laughed heartily and Tim joined in, seeing the funny side after his initial fright. It was the best laugh they'd had in what seemed like ages.

'I'm just going for a quick slash,' Tim said, still chuckling. He moved to the edge of camp and around the side of a big tree with a rich brown bark. Just as he unzipped his flight suit, something wet dropped from above. It wasn't rain or dew so, curious, he leant over to look. A thick, congealing black liquid had splattered onto a large, broken leaf. Puzzled, Tim bent closer and further drops fell from above, one smacking down onto the top of his head where it stuck in his hair. It felt warm and Tim felt his stomach slide as he quickly looked up. At first he saw nothing, but then a large shape lowered itself down onto a wide branch high above him and swayed unsteadily.

Badly wounded as he was, Slothra was still horrible to behold, and Tim gazed in horror at the deep, festering gouges in his leg which leaked the thick black blood. He was holding what looked like a bow.

Tim leapt back so quickly he nearly fell, and sprinted back to Gar-ran as a wooden arrow whipped over his head.

'Slothra! He's got a bow!' Tim shouted as he ran.

Wasting no time in talk, Gar-ran pressed one of the last two mini-bombs into Tim's hand and they sprinted back along the trail.

'Come on!' Gar-ran yelled. Tim tried to do so, but his rucksack snagged on a branch and pulled him back. He yanked it free as another arrow smacked deep into the thick trunk just above his head. He was desperate to unleash the bomb, but already Slothra had moved into cover. Tim ran on, the pain in his knee reverberating throughout his leg. He caught up with Gar-ran and they slashed their way through the overgrowth. They were off the trail and plunging back into the jungle's heart.

After several minutes, Gar-ran crouched down by the base of a massive, sprawling tree and signalled Tim to join him.

'Run in zig-zags as best you can and then run normally. Keep breaking up the pattern and he won't be able to get a bead on us. Can you keep going for a little while?' Gar-ran whispered into Tim's ear.

'Yes, yes I think so,' Tim whispered back. His knee really hurt. Gar-ran helped him up and they stumbled on again, sometimes zigging to the left or darting hard to the right and then straight again. It was exhausting, but no more arrows fell close. Tim was edging closer to panic. *Why doesn't he just die?* The bounty hunter seemed indestructible.

They stopped again, sheltered by a tall fern. Greedily, Tim gulped down some water and scanned the trees above. They listened for a few moments.

The jungle, usually so full of life, was now unnaturally silent. They'd been stationary for too long so, after exchanging an anxious glance, they burst up and off again.

They were moving through a large area of bracken when Gar-ran crashed down. For an awful moment Tim thought he'd been struck by an arrow, but then saw the fallen branch that had tripped him. Gar-ran sat up, panting for breath.

'I dropped my bomb.' His voice was a raspy whisper. Tim knew the bomb hadn't been armed or it would have detonated already, but it meant they were down to one, plus the machete. Gar-ran had been lucky not to fall on it as it lay only an arm's reach away. Tim grabbed it and passed it over.

They were exposed and Tim's heart was hammering like a demented drummer. Slothra could be anywhere. Gar-ran staggered up, and a leaf fell, lightly brushing Tim's shoulder and making him jump wildly. He looked up just in time to see Slothra throw the vine leaf net. It was a bad throw though and snagged on a small branch. The hunter reached down to free it but his leg gave way and he toppled thirty feet down, hard into the forest floor.

Tim pulled out the small green bottle Gar-ran had given him that morning. He waited, turning almost rigid with apprehension and caught between the urge to keep moving and curiosity to see if the beast was down for good.

'Do you think ... ?' Tim began.

'We have to be sure. I'm fine now. I'll check. You wait here.' Gar-ran crept forwards.

'I'm coming with you,' Tim muttered.

'All right, but keep back.' They stalked through the deep bracken. Sweat trickled heavily down Tim's face but he ignored it. Slothra lay on his back, his head turned to one side. He looked dead, and smelt rancid. Gar-ran moved closer though and aimed the tip of his machete close to Slothra's chest. Tim looked away, not wanting to see the killing thrust.

Gar-ran yelled, but in pain, and Tim spun around to see Slothra crushing Gar-ran in a bear hug. He ran forwards.

'No, stay back,' Gar-ran gasped, his face contorted. Slothra looked round, but too slowly, and Tim sprayed the content of the bottle full in his face. The bounty hunter reared back, releasing Gar-ran, and sank down coughing, spluttering and making a terrible choking sound, as he furiously wiped his face and eyes.

'It works!' Tim exclaimed, his voice high-pitched with fear and excitement. After the discovery that Slothra had an overwhelming allergic reaction to the coke soft drink, Gar-ran had managed to stockpile many bottles of the fizzy drink. He'd then found a way to produce a synthetic version in his lab to use as a weapon, but which up till now was untested.

Meanwhile, Gar-ran had staggered up and was looking frantically for the machete. He found it just as Slothra reared up and threw himself towards Tim. Swinging wildly, Gar-ran ducked and thrust the blade deep into Slothra's chest, then quickly stepped back.

Tim watched, horrified, as Slothra tottered, then slumped to his knees and pitched face forwards.

'He's done,' Gar-ran said simply.

Tim stood there horror-struck. *Is it really over?*

Gar-ran patted him on the shoulder. 'Let's go.'

Slowly, they made their way back to the trail.

Thirty-One
Loose Ends

It was late morning when they reached the ship. Tim was about to dash ahead when Gar-ran restrained him.

'Wait. The area may be booby trapped.'

Tim's smile faded as he stood stock-still and took in their surroundings. Nothing looked any different from the other miles of jungle they'd trekked through, but with the leaf litter so thick, it was impossible to tell what may be hidden underneath.

'The only way to be sure is to bring the ship to us.' Gar-ran withdrew the controller and held it awkwardly in his bound hands as he typed in the ignition code sequence. There was the familiar hiss as the thrusters engaged and the ship surged up. Heavy drops of water ran down the silver flanks as she ascended to twenty feet. To Tim she looked magnificent and he'd never been happier to see her. Under Gar-ran's direction she sailed over until directly above their heads. He inputted another code and the ship slowly lowered, blocking out the light from the clearing overhead.

'It's coming down on top of us,' Tim said with some concern.

'Yes, move back, keep to the tracks we made. It's the only way to be sure.'

'Ah, OK.' Tim moved out of the way as the ship touched down. There was a popping sound as the airlock disengaged and the door slid open. He looked at Gar-ran, who nodded. Without a word, Tim quickly went up the slope and inside, heading straight for his seat in the command hub. He plonked himself down in the co-pilot seat and let out a deep sigh of relief. He ached all over but stood up as Gar-ran appeared in the doorway and Tim remembered about his hands.

'Sorry, I forgot.'

'That's OK. I have the tools to get them off in the weapons cache, but I'll need your help.'

'Sure, let's go.' Tim led the way down the corridor, hobbling slightly. He placed his palm on the ID sensor and the security panel slid up and they stepped inside the small room.

'There, those ones,' Gar-ran indicated a brass-coloured hand tool that reminded Tim of a large pair of garden secateurs, the sort of thing his mum used for pruning jobs in the garden. They were incredibly sharp and he was able to easily cut off the cuffs, which fell to the floor with a clonk.

'Much better.' Gar-ran gently massaged his wrists, which were red and sore.

***

Forty minutes later, Tim was alone in his room. He'd showered the filth of the rainforest off and applied cream to his cuts before changing back into his Earth clothes. Feeling fresh again, he headed back to the command hub. Nerissa's smiling face beamed from the viewing screen and Tim smiled back as Gar-ran came in.

'I'm going to have to replace the shield generator.' Gar-ran looked frazzled.

'Can I help?'

'You can watch if you like?'

'OK. Is it a big job?'

Gar-ran flexed his hands. 'May take a while.'

Tim knew he wasn't going to be much help as he knew nothing about electronics, or whatever system the Scarab used, but he could keep Gar-ran company at least, and it was better than just hanging around.

***

After an hour Tim's stomach was rumbling. Gar-ran poked his head out from a cupboard that was full of different-coloured cables.

'Go and get some food. I'll join you when I can.'

'If you don't mind?' Gar-ran waved him away and Tim darted off. He was famished.

***

Later, they met up in the command hub. Tim took his seat and the straps emerged to secure him. Gar-ran rapidly inputted the launch sequence and engaged the viewing screen. They soared up and, within two seconds, were above the canopy and once more viewing an endless sea of green treetops.

'Just one more thing left to do. It can't be far away,' Gar-ran said, almost to himself.

'What can't?' *Have we left something behind?*

'Slothra's ship. We must destroy it before we go. Do you remember how to start the scanning sequence?'

He had to think for a moment. 'Ah, yeah I do.' He typed the commands into the panel before him and there was a faint hum as the three lights above the small monitor turned a deep amber colour. Following Gar-ran's instruction, he fine-tuned the settings to alert them when the ship was located.

They flew in an expanding square pattern and it took the best part of an hour before the alarm triggered. Gar-ran homed in on a break in the canopy. Nerissa was able to generate a 3D image of the clamshell-shaped craft. Gar-ran locked on and took the Scarab up another 200 feet.

'D'you want to take the shot?' he asked.

'Can I?' Tim was surprised, but delighted. He pressed the engage button and a single, laser-guided missile streaked down. There was a slight pause before the gust of orange flame and thick black smoke plumed up from the forest floor.

'Done,' Gar-ran said, his expression hard. They surged up and Tim closed his eyes.

Gar-ran set a course to take them to the outer fringes of the Karanagan system before they called it a day and headed to their quarters. Tim barely had the energy to get undressed and fell into a dreamless sleep the moment he laid his head down.

Thirty-Two
Preparations

‘**M**orning Tim. Sleep well?’

Tim nodded, stifling a yawn. He was still tired, but on the whole much better.

‘Well we're homeward bound at last. It's thanks to your efforts we've made it this far,’ Gar-ran said as he spooned some eggs and bacon onto Tim's plate.

‘It was a joint effort,’ Tim replied as he attacked his breakfast. They'd really learnt to work as a team, especially in the last few days.

‘How soon can we get there?’

‘We have to be there in six days. The day before the portal will be opened at the latest.’

That didn't seem bad at all. He'd lost track of how far from home he was; the distance must be practically incalculable in terms of miles. He could hardly wait to get back, but didn't want to think about it too much as there was so far to go, and he didn't think he could bear any more interruptions to their journey.

'What exactly will we be doing when we get there?' This was something that had been bothering him. Everything so far had been building up to this next stage, and now that it was nearly here, he wasn't sure about what would be happening, or his role in it.

Gar-ran placed his cup down and looked serious. 'First, I have to reassemble the dimension bomb and get it working. That's number one priority. When we actually get back, I want to try to find out exactly who's behind this scheme to open a portal and allow Mephango, and goodness knows whatever else, through. Then we've got to stop them before it's too late.'

Tim felt a chill at the words 'whatever else'. Were there more demons? As if one wasn't bad enough. He remembered something from earlier.

'And you think it could be to do with that Dell guy, the one you chased?'

'Karron-Dell, yes. If he survived the crash then he might still be out there.'

Tim nodded. 'So, if he's still alive, and we can stop him, we might not need the bomb?'

'Yes, that would be ideal, but I'm leaving nothing to chance.'

***

It took Gar-ran four days of constant work to repair and reassemble the dimension bomb. Cleaning the segments alone took half a day, then much of the interior circuitry had to be replaced, and several times Tim heard Gar-ran cursing to himself as he passed by the lab. Finally, all segments were assembled and electronically charged overnight, and on the morning of the fifth day, it was ready.

'Looks great. Bigger than I expected,' Tim said as he peered close. Reassembled, the device was the size of a grapefruit and shone in the bright lights of the lab.

'It's very cleverly designed. You see those little levers on each side?'

Tim nodded.

'Each of them has to be locked into place. That's the arming mechanism. Then once it's in proximity to Mephango, it detonates, opening a counter-portal which will force him back to his own realm.' Gar-ran's eyes shone with conviction, and Tim smiled. Gar-ran was convinced, but the problem was there was no way to test it until the critical time. *What if it doesn't work?*

He kept his opinion to himself though. Gar-ran had hardly slept the last two days and he didn't want to spoil the moment.

Twenty-four hours till Earth-fall, he could hardly believe it. He wasn't sure how he felt. A mixture of excitement and fear as to what would be coming next.

Nearly home though. Not that he'd be going to his actual home yet. Gar-ran had explained they'd be heading to the national park in Snowdonia, scene of the mysterious disappearances that had been in the news, and the area he was sure the portal would be opened. It was a huge place to search, but no doubt the marshal had a plan.

However, just to be back on his home planet would be wonderful. Home planet seemed a funny term and Tim smiled to himself as he thought about it. How many planets were out there really? He'd seen a few, and they were all different. How many must Gar-ran have visited during his service? Perhaps one day Gar-ran might take him to other places, like Nectar-3, rather than the jungles of Karanagan.

They were taking a slightly different route on the way back, to avoid the asteroid belt and then pass close to Mars before the final rush onto Earth. It was early evening before Gar-ran came on the intercom asking him to come to the lab. Welcoming the distraction, Tim flung aside the mag he'd been trying to read, rolled off his bed and hurried out.

He slowed as he entered the room and his eyes struggled to adjust to the near darkness. Suspended over the table was a 3D holographic image of what looked like a mountain range.

'Is that Snowdonia?'

'Yes, and this peak here is Mount Snowdon. However, this is the area I want to concentrate on: Lake Glaslyn. This is where Nerissa detected the greatest energy output.'

'A lake?' Tim was surprised. He'd been imagining wild, rugged countryside, perhaps with Karron-Dell holed up in a secret mountain lair. A plain old lake wasn't the same.

'Not just any lake though. Glaslyn crops up in folklore and legend time and time again. This is the lake King Arthur's sword Excalibur was thrown into when the king was dying, and a ghostly white arm rose from beneath the water to catch it. The Lady of the Lake.'

'Cool, I've heard of that, and I used to watch *Merlin* on TV.' This was more like it, Tim thought.

Gar-ran smiled, and continued. 'And this is also meant to be the grave of a fearsome monster called The Afanc, which preyed on the people in the nearby village. Eventually they were able to capture the beast and it was dragged in chains to here, where it was drowned.'

Tim's eyes widened as he imagined the scene. *Why don't they cover things like this in school?*

'So, it could be our turn to become part of the legends?' That was something Tim hadn't considered.

Would he and Gar-ran's adventure one day become part of British folklore?

'Yes. Except this legend is all too true. I have a theory that Glaslyn might be a natural conduit point between Earth and other dimensions. Sometimes a portal might open naturally and only for short periods. I suspect that the one we seek has found a way to open the portal and bring forth whatever lies on the other side.'

Tim was silent for a few moments as he stared at the map. 'Gar-ran, do you think we can stop whoever's behind this, before the portal is opened?'

'I hope so, but it won't be easy. If Karron-Dell is behind this, he's as ruthless and cunning an enemy as you could ever want.'

Tim mulled over this disturbing theory. 'So, they'll probably be waiting for us?'

'We'll have to assume so, yes.'

We have the advantage of the Scarab and Nerissa though, Tim thought.

'Well, we've done well so far, against the odds …'

'Yes, yes, we have, and if we can retain the element of surprise, we'll have a good chance. The ship will be invisible to anyone on earth so I'm planning on us being able to do a close reconnaissance.' Gar-ran looked and sounded confident and Tim felt encouraged.

'How long now?'

'We should make Earth-fall in seventeen hours. Get some rest.'

Tim nodded and headed back to his quarters, but sleep was far from his mind.

Thirty-Three
Earth-Fall

'**N**ot more rain,' Tim said as he watched the downpour on the viewing screen. They were three miles above the Nantlle ridge in Snowdonia. Tim's initial elation at being back on Earth had diminished somewhat at the prospect of being drenched again.

'Well, Snowdonia is one of the wettest parts of the UK,' Gar-ran grinned. 'At least we won't have to camp out this time.'

'That was the best bit.' Tim sank back into his chair. He was doing his best to contain his apprehension. Once they'd entered the atmosphere above the UK, Gar-ran had tuned into various news broadcasts. They'd listened to two reports of mysterious lights in the sky above North Wales, and people were advised not to walk in the national park alone following the still unexplained disappearances.

It was 3 a.m. and time to begin their descent. Gar-ran was about to say something when, all of a sudden, the ship started shaking violently.

'What's happening?' Tim asked, alarmed. They were rattling around so much, he could hardly see straight.

'I don't know. We're losing power! Nerissa?' Blue streaks of light crackled across the viewing screen as if they'd flown into a violent electrical storm. Nerissa's face appeared briefly, looking anxious, then the screen went blank.

They were losing altitude fast. Too fast. Tim sat there feeling helpless. He knew the basics of flying the ship, but all his instruction so far had been under calm conditions. Gar-ran was hammering commands into the console and he felt the ship begin to level out, but they were still going down fast. He gripped his seat and braced himself. The impact was tremendous, but his seat restraints held, preventing him from being mashed against the console. It was still horrible though as they skidded for some time before jerking to a halt.

'Are you OK?' Gar-ran asked, his long hair looking wild.

'I think so.' Tim felt breathless; his heart thumped painfully. *Is this a panic attack?*

'What happened? Why did we crash?' The seat restraints had disappeared and he was able to sit forward.

'Some kind of attack, Nerissa?' Gar-ran asked, but there was no response.

'Hang on a minute.' He punched in a command and the viewing screen blinked on again. Six figures clad in black and carrying rifles were running towards them fast.

'We need to go now. Move it, to the airlock. And check your weapon.' Tim sat there bewildered and looked back at the running figures on the screen. Everything was happening too quickly. Then he leapt up and sprinted to the airlock, Gar-ran close behind. He pulled out his laser pistol, checked it was charged and the safety setting engaged.

'Who are they?'

'Don't know. We've got a head start on them but we've got to go as we're sitting ducks here.'

Tim was about to ask why they didn't just sit tight and use the ship's weapons but then realised that if whoever was out there had the technology to locate and bring them down, they were probably outgunned anyway. That was a scary thought. The airlock popped open and he shot down the ramp. A full moon lit the night sky. Together they ran hard towards a low hill.

'Keep going over the hill,' Gar-ran said, Tim was nearly over the brow of the hill when something hit the earth next to him, sending up a tiny spray of mud. They were being fired upon!

'Keep going!' Gar-ran yelled. The grass was thicker on the other side and slippery and they were forced to slow down to avoid a nasty tumble. They just got to the bottom when a blinding white light halted them in their tracks.

'Stay where you are and throw down your weapons!' a military-sounding voice somewhere in front of them shouted.

'Drop your weapons or we will open fire!' the voice barked.

Tim looked at Gar-ran, who nodded. Reluctantly, he let the pistol drop to the ground. Gar-ran did the same.

'Hands up and kneel down!'

They sank to their knees, still dazzled by the light.

Four figures approached. As they got nearer, Tim saw they were all armed. The men were dressed in black and wore heavy boots. One man covered them with his rifle while the other three grabbed him and Gar-ran and forced their hands behind their backs and tied them with what felt like zip ties. They were then hoisted to their feet.

Someone else approached. Blinking against the glare of the light, it took Tim a moment to see the powerfully built figure clearly. He was tall and also dressed in black military fatigues. This only seemed to emphasise the unnatural pallor of his skin, which was chalk white, heavily wrinkled and in contrast to his terracotta-coloured hair and eyes. Tim tensed as the stranger fixed his gaze on him.

Gar-ran though was the first to speak.

'I knew it. It could only have been you, Karron-Dell.'

The man stopped and stared at Gar-ran in astonishment. He quickly regained his composure and smiled, but there was little humour in his expression.

'It's been a very long time since I used that name. I am known here as the designer. And you are?'

'I am called Garreentius Neva, and I have searched for you for a long time.'

There was a note to Gar-ran's voice that Tim hadn't heard before and he turned to him, but Gar-ran was focused only on Karron-Dell.

Karron-Dell chuckled and was about to reply when he stopped and stared at the embroidered motif on Gar-ran's tunic.

'You're one of them? On your own?'

'We are everywhere,' Gar-ran said and smiled pleasantly. A flicker of alarm passed over Dell's face before he got control of himself.

'Well, marshal, I'm glad to see you. Thank you for bringing me a ship. I hoped more of your kind would come to witness the coming horror, but you'll have to do.'

Tim watched, feeling hopeless as rage and hatred contorted Dell's face and he swung a vicious kick at Gar-ran, striking him hard in the chest, sending him sprawling backwards.

'Leave him alone!' Tim tried to jump up, but two strong pairs of hands held him.

'Forty years!' Karron-Dell screeched as he kicked Gar-ran again.

'Forty years I've been here! A lifetime wasted on this backward world because of you and your kind!' Gar-ran tried to stand up but the third kick knocked him flat.

Despite the pain, he stared coldly at Dell, and Tim felt a surge of pride.

'It was better than you deserved,' Gar-ran growled.

Dell stepped forward again but stopped short and, with a visible effort, got control of himself. He turned to Tim.

'I was beginning to think we would never meet. My congratulations on avoiding Slothra and making it this far; you've both done very well.'

He paused as if assessing them both. 'It took me a while to realise what you were after and why you needed the boy. And I have to say, when I made the connection, it didn't seem possible. Who would ever have believed a segment of the fabled dimension bomb would be here? And you managed to find the other pieces, I take it? Extraordinary. Still, they won't help you now.'

Two soldiers stepped forwards and hoisted Garran up.

'How did you detect us?' he asked.

Dell turned around as a smug smile lit his face.

'From Slothra's reports I realised your ship must have a cloaking capability and normal tracking would be next to impossible. So, I was forced to become creative. A craft such as yours may be invisible but it still generates an enormous amount of energy, and that can be tracked. I located you the moment you came out of orbit. I deduced you would come here, drawn to this place as I was by the old legends and the history. My men have been ready for days.'

He indicated the large, open-deck truck that rumbled into view. On the back was fixed what looked like a sophisticated satellite dish manned by two more soldiers.

'Getting you with the first blast was more luck than anything really. If you had been going any faster, we would have missed.'

There were a dozen soldiers surrounding them. Tough, grizzled men with hostile expressions. *Who the hell are they? And how could it have gone so wrong, so fast?* Tim thought as he was dragged up. Dell turned to one man who was older than the others.

'Major, take them to the platform and detail four men as guards. Send another three men to me while I inspect the ship. And don't underestimate these two. They may not look like much but they've caused me plenty of trouble.'

'Yes sir.' The Major gave the order and Tim was frogmarched with Gar-ran to a large wooden structure on the edge of the lake. There were steps up to a wide platform which extended several feet out and directly over the water.

'Gar-ran, is that Lake Glaslyn?' Tim whispered.

'Yes ...'. Gar-ran was about to say more when a soldier hit him hard in the back with the butt of his rifle.

'No talking.'

Gar-ran gasped with the pain and Tim felt guilty. He looked out over the water. Glaslyn looked bleak and sinister and black as tar in the moonlight. The rain had stopped and a faint breeze rippled the surface.

Reluctantly, they climbed the steps. It was colder on top but for the first time they had a clear view of their surroundings. Positioned on opposite sides of the lake were what appeared to be two large searchlights. A series of thick cables from each light ran backwards towards what Tim presumed to be a sophisticated generator. A rifle-toting soldier stood close by.

'Down. No talking,' said one of their guards, forcing them into a sitting position. The rain had stopped but the platform was still slick with water. After twenty minutes, Tim could feel it begin to seep through his flight suit. *What next?* he wondered.

Thirty-Four
Point Of No Return

K arron-Dell cursed. There seemed to be no way
to gain access to the ship. He shouldn't have
been surprised really. It wouldn't be much of a
prize if its defences were easily breached. Still, the
desire to drag the marshal over and *make* him open it
up was almost overwhelming. He turned away
abruptly. He'd waited years for this day. A few hours
would hardly matter. In fact, the next couple of hours
should be the most satisfying he'd ever spent on this
miserable planet. He checked his timepiece and
smiled. Not long to go.

***

The stairs behind creaked and Tim turned
around to see Dell, flanked by two soldiers, stride onto
the platform. He walked straight over to Gar-ran.

'Give up your controller and the access code to
the ship.'

Gar-ran held the designer's gaze but said
nothing.

'Very well. We'll do it the hard way.'

Two soldiers grabbed Tim and roughly hauled him up. The designer strode over and in one smooth motion drew the semi-automatic pistol from his side holster and held it to Tim's head. The barrel was cold and Tim flinched slightly as the metal pressed into his temple.

'It's only an Earth design but it's effective.' Karron-Dell's voice rang with confidence. He was enjoying himself.

'Don't do it, Gar-ran!' Tim tried to move his head.

'It's all right, Tim. It's in my left pocket,' he said to the nearest soldier. Keeping his gun trained on him, the soldier unzipped the pocket and threw the controller to Karron-Dell, who caught it one-handed.

'Well?' he said.

'Twelve, zero, one, one,' Gar-ran said, his voice flat.

The designer frowned slightly and then slowly smiled. 'The relative atomic mass for Carbon. Ingenious.' He shoved Tim down and turned his back, missing the slight smile on Tim's lips. Dell stalked to the edge of the platform and spun around to face them.

'In one hour and twenty minutes the sun will rise. The portal will be opened and Mephango will come. You two will have a prime view. I wish I could stay and see the destruction of this world but I have bigger plans and other scores to settle. The other marshals will come no doubt, but they will fail. And I'll be far away. With my team, of course.' He nodded to the soldiers.

'He's lying. You'll die here if you listen to him.' Gar-ran looked up at the closest soldiers.

'Don't waste your breath. My men are loyal. They know they'll be rewarded. Here on Earth, they're outcasts, unrewarded and forgotten by the countries they served and shed blood for, but in the places we will go to, you will all be kings!' He raised his voice to a shout and knelt down beside Gar-ran.

'Know this, when the time comes. You are to blame. If you and your colleagues hadn't dogged and hounded me along every step and ruined every one of my enterprises, none of this would have happened. But you forced me here to rot and stagnate in a primitive backwater for forty years. But, for everything there is a price to pay, and you will bear witness to the destruction of these people and their precious planet.' He stood and smiled malevolently.

'Keep a close watch on them, Major Anson.'

'Yes Sir.' Anson nodded. The designer walked away, flanked again by two guards.

***

Tim racked his brain for some kind of plan to get out of there and back to the ship but, as the time slowly ticked away, he began to feel desperation stealing over him. He wasn't allowed to communicate with Gar-ran and the Scarab was over 100 yards away. Their hands were tied and they were exposed in full view to a dozen heavily armed soldiers under the control of a psychotic alien who was bent on revenge. Not a good day out. He wouldn't let himself give up though; they'd made it this far and, after all, he was on home territory. That must count for something.

Slowly, almost imperceptibly, the sky to the east began to lighten and he could feel the tension in the men around them. Major Anson walked to the front of the platform. Suddenly, Gar-ran spoke.

'Tim, be ready, we'll need to ...'

'SILENCE!' Anson bellowed, his hand dropping towards his sidearm.

Below, Karron-Dell watched the sky. Just a few more minutes. It had taken him years to design and build the electropulse generators which could fire and sustain the frequency needed to tear the portal wide and keep it open. Was it fear he could feel in his gut now, or excitement? It didn't matter really. He raised his arm high and then dropped it again. On either side of lake his men threw the switch and the great round lenses of the pulse generators blazed brilliantly.

***

Watching from above, the lake seemed to glow and shimmer. Tim heard footsteps and Karron-Dell strode triumphantly onto the platform. The sky was reddening and, far away, Tim could hear the faint song of a bird.

'Now to complete the ritual. Mephango must be tempted with blood, a little taste of what's in store for him.' The designer grabbed Tim by the collar of his flight suit, making him gasp, and dragged him forward to the edge of the platform. He struggled hard but was forced into a kneeling position facing out across the lake. His eyes widened as Dell produced a large and very sharp combat knife.

*****

The sky was brightening with every minute and Lake Glaslyn was bathed in a shimmering white light. A fine mist was spreading all across the surface of the water with unnatural speed.

'Mephango! Great One, Lord of Destruction, we welcome you!' Karron-Dell's voice rose to a shriek. 'Accept this small offering and join us. Come to us!'

Tim winced as the blade cut along the side of his neck. Immediately the blood ran down and dripped into the lake. Karron-Dell dropped the knife down into the water where it disappeared into the glowing mist. Now that he had gotten over the initial shock, Tim realised with relief that the wound wasn't deep, just a long nick, although it was horrible to feel his blood trickling away and not be able to do a thing about it.

Gar-ran had cried out when he saw the knife, and Tim sensed Anson had moved nearer. The air above the lake crackled and shimmered.

'He comes, he comes!' Karron-Dell roared.

In the very centre of the lake, something began to form. The soldiers manning the electropulse generators took a step back as their hands strayed towards their sidearms.

'Anson, help us, before it's too late.' Gar-ran sounded frantic and Tim tried to twist around, but Dell smacked him around the head.

'It's already too late, behold!' Karron-Dell pointed outwards.

The creature hovered above the lake surface and slowly began to uncurl to its full height. Even from the distance of the platform, Tim realised it must be at least 100 feet tall. It stood upright on two enormously powerful legs and Tim shuddered when he saw the creature's cloven hooves. Its arms flexed and stretched, powerful muscles rippling beneath the blue-black skin. Spines and spikes of different lengths protruded from its back, like grotesque living stalagmites. Most frightening of all though was the demon's head. Two great, curling horns framed Mephango's face. His eyes were pillar-box red glowing slits and the six thick tusks which grew from his lower jaw were chipped and pitted with age but still fearsomely sharp. Slowly, he turned his head towards the platform.

'Watch, it begins!' The designer's voice was high and bright with excitement as he moved to the far edge of the platform.

***

Gar-ran stared hard at Anson in silent appeal and saw the truth dawn in his eyes. Quickly, Anson moved behind him and cut through the zip ties, freeing Gar-ran's hands. He freed Tim just as Karron-Dell spun round.

'Fool.' Anson stood and was about to speak when the designer shot him in the head. The two other soldiers reacted a fraction too slowly and Dell finished them with a single shot each. Gar-ran threw Tim the ship controller and hurled himself at Dell, knocking him down.

'Run, Tim, get to the ship!'

Tim bolted away. He glanced back for a second to see Gar-ran frantically grappling with the designer, before hurtling down the stairs and across the wet ground to the Scarab.

***

Karron-Dell swung his pistol like a club but Gar-ran just raised his arm to block in time and punched him hard in the face. With both hands he grabbed Dell's wrist and slammed it down against the platform. The pistol skidded away and dropped into the lake. Enraged, Dell shoved Gar-ran off him and jumped up, drawing back his leg to deliver a massive kick, but then he slipped. The platform was slick with rain and blood. His arms windmilled around as he fought to regain his balance but he was already falling backwards into the seething waters of Lake Glaslyn. Gar-ran dragged himself up and stumbled down the stairs towards the ship.

***

Like a spider on its web, Mephango felt the ripple as Karron-Dell crashed into the water. He fixed his attention on the tiny figure climbing the bank of the lake. The one who had summoned him.

***

Tim typed the correct airlock activation sequence again as he fought to get his breath back. The code Gar-ran had given the designer was missing two key numbers. Why wasn't it opening? He turned back and saw Gar-ran stumbling over the ground still forty feet away. With a soft hiss the airlock opened. 'Gar-ran, hurry!' he yelled. He looked out across the lake. The demon somehow seemed larger than ever. Gar-ran, panting with the effort, finally caught up.

'Get the bomb. I'll try to get the ship online,' he gasped. Tim raced through the airlock.

***

Karron-Dell hadn't run far before the shadow fell over him. He stopped, turned and looked up. For once he was lost for words. Jumbled thoughts raced in and out of his mind but he couldn't articulate them. He stared up and raised his hands in supplication. The great horned head bent to look at him and Dell froze. He couldn't move an inch, not even as the great cloven hoof rose above him.

'Wait!' But there was no time left, none at all. Just an immense weight crushing down on him and blackness falling all around, and then nothing.

***

Tim ran to the command hub. He had the bomb. 'Do you need help?'

'Nerissa's still down and a lot of the systems offline. Damnit! We don't have time for this.'

Tim ran to his chair and activated the viewing screen. The image was scrambled but then cleared. Mephango was much closer.

'What happened to Karron-Dell?'

'He went into the water. I didn't see after that. Come on, come on …'. Gar-ran frantically typed in lines of code, but nothing engaged.

Tim suddenly knew that if they stayed where they were, they would both die. He looked at the viewing screen again. Mephango would soon be upon them. He made his decision.

'I'm going out there, I think I can stop him.' He ran towards the door.

'No Tim, wait! I'll come with you.'

'Look after the ship.' Tim turned and sprinted out, leaving Gar-ran staring helplessly.

In the airlock, Tim thought he was about to throw up. He'd never felt so afraid before. Taking a deep breath, he armed the bomb, which began to vibrate faintly. If he could lure the demon away from the Scarab, at least Gar-ran would have a chance then. He took off, running hard.

He became aware of a faint whispering. A soft, compelling voice urging him not to be afraid. Reassuring him that everything would be all right. The Lord of Destruction only punished the evil-doer. An innocent boy like him had nothing to fear. He shook his head to clear it and saw the demon was almost on top of him. A great clawed hand reached down and he only just managed to dart out of the way. He had to get more space.

He ran as hard as he could but still felt the voice again. It was as if there was always someone behind him whispering in his ear, telling him not to fear. Lord

Mephango admired his courage. If Tim would only cease his senseless struggle, they could join forces, purge this world of evil. A new golden age could begin here and now, but he must lay down his weapon and surrender. He knew it was all lies but the voice was so compelling, so reasonable, he almost wanted to stop and listen properly. He felt himself slowing, and at that moment, Mephango charged.

***

On board the ship, the control panel lit up and Gar-ran punched in the ignition sequence. The whole ship juddered violently, but slowly began to rise.

***

Mephango bore down on Tim like a laser-guided missile and there was nowhere left to run. He felt faint. The demon churned up great clods of earth as he galloped towards him. Tim leant back, took a breath and hurled the dimension bomb as hard as he could.

It looked so puny as it arced threw the air. Tim's heart sank; it was like throwing a tennis ball at a whale. He closed his eyes and something knocked him back like an invisible wave. A great bloom of light engulfed Mephango and he screeched as thin blue lines of electricity danced around him. It was a terrible, searing sound and Tim clamped his hands against his ears. The air around the demon shimmered and he gave a great bellow of rage and frustration as he was dragged upwards and backwards. There was a muffled explosion and a cold wind blasted Tim, making him shudder. When he opened his eyes, the demon was gone. Nothing remained except a swathe of scorched grass.

Tim pushed himself up and stumbled towards it. The surface of Lake Glaslyn still glowed with a brilliant white light, like a mirror in the sun, and as Tim watched, the glare intensified. Squinting, he saw with a dawning horror something else was taking form above the lake. Of course! The portal was still open. Whatever else was on the other side could still come through. The Scarab appeared overheard and Tim pointed frantically. The only chance was if Gar-ran could destroy the generators on the other side of the lake. He ran to the water's edge. Something hit the first generator and it exploded in a fiery roar. Tim looked up just in time to see the second missile fire. It struck the second generator, obliterating it with a huge boom. There was a brilliant flash, like a blast of sheet lightning, and the thing that was forming dissipated like smoke in the wind. Tim sank down and said a prayer as, slowly, Lake Glaslyn returned to normal. He was still kneeling there when Gar-ran came alongside him.

'We did it, Gar-ran.' He felt empty inside, nothing at all like he'd imagined he'd feel. Gar-ran, too, looked sombre.

'Yes, we did.' He placed a hand on Tim's shoulder. 'You've done a great thing today. I know it's been hard, but it's all over now. Come on inside. It's time to go home.'

Epilogue

There was no sign of the surviving soldiers, but Gar-ran retrieved what was left of Karron-Dell's body and placed the remains in cryrostasis in the lab. He then carefully dabbed some healing cream on the cut on Tim's neck and applied a large plaster. They moved to the command hub and took their usual seats.

'So, how much more of the summer holidays do you have left?'

Tim had to think for a moment. 'A couple of weeks.'

'Time to rest up and relax then. You've certainly earned it.' Gar-ran smiled broadly. He looked better, Tim thought. He was also feeling more like himself. It was as if they'd both turned an enormous corner after a long and difficult race and the finish line was just ahead.

'I can't believe I'm actually going home. Feels like I've been away forever. What will you do now?'

'I'll be sending a full report to marshal command and clear things up here as best as possible. They'll want to come and see for themselves, I'm sure.'

'How's Nerissa?' She'd missed all the action.

'Still offline, but I'm sure I can get her back up soon.'

Tim nodded. He'd have liked the chance to say goodbye to her. He voiced a concern that was bothering him.

'Gar-ran, will we ever see each other again? Or are you going to wipe my memories like we had to do with Josh?'

Gar-ran frowned, looking surprised. 'No, no I'm not. We're a team. Of course, we'll see each other again. We're friends, aren't we? And there's still a lot of flying to do and learning about the ship, if you're interested?'

'You bet, that would be great.' Tim definitely wanted to be able to fly the Scarab.

'We have a deal then.' He smiled and Tim relaxed and sank back into his seat. He suddenly felt very tired, but happy.

It was mid-morning when they landed back at the beach. Tim had asked to be dropped off there as he wanted some time to walk and think things through before going home.

He felt reluctant to go. He was thrilled to be back but, at the same time, life was never going to be the same again. He'd grown up a lot and the world would always seem different to him now. But despite all the upheavals and traumas, he had been on an amazing adventure and found a true friend and mentor in Gar-ran. They stood in the airlock. Tim was dressed in his normal clothes.

'Goodbye for now. I can't thank you enough, Tim. Truly. I'll be in touch though before the holidays are over to see how you're settling back in, and you can reach me anytime if you need me, or if you just want to talk.'

'OK, well I'll see you soon then and thanks … for everything. For getting me home again.'

They shook hands and Gar-ran clasped him on the shoulder, activated the airlock and Tim stepped out. The sun was shining and there was a slight breeze blowing in from the sea. It was going to be a beautiful day. He stepped onto the beach, smiling as he smelt the salt air and heard the cry of the gulls whirling overhead. He walked slowly at first, relishing the feel of home ground beneath him and gazing around. Then he began to jog, the pebbles slick and crunchy under his feet. Then he was running, running hard with the wind behind him, feeling as light as air and grinning from ear to ear. Home. Home at last!

Neill Hoskins lives in the beautiful county of Dorset on the south coast of England. He originally trained as an actor and lived and worked in London for many years before recently moving back south. This is his first book in a planned series of adventure stories. When not writing Neill enjoys basketball, karate and spending time with loved ones.

www.neillhoskins.com

CPSIA information can be obtained
at www.ICGtesting.com
Printed in the USA
BVHW051959070223
658066BV00002B/4